Stephan Collishaw

Stephan Collishaw was born in 1968. He lives in Nottingham and is a teacher. He was awarded an East Midlands Arts Bursary for *The Last Girl*, which is his first novel.

Stephan Collishaw

The Last Girl

SCEPTRE

First published in Great Britain in 2003 by Hodder and Stoughton
A division of Hodder Headline

A Sceptre paperback

1 3 5 7 9 10 8 6 4 2

A CIP catalogue record for this title is available from the British Library

ISBN 0 340 82692 4

Typeset in Sabon by Palimpsest Book Production Limited,
Polmont, Stirlingshire

Printed and bound in Great Britain by
Mackays of Chatham plc, Chatham, Kent

Hodder and Stoughton
A division of Hodder Headline
338 Euston Road
London NW1 3BH

For Marija

I

Jolanta
Lithuania
Mid 1990s

Chapter 1

I smoked the cigarette down to the very nub, until it almost scorched my lips. Through the blue veins of smoke I glimpsed her as she walked down the narrow alley. In her arms she held a child. My insides wrenched, suddenly, sharply. She held the child so tight against her breast. It was that, perhaps, that caught a ladder in my heart.

The café was called Markus and Ko. I had been reading the poems of Marcinkevicius.

> *I love you with hands black from crying,*
> *I love you with darkness and death*
> *forgetfulness and light*
> *with the low grass on a sunken grave*
> *I love—*

I stubbed the cigarette out in the saucer of my coffee cup and struggled up, pushing my arms clumsily into my jacket, which tore as my fingers caught the thread of the lining. I hurried out into the cobbled alleyway, glancing down the street after her. The tops of the buildings were washed with brilliant sunlight, but at street level it was gloomy. She had not gone far. Behind me, from the bar where he had been standing, the waiter called out. I had not paid. I paused a second, snagged by the authoritative tone of his voice, but the young woman was walking fast. I followed her, my heart racing. She had reached the corner by the time I caught up with her. In the door of the café the waiter stood calling after me. Hearing the commotion, the woman turned, her dark hair sweeping across her shoulder as she flicked her head. The baby lay quiet in her arms.

I have an old Russian camera, a Triplet 69.3, presented to me by the university twenty-odd years ago on my fiftieth birthday. This morning I had picked it up as I left, struck by the quality of the light which nestled in the tips of the waking trees and caught in the tangle of church spires above the city. I stood on the corner, foolishly, with the shout of the waiter echoing from the stone walls, and the woman looking at me as if I was a madman.

'Can I take your photo?' I asked.

'My photo?' she said in Russian, a frown creasing her brow.

I put the camera to my eye and took one hastily, before she had a chance to refuse. I managed to get the baby in the frame too. It slept on completely unaware. My finger trembled as it pressed the shutter. She turned then and walked off at a smart pace.

The waiter caught my arm. I had not heard the sound of his approach as I stood watching her figure recede, my mind skimming back across the years, my chest heaving as I struggled to catch my breath.

'You didn't pay,' the waiter said abruptly.

'I haven't finished,' I said, turning to him.

'You have now.' His hand thrust out for the money.

'For kopecks you want to be so rude?' I asked.

'Just pay.'

I live in a small apartment not far from the café. Originally the apartment had been bigger, with three rooms, but I live on my own and what do I want with so many rooms? I sold one to the family in the next apartment. As soon as the money was on the table the young man was around with two friends, knocking a hole in the wall and sealing off my doorway with some crude brickwork. I'm not complaining, God knows I need the money badly enough.

Often I sit by the window of my apartment and look out over the courtyard. In the summer the trees canopy the whole area, and in the autumn they turn a beautiful bronze. On the benches beneath the trees I see my neighbours gossiping or knitting, or staring vacantly out into the world that has changed so much they no longer recognise it. Sometimes I go and talk with them but more often than not I just sit and watch from the window.

When I arrived home that day, my head was pounding and I found it hard to breathe. The excitement had been too much. I felt unaccountably distressed and a little bewildered by what had happened at the café. I sat down in a chair by the table for a while and had another drink. My hand continued to tremble and I spilled the hot coffee, scalding myself.

I have a small darkroom in the bathroom. I took the film and developed the picture of the girl. My fingers fumbled stiffly with the coiled film. It wasn't a good shot. I had not had time to focus it properly and it was slightly blurred. It looked as if she was carrying a small sack of potatoes rather than a child. I pinned it to the wall by my writing desk. Her startled eyes looked straight out from the photograph, into my own. She stared at me with such confidence, such affront. I sat at the desk for a long time just looking at that poor image of the girl on my wall.

Later I took the creased book of Marcinkevicius' poems from my pocket. As I read, I felt her watching me. That was a good feeling. It was a comfort to have her eyes on me as I turned the pages.

In the hours when I should have been writing but couldn't, when the books lay unread on my desk, I stared up at the photograph of the Russian woman and her child on my wall.

I might have been able to believe that my action was simply the result of a moment's madness, if the same thing had not occurred a week later.

I was sitting on a park bench in Ghetto Square when once more the sight of a young woman struck me painfully. She walked slowly across the grass towards me looking down at her baby in its pram, oblivious to my presence. She cooed softly down to the child, soothing it. Her long brown hair was tied neatly back behind her head. Her hands rested on the handles of the pram.

She paused for a moment about ten paces from me. I took my camera from the wooden bench by my side. My heart beat disturbingly as I raised it to my eye. I felt as if I was committing a crime. Focusing the lens with shaking fingers I took the photo quickly. The click of the camera exploded in my ears and seemed to carry across the grass of the park, drowning the sound of cars rushing by. She did not look up. I placed the camera back on the bench beside me. I felt flushed and ashamed.

A moment later she straightened up and continued once more on her path. She passed within a few feet of me. Her scent cut into my nostrils. Her coat rustled against her legs. There had been something about the way she had looked down at the child that ruffled my heart. As soon as she had disappeared from view, I clutched the camera and hurried back to my apartment. Arriving breathless once again, I threw my keys onto the table and took the camera into the bathroom. Standing over the sloshing fluids I watched the blurred image slowly appear on the paper.

When the print was dry I unhooked it from the line in the bathroom and pinned it to the wall beside the Russian. They hung there together on the wall: two mothers, both young and undeniably pretty. The Russian was dark with long hair and this new one was just a little lighter. While the Russian stared out of the photo, challenging, the other gazed down into the pram, unaware.

For a full hour I sat at my desk and stared up at these two photographs. One by one I smoked a packet of twenty Prima cigarettes. The lines of Marcinkevicius winged like dark angels above my head; I love you with hands black from crying. With darkness and death. The earth, I felt, was beginning to shift, and the long dead were stirring.

Chapter 2

My apartment is along the back of Vokieciu Gatve, German Street. This is now becoming a desirable place to live; it was not always so. If you leave my flat and walk for ten minutes you come to Ghetto Square, or the Square of the Sacrifice of the Ghetto. This is a walk I take often in the mornings. After crossing the square, I can take a choice of streets, but almost always chose Zydu Street – Jewish Street – a narrow lane typical of the ghetto. The plain four-storey buildings curve with a fluidity and beauty that the Soviet architects were completely incapable of understanding. This strikes me always. The old town has grown out of nature; it bends to the shape of the rivers that run through it, it listens to the shape of the hills. It winds and flows and hugs the earth as though it were lichen, a beautiful moss spread across an ancient log.

There are no trees or flowers on Jewish Street, just the plaster and brick of the houses and the cobbles on the street. In the autumn there are the leaves, crinkled and brown, which blow here and catch in crevices. But there are no flowers. Even so it is not barren. Not sterile like the housing projects of the Soviets. The shape of the street is like a river, like a hill.

At the top of Jewish Street, as it suddenly halts in the car park behind my apartment, amputated, there is a statue of the Vilna Gaon. I stop there and run my fingers over the Hebrew script I cannot read. At its other end Jewish Street runs out into a small triangular junction, the confluence of rivers, the veins of a leaf. Here it runs into Gaon Street and

8

I follow that, down the hill, past the buildings that are now being carefully restored.

The ghetto is flourishing. For years these streets bore little sign of what they had been. They fell silently into decay. Windows gaped, empty sockets, great weeping holes. Buildings bereft of their owners, of their past. Now the plaster is renewed, the floors are retimbered. The roofs are retiled and the cobbles are relaid. The façades are repainted and walls wear signs recounting the history of the ghetto. But for years those decaying broken-backed buildings were signs. Now they are gone and we have smart boutiques, restaurants and Western cafés.

There is a doorway, here, where often I pause. The lintel sags and rusted hinges hang from the doorpost. I peer in, straining my eyes against the darkness, as though searching for something in there. There is nothing. Only the damp sour scent of decay, stale air. I was stood at the door early one morning, gazing blankly in, when my eyes caught a movement in the gloom. I stepped back, afraid. A dog emerged. It stared at me startled, then loped away. My heart began to pound as I continued with my walk. What did you think it was? I chided myself, the spirit of the dead stirring in the darkness?

On Gaon Street a plaque relates how the Jews were marched out of the ghetto through the gates that used to stand here. They left their homes for the forests outside the city, for the deep forests from which they would never return. To Ponar.

Gaon Street opens out into a square. If you look at the old maps it becomes clear that these spaces are wounds; that once synagogues stood here. This space is now the Square of the Sacrifice of the Ghetto. Each morning, when the weather is good, I come to sit here and think of all the stories that could be written.

I used to write. Twenty years ago I wrote. I taught at the university and published my poems and novels. But now I cannot. I sit at my desk in front of my typewriter but no words come. They have left me. Instead I reach up to my shelf and take down Marcinkevicius or Miloz. But I cannot write.

On my way home I stop once more by the bust of the Vilna Gaon. I rub the script and feel the Semitic curves beneath my fingers. I feel the cool hardness of the stone, the sharpness of the edge of the script carved with such care, such brilliant precision. That was how I used to feel about the words of my poems. They were carved with precision.

I have a sketch of the Gaon above my desk, alongside which I have pinned the photographs of the young mothers I saw in the street. His long, full beard flows down over his chest. His nose is crooked. His eyes are large almonds suffused with benign wisdom. What strikes me though, when I look at this picture of the Gaon, is the deep, single crease that lines his forehead. That crease speaks to me. It speaks of the concern of a scholar, the concern of a saint. I imagine he must have looked more wasted than this. Certainly he looks thin, and there are bags beneath his beautiful eyes, but still I imagine in his poverty he was more stooped, that his beard was not so full and healthy, that his cheeks sank deeper.

Eliyahu, the Gaon, was born wise. He was born at Easter in 1720. By the age of three, legend says, he knew Chumash and the Siddhur by heart. By four he was expert in Kaballah. By six he was debating with learned rabbis and Talmud scholars.

The streets of Vilna were busier then. These narrow alleys with their uneven cobbles were, in winter, lost beneath rivers of mud, in summer carpeted with dust. The streets rang with the noise of horses and the rasp and scrape of metal cartwheels on the stones beneath the dirt. Men crowded these streets, talking, singing perhaps. Arm in arm they made their way to the Beth Midrash, to their job in the glass works. Women leaned from the window shouting to neighbours, to their urchin children begging from passers-by. The narrow alleys rang with the sound of Yiddish.

When he was older, his wife went out to work and Eliyahu studied. He studied always by candle, keeping the shutters firmly closed against the world. Blocking himself off from its noise, its fun, its temptations, even from its light, he created a new world to inhabit, a world shared by other scholars before him, a world raised out of the letters of Talmud, Torah. A world of words.

He tormented his body, depriving it of sleep. Of nourishment. Instead of meat, he fed himself bread soaked in water and this, even, he opened his throat to, letting it pass down without touching his tongue to deprive himself of the pleasure of its taste. Working in his cold room with his bare feet dipped into a bucket of cold water he wrote words of wisdom, words that would be cherished by thousands after him.

But this city is no longer his city, despite this bust and the signs and the streets and squares named after him. It is not his city or the city of his children. The city has been cleansed of them. Cleansed. What a bitter taste that word has when we roll it on our tongues. Yet still I feel that their ghosts linger, in the odd neglected building. Whispering.

Chapter 3

A madness descended upon me. Those hours I was not at my desk surrounded by scattered books and papers, by saucers overflowing with ash and cigarette butts, I was wandering the streets of Vilnius with my camera. The women I photographed were mothers with small children.

At first I took the shots surreptitiously. Sitting on a bench in the park, my camera at the ready, set for the right distance and the right light, I waited. Hidden behind my copy of the *Lithuanian Morning*, I pretended to be engrossed in the innumerable political scandals which in truth depress me heartily, and which I avoid. On most other benches were pensioners like myself, some talking earnestly, others gazing away blankly, across the grass, lost in their memories. By mid-morning the mothers would come, drawn out by the warmth of the sun. Unobtrusively I would pick up my camera, take the picture, and disappear once more behind the newspaper.

Later I grew more courageous. I approached the women to ask if they minded me taking the photo. The fact that I insisted they had the baby with them, preferably in their arms, relaxed them. After the first few attempts I invented a story. I was a newspaper photographer taking shots of citizens relaxing in the park. I did not have to go into details; it was enough to call myself a reporter.

There were times of course when it was hard for me to tell whether the young woman was the mother or a nanny, but this was important to me. I took time to engage her in conversation, ask about the child. It was important that she should be the mother; the picture would lose its authenticity if she were not.

After I had taken on the role of photojournalist the whole thing seemed less mad, less questionable. I began to defend it aesthetically. In fact, as I continued, I took more time posing the shots. It was only those first photographs that were rushed and blurred. Later they were of a good quality. Often I shot in black and white, but I also experimented with colour. The women were happy to pose on park benches or standing beneath the emerald canopy of old trees.

One Friday evening I hurried to the library and took out a lavishly illustrated text on the development of Western art. Late into the night, I pored over the pictures in the dim light of the apartment. Centred in Daddi's Triptych of 1348 is a rosy cheeked, fair-haired Madonna. The infant God nestles in the crook of her left arm. It is a painting of wonderful warmth and tenderness. It is not the shining gilt that draws the eye. Neither is it the image of Christ glorified, or Christ hanging grey from the cross, scarlet blood spurting from the wound, spraying his disciples. The dying Christ is pushed to the side. In the centre of this image, under the dark sky glittering with golden stars, before the beautifully worked red and yellow backdrop, is the simple picture of a woman looking down with gentle indulgence at the child nestled in her arms. While she cradles with her left arm, her right hand lifts and gently strokes the baby's chest. And he, the young child, looks up with equal adoration at his mother. He lifts, too, his right hand, as if to caress the cheek of his mother. The apostles linger at the feet of the mother. Here, one says, looking straight out of the frame at us. Here, this is what you have to look at, this is what is important. Yes, this is to be the object of our worship, the mother and the child.

Chapter 4

It was in the silence of a church, on a day when the sun cut particularly cleanly across the nave, illuminating as it did the head of Mary, the Mother of God, that I saw my last girl. The church of the Holy Mother of God stands on a hill towards the river. It is a little farther up the road from the beautiful, gothic St Anne's and Bernadine's. It is not so impressive, but when sitting at this desk not writing a word for days on end is sending me crazy, I go there to sit in the perfect stillness. To look at the way the light can slice the darkness. To admire the beauty of enclosed space. The quality of silence.

For years I have tried to pray, but I cannot. The words simply do not come. I get to my knees and lift my eyes to the picture of our saviour, but I am unable to get beyond this point. Instead I kneel in silence.

I thought my photographic obsession was burning out. I had not taken a picture for over a week and felt no desire to do so. That very morning I got up with something approaching energy and optimism. Whilst boiling water on the old stove for a coffee, I sat at my desk and opened my large jotter. For one whole hour I wrote. The words poured out with a vigour and freshness I had not felt for years. And then they dried up. It was like a fleeting, cool shower in the desert. The bright mood with which I had awoken dissolved in a flash.

After boiling the kettle once more and sipping my way through a good too many coffees, I slammed the jotter shut. It is a mistake to try to force the words. Like a butterfly they flutter on, somewhere farther out of reach with each swoop

14

of the net. I had pushed too hard. I should have been content with those words that I had got down, those thoughts that I had managed to frame with my clumsy scribbling.

Angry and trembling with the effect of too much caffeine, I paced the small room. Through the wall that used to be a doorway into my second bedroom, my neighbour's small child kept up a consistent high-pitched wail. I clenched my fist hard. I needed to walk.

I pulled on a light jacket and slammed the door of my apartment behind me. The dirty windows prevented much light from entering the stairwell and I descended the stairs with customary care. The air outside was warm. My old neighbour, Grigalaviciene, was sitting on the bench outside the doors, knitting in the sunshine. She smiled and nodded and seemed about to create a space for me to sit by her. I paused and looked down at her. Her grey hair was thinning and her skin creased softly. For a moment I considered sitting with her, but I knew from experience that once she started talking there was no stopping her and I was in no mood for conversation. I nodded and, buttoning my jacket, moved on briskly.

The air in town was fresh. It was a pleasant day for a walk, the sky was beautifully clear. The colours seemed to palpitate under the sun's warm fingers. I had half a mind to sit in a café, but the amount I had already drunk put me off. I walked quickly, feeling the movement relax me. I tried to divert my mind from my writing. As I paced down the narrow lanes I played a game that I have played for years. Looking out for a notable person I tried to decide which novel they were from. Almost immediately an old man hurried up the street towards me. He kept to the shadows as though he wished nobody to see him. He looked sixty or more, though perhaps, upon closer inspection, he might have been younger. He had a doleful, careworn face. He presented me with no difficulties at all. This was obviously Balzac's poor Goriot. In his pocket was some jewel he was hurrying to sell to raise money for his daughters. A man being slowly killed by his love. Love's monstrous, plump fingers beckoning him on, always on, to his death. I shook my head. I love you with darkness and death.

The church seemed empty when I came to it. I allowed its cool darkness to swallow me. I crossed myself, fingers following the worn, ancient ritual, finding in it a certain comfort. For so many years we were denied this. I sat on a pew at the back of the church, my head bowed. Though I could not pray, the church in itself, in its silent space, created an atmosphere of prayer. Just to sit there in silence was to be in communion with something greater, even if that greatness was only the purity of the silence and the way that the sunlight cut through the stained glass of the window.

As I sat with my head bowed I heard footsteps entering the church behind me. A woman's heels clicked on the flagstones and the church door thudded softly. The clicks stopped momentarily and I heard, not far behind me on my left, the soft rustle of a dress as she genuflected. In the silence, also, the delicate breath of a child as it sighed. The heels clicked past me, and from where I sat, head bowed to the floor, I saw her legs stride by. The muscles in her calves tensed beneath her stockings. I watched as she walked down the aisle to the altar. She sat the small child on the front pew and approached the altar alone. She knelt before it and crossed herself and buried her head in her hands as she prayed.

I watched her as any might that sat in that silent space, alone. She knelt before the altar for at least five minutes and perhaps the thought that was uppermost in my head was one of wonder at the young child who through this entire period uttered not one sound.

*   *   *

She turned then and picked up the child. She hugged it to her and kissed it. She did this in such a natural way as if they two were alone in that space, as if she had not noticed my presence. Tucking the child onto her hip she turned back up the aisle. In the dimness of the church it was difficult to discern much of her appearance from the back pew. To make it more difficult she was wearing a collar that rode up high around her face, obscuring it. She was about five feet from me when she stepped into a pool of light that fell from a high window.

Her face was illuminated with the suddenness of a revelation. My heart froze and my hand flew to my mouth. She heard my stifled groan and noticed me for the first time. There was a look of surprise in her eyes. Our eyes met and her step faltered for the smallest part of a moment. That look was fifty years old. It cut me to the quick. In that moment the madness of my photographic craze became clear.

She walked quickly past. I remained in the pew, my heart racing. My face burned and my thoughts scattered across the decades. I faintly heard the clicks receding behind me and the soft thud as the door of the church closed behind her. A sudden panic took me then. I stood up and hurried to the large wooden doors. In the darkness I stumbled on some loose matting and fell with a crash, hitting my face. I sat in the darkness, rubbing my head.

Outside the church she seemed to have disappeared. My eyes darted around searching for her. And then I saw her. She was pushing a colourful pram down towards the corner of Maironio Street. On this corner was the gated entrance to the park. As I watched she turned in through the gates. I set off after her, not hurrying, comfortable in the assumption that she would be there when I arrived.

Sure enough, turning through the gates, I saw her kneeling

beside the sandpit. A small café was open, but deserted. A middle-aged woman swept the dust behind the building. I wandered to the serving hatch and called into the back. There was no immediate response. Eventually I heard the scuff of old shoes on the tiles. The woman appeared indolently behind the serving hatch. For as long as possible she ignored my presence.

'Well?' she muttered finally.

'Coffee,' I said.

She pulled a chipped cup from a pile that was drying and threw it beneath the machine. The machine hissed and steamed as angrily as she did. She slopped the drink onto the counter in front of me. Even though it was nowhere near full, still it managed to spill over the side. She stood there looking at me, not bothering to inform me of the price. I put a Litas note on the counter, which she snatched up. In the Old Town they are politer now. Tourism has forced a change. After all we're Europeans now, not Russians. It was comforting then to find this woman still serving the coffee as I had always had it served, without the smile, without the pleasantries that mean nothing. I smiled. She grunted. She turned and went back to her sweeping.

I sat at a dirty table and watched the young woman. She played for a long time. It was difficult to see much of her from behind. Her hair was long and dark, as the Russian girl's had been. That did not escape me, of course. I saw the meaning in that. I realised what it was that had made me run out into the street, then, to see her. But with the Russian girl it had only been the hair, the hair and the baby. I had started searching for the wrong thing, then, looking for all those young women with their babies.

It had taken that flash of her eyes in the light of the church. That momentary vision had sped me back across the years, years full of movement, ambition and energy. Full of writing and arguing and desperate forgetting. And I had forgotten. I had forgotten and continued to forget with the same fury. Continued to bury, to cover over, though I was no longer aware why.

I wanted her to turn so that I could once more see those eyes. Her eyes. To check whether it had been the light, the church, the strange madness that had possessed me for those last weeks. But she did not turn.

After a while she straightened up and pulled the baby from the sand. She held it up for a few seconds, drawing it close to her face. The baby was moaning. It struggled slightly against her embrace. She spoke to it in a voice that was no more than the faintest of murmurs. She kissed it and, faintly, I could hear that, too, the smack of her lips on the soft flesh of the child's cheek.

Quickly then, she bent and laid the baby in the pram. She did not pause. It was as if she had suddenly remembered something and realised that she had to rush, though she did not look at a watch. She pushed the baby down the path, past the tennis court, back through the green pathways of the park to Cathedral Square.

I followed her at a distance, longing to see that gaze once more.

Chapter 5

At the peak of the cathedral, a large new golden cross sparkles in the sunlight. A brighter echo of the three white crosses that top the green hill behind it. These newly re-erected crosses stand, a memorial to the first missionaries to venture into these last pagan reaches of Europe. For their pains, they were murdered and their bodies dumped in the river that flows at the foot of the hill. Or so the legend goes.

Monuments come and go. Now, we, the last of the pagans, rebuild monuments to our dear Catholic faith. We are eager to seem Western after years of being forced to face east. The communist heroes we were surrounded with have all gone. Lenin Square, where he stood so proudly, is now Lukiskiu Square. Lenin has gone, lying broken, no doubt, on some waste ground. This city is a master in the art of reinvention.

It's not just the monuments that have gone. The street names too have disappeared. Good Lithuanian heroes have replaced all those good communists. Those massacred by the Russians in '91 are on the street plaques now. The KGB offices are now a museum. The nationalists call for a full indictment of Soviet war criminals. To listen to them, to see this disassociation, would make you think that none of them had been involved with our country for the last fifty years. Ah yes, we are masters at reinventing ourselves, at distancing ourselves from what we were.

But this was once a Jewish town. It is hard to imagine that now. Before the war nearly a third of the population was Jewish. Synagogues huddled in with the churches. The rustling of the pages of the Talmud vied with the clicking of the rosary. What evidence of that is there now? The communists had no use for the niceties of fact. The Jewish dead were subsumed into the general toll of the victims of fascism.

It's still possible, though, to see the remnants of that old city. Often I walk up towards the train station. In one of the dirtiest streets, where the buildings are crumbling with neglect, is an old Jewish school. It stands, like a rotten skull, its windows cavernous holes. Daring to enter beneath the slumping brickwork it is still possible to see the Hebrew script on the walls.

When I found that I could no longer write I turned my time and attention to studying. My teaching at the university kept me abreast with literature, but for myself I read what I could of that other city I inhabited. The ghost city. The city of spirits. The darkened shells, the neglected parts of town, the spaces that stand strangely vacant. I read of the Gaon, I read Mera's writing. I read of the Jewish Vilnius destroyed by the Nazis.

She crossed Cathedral Square in the direction of Gedimino Prospect. I followed at a little distance; I had no camera, no façade behind which I could approach her. Without that mask I felt a little lost, I had become quite dependent on it in my relations with these unknown women. When she stopped, waiting to cross the main road, I lingered under the canopy of trees. She crossed without looking back. Why should she?

I hurried after, obscured by the crowds that pushed along the pavement. A trolley bus trundled along the cobbled main street. She moved forward, collapsed the pushchair, taking the baby in her arms. A man held her arm, steadying, as she boarded. A wave of panic tightened my chest. I lurched forward and slipped through the back doors of the trolley bus as they were closing. The doors, catching on my arms, sprang back open. Breathless, I pulled myself aboard. I grabbed the handrail. I did not look to see where she was, fearing I had drawn attention to myself.

There were no free seats and I was forced to hang on as the trolley bus picked up speed down the uneven road. At the corner it slowed, its two tentacles feeling tentatively for the electric wires. Looking along the bus I could see that she was close to the front, the baby on her lap. She gazed ahead of her. There was no mistaking the similarity. It was not just the physical features; it was the quality of that stare. As though she was pondering on something. As though she was able to see into the future and knew that it was bleak.

A pain stabbed my heart. Not a poetic pain, a genuine physical one that almost made me gasp. The last time I had seen that look I had turned from it. Had turned my back upon it. I pressed my forehead against the cool window.

The trolley bus swung out of the busy Old Town streets and headed north to the district of Karoliniškiu. Winding up the hill the bustle of the city dropped away. The road climbed through green hills, the trees of Vingis Park spreading a green balm through the scattered apartment blocks.

At the top of the hill, she got up suddenly. Holding the baby in her arms, she pulled the pushchair awkwardly from the trolley bus. I alighted after her and, feeling bold, offered to help put up the pushchair. She smiled. I bent over the colourful chair and struggled with its complicated locking system. In the end she was forced to bend and flick a small red lever I had missed. The chair folded out into its proper shape. She thanked me. I lingered; she had not even looked at me.

When she straightened up, the baby strapped into its seat, our eyes met with a sickening jolt, with a sense of indecency. Feeling this too, perhaps, she quickly lowered her gaze. She turned and walked away. I watched her figure receding. How must she have felt, when I turned from her? When I could not look at her, unable to bear the truth that eyes cannot help but tell. Could not bear that intimacy of eye nakedly appealing to eye. How did she feel as I turned my back? Did she stand and watch my figure recede down the street? My back which refused to turn, even for a last look?

I followed her. She did not glance back so I presumed her unaware. In truth I may have exaggerated our contact. It is quite possible that at this time she was completely oblivious to me, that in fact each time we had seen each other it was I seeing her rather than she seeing me. I rewrite this history like all historians of my city.

She turned inside an apartment block. Unless she lived on one of the lower floors she would be taking the lift, assuming it worked. It would have been impossible for me to follow her further without really drawing attention to myself. I loitered on the dirty broken pavement outside the doors. Inside I heard the lift creak and groan as it made its slow way down through the centre of the building. The creaking stopped and the doors rumbled open. Moments later the creaking started once more. For a long while I stood listening to its groans as it climbed, seemingly, endlessly higher.

Before taking the trolley bus back to the centre I bought a copy of the *Lithuanian Morning*. Right wing politicians fulminated over the proposed opening of a park of Socialist era statues. The idea that Lenin and Marx would once more raise their ugly heads in the land, even in the noble capitalist cause of getting tourists to part with their money, was too much for them to bear. The past was dead, why resurrect its leaders?

In the centre it began to rain. A light refreshing rain. I trudged back through the busy streets. The dead do not like to lie silent. We write over and again, but the pages are too thin and finally the past texts begin to show through. Ghostly words can be seen beneath our fresh ink. As I wandered up the hill into the confines of the old ghetto I heard the fragile melody of the dead whistling through the scaffolding.

The next day I lay in bed late. My head throbbed and I knew that I was going to come down with a cold. I poured a liberal dose of vodka into my coffee. For the rest of the day I sat in my chair barely moving, an old sheet wrapped around me. I looked out across the trees in the courtyard. The fine weather had broken and a soft wind blew the light rain in flurries against the glass. My breath steamed the glass as I looked through it. When the vodka was finished I found, to my disappointment, that I did not have another bottle. In the evening, consequently, I moved on to the bottle of sweet cherry brandy. When I awoke the next morning it was still raining and my cold was worse.

Chapter 6

On Thursday morning I woke early and cleared out the bottles from beneath my bed. I washed and shaved, as well as I could, considering the shaking of my hands, and chose from my wardrobe the cleanest of the shirts. The rest I packed into a bag to take to Svetlana on Sv Stepono who does my washing. I emptied the ashtrays into a small plastic bin and sat by the window waiting for the dustmen to arrive. At ten thirty I heard the long vulgar blast of their horn and carried the rubbish down the stairs with my neighbours. Grigalaviciene nodded at me sternly; she could smell the cheap brandy from the distance of a floor. I smiled at her. She turned her back and huffed her tidy rubbish bin down to the lorry.

When I had deposited my bag of clothes with my woman on Sv Stepono I caught the number thirteen trolley bus from Gedimino and took the ride up to Karoliniškiu. The weather had improved a little. The rain had held off since the previous afternoon, and the clouds flew high and unthreatening. A wind blew, catching paper bags and tossing them into the air, taking the trees and giving them a good shake. At the junction with Seliu, as the road turned up the long hill between the green banks of grass, I was tempted to get off the trolley bus, to nip this madness in the bud and go take a stroll in Vingis park. A walk under those large old trees would do me more good, I thought. In years past they had helped me with my writing. Often I used to catch the trolley bus out and walk there. But I stayed on, to the top of the road, and got off where she had.

I had not gone there following any kind of a plan. I did not know which was her apartment, and even if I did I could hardly just go and knock on her door. Instead I sat on a bench opposite the apartment doors, having little hope that she might appear. My bench was on the edge of the playground and a woman with her grandchild soon joined me. She waved the child away. Go and play, she told the child. Go and swing. The child wandered off to the broken play things; a roundabout that swung in a loop taking you from ground-scrapingly low to high in the air in its circle, a swing that sagged dangerously in its seat and a bare metal rocket climbing frame mocking Soviet dreams in its austere dilapidation.

I watched the child kicking at the damp soil. The grandmother sat on her bench for a while looking around for some one to talk to. When I avoided her eye she grew bored and shouted for the child to come. I stayed there, watching the figures emerging from the doorways. The first drops of rain had started falling when I finally moved.

I walked past her doorway, then, impulsively, turned back and entered. I called the lift. I travelled up to the top floor and stepped out. Four doors stared back at me blankly, anonymously. Was she behind one of them? There was a sound. A door handle and a man's cough. I quickly stepped back into the lift and descended.

On the way home I bought a bottle of cranberry spirits to help the cold. I bought the paper and at the small stall opposite the cathedral that sells religious items I picked up a thin book on icons. In my apartment I laid the book open on my desk, running my thumb down the centre of the spine, flattening it open on the page of a Madonna and child I had not seen before. I took a razor and sliced the picture as neatly as I could from its spine. I stuck it to the wall with my photographs and, sitting back with my glass of Bobeline, compared them.

This Madonna, I thought, was not sad. She was melancholic, but she was not sad. Did that painter not feel the pain of knowing your child is lost? Did he not want to vulgarise his goddess with such emotions as those that Marija felt as she gazed at her baby and knew with God-given knowledge that he had to die? That fearful knowledge I knew from her eyes. Knew and yet was able to turn from. I say that, and yet each night those eyes are upon me now and try as I might I am not able to turn from them.

The next day I had barely arrived at her block when she emerged without the child. She turned and walked quickly across the park towards the trolley-bus stop. I followed her. The wires clicked and whistled, a trolley bus trundled through the traffic so that we were forced to break into a run. Its doors had opened by the time we reached it, she before I. I felt sick from the exertion as I grabbed hold of the rail and pulled myself inside. The doors swung shut with a heavy thud. I closed my eyes and gasped, trying to recover my breath. The trolley bus lurched out into the traffic and immediately picked up speed, forcing me to hold tight to the rail to stop myself from falling.

Opening my eyes I noticed she was watching me. She edged across her seat to give me space. I saw a look of concern in her eyes and realised that she saw me as an old man, frail and weak. I straightened myself up. I wanted to banish that image, but as I lowered myself carefully onto the seat beside her I was aware of the smell of spirits that clung to me. I saw the heavy thickness of my hands and the brown, old coarseness of my skin, the veins bulging up like ruts in a country road. I noticed the thin worn quality of my trousers. I tried to smooth them with my hand.

Her hand was on her knee. As I smoothed my trouser leg her long fingers rested delicately only inches from my own. Her skin was smooth and pale. Her nails were clean and short. There was no movement in her fingers, no tremble, no shaking as there was in my own. Her leg was thin too. My eyes gazed at our two hands resting now almost side by side, only a fraction of space apart. Only a fraction and yet how great was that gulf, how many years, how many different things kept me from sliding my own blunt old finger those few inches and touching the tips of hers. It has been too long, and though she appears to me as clear as crystal each night, even though now I can close my eyes and picture her, it is not possible to reach back across the years and change that moment, to reverse it. It is done and she is gone. The distance is too great.

'Only just made it,' she said.

'Yes,' I said, looking up into her face. Not the eyes, I could not look into those eyes. She was still looking at me and I traced in her voice a note of concern, a delicate probing to ask if I was all right.

'I'm getting too old for running,' I laughed.

She laughed, 'It's not so easy for me.'

'You're the picture of health,' I said. 'It does you good when you're so young.'

'I don't feel so young.'

I dared then to look beyond the fresh pink of her flushed cheeks, beyond the smooth curve of her nose and the soft hair that downed her face. Beyond the thick, dark eyebrows to her eyes. She was smiling; smiling with her eyes, though there was barely the trace of a curve on her lips. A prickling sweat broke out on my forehead.

My fingers trembled beside hers. Mine blunt, hers elegant. The sun shone through the grimy windows, warming them. And then, on a corner, the trolley bus rocked awkwardly, causing her to lean against me. Her thigh pressed against mine and the tips of our fingers touched as she tried to balance herself. We withdrew immediately. I smiled and she smiled too, before turning and looking out of the window. We were descending the long hill, the green banks rising on each side of us, the trees barely moving in the breeze.

We did not speak again. The trolley bus fought its way through the traffic into the centre of the Old Town. She got up as we lurched slowly into Gedimino Prospect. I let her past me and then followed. When she turned, I looked studiously out of the window as if my getting off had nothing to do with her. She walked swiftly down Gedimino and into the department store. I stood for a moment debating then crossed the road and entered the new American restaurant, McDonald's. It was crowded and I had to wait in a queue to be served. I sat by the large plate-glass windows and watched the department store doors. She did not reappear. Maybe, standing in the queue, I had missed her. The coffee was tasteless and the seat hard. I did not stay long.

I dreamed of her that night. She was walking down the road with her child in her arms, imploring me. I could read in her eyes the fear and desperation. I saw too, in the corner of my eye, the men approaching. I turned my back. But each time I turned she was in front of me again, and behind me the men drew closer. I awoke a number of times but each time my eyes closed heavily again, I had to turn from her once more. In the morning I was exhausted.

Shortly after sunrise I pulled on my coat and walked across the grass, beneath the trees, to the top of Zydu Street. I stopped by the bust of the Gaon and rested my head against the cold stone. My blunt fingers felt the sharp edge of the engraved Semitic sentences. I tried to find words to say to him, but I couldn't. I stood for some time, my back resting against him, glad to have that solid presence behind me. I smoked three cigarettes one after another and then went home.

The next time I saw her was in fact quite by accident. She

was again pushing her child. I had been in the bookshop on Gedimino when, through the window, I saw her pass by. I slipped out of the store and hurried after her. I caught up with her at the door of the McDonald's restaurant. I was able to hold it open for her. Only then did I affect to recognise her. 'Hello,' I said. She smiled, remembering me.

'You're eating here?' she asked somewhat incredulously.

'The coffee's good,' I lied.

'The coffee's terrible,' she laughed.

'Well, maybe I can buy you a cup of America's worst coffee?' I asked. She smiled but seemed to hesitate.

'Why not?' she said.

Sitting once more by the plate-glass windows, I was able to watch her now across the table. She spooned yogurt into her child's mouth. The baby was blonde. Her small blue eyes sparkled clearly. She watched me while her mother fed her. She was not at all like that baby. That had been dark, its skin sallow and its hair fine. It lay quietly in its mother's arms, in the dark Vilnius alleyway. Had it ever grown?

'And what's your name, young lady?' I asked to clear my mind. The baby looked at me suspiciously, continuing to eat the yogurt fed into her mouth.

'Rasa,' the mother answered for her.

'Rasa, a good Lithuanian name,' I said. 'A beautiful fresh droplet of dew. And yours?' I asked.

She hesitated a moment again before answering. She looked into my face, as if she would find there whether to trust me or not. 'Jolanta,' she said. So there it was. Jolanta. Not Rachael. Jolanta. I breathed in deeply, inhaling that name which was not her name, allowing it to fill my lungs with a fresher air than the putrid air of painful dreams.

'And you?' she asked.

I stood up formally and held out my hand. 'Steponas

Daumantas.' She took my hand and I pressed it. I held it a second. 'Very pleased to make your acquaintance.'

She nodded and withdrew her hand. 'Very pleased to make your acquaintance too,' she said, ironically, but with humour and a smile.

'And what do you do, Mr Daumantas?'

I laughed. 'Me, I'm an old man, a pensioner. What did you think I was, a soldier?'

'You don't look so old and anyway, age is in the mind,' she said with the simple-minded confidence of the young.

'I'm old in the mind too.'

'Well, what did you do then, Old Mr Daumantas?'

I toyed with the idea of lying, of creating another person for her. Her eyes were upon me and I did indeed once more feel young in my mind. If being young means confusion and stuttering nervousness.

'I am, I was a writer,' I corrected myself.

'Was?' she asked. 'Surely that's one thing you can do no matter what your age?'

'Sometimes it is, sometimes it isn't. I find it hard now,' I said, wishing I had not introduced the topic. It trespassed on an area that was far too closely related to why I was sitting in front of her.

At that moment the baby shouted angrily. The spoon of yogurt, which had remained for the past few moments suspended in mid-air between tub and mouth, found its way to its destination. Jolanta fed the baby quietly for a moment. Then she turned back to me and said, 'Perhaps, then, you could help me?'

'Help you?' I asked, taken aback. 'Of course. I would be delighted to help you.'

Tiring of our chatter Rasa began to cry, demanding attention. Jolanta lifted her up and shushed her. She wailed loudly. I waited patiently but the baby was not at that moment going to let us finish our conversation. Jolanta glanced at her watch, awkwardly, holding the baby in her arms.

'I'm late,' she commented to herself as much as to me. She stood up. 'I'm sorry,' she said. 'I have an appointment now. Would you seriously be willing to help me?'

'Of course,' I assured her, standing too.

'Perhaps we could meet again?' she asked a little nervously, as if she felt that she might be imposing upon me.

'I would be delighted,' I said. 'Would you like me to take your telephone number and call you?'

'No,' she said quickly. 'No, no need. We can meet again tomorrow if you are free?'

'Yes, I will be,' I said.

'Shall we say here then, at twelve?'

'Perhaps I could take you somewhere a little nicer for lunch?' I suggested. I indicated the polystyrene cup. 'The coffee here really isn't drinkable.'

'That would be nice.' She smiled. Her eyes were beautifully bright. My heart pounded. Foolishness, I said to myself once more. Pure foolishness.

Chapter 7

Svetlana on Sv Stepono had cleaned my shirts. She took the few Litas I offered her, slipping them into her palm, folding her fingers over the crumpled notes. She was obviously in need of the money but seemed embarrassed to take it from me. She insisted I stay for tea. I sat on the edge of the rumpled bed, which in the daytime served as both sofa and wardrobe for her teenage son's clothes. The windows of her cramped room were mercifully small. Only one pane of glass was unbroken, the others were covered with plastic bags from one of the new supermarkets in the city. I doubted she shopped there. I had given her one of the bags with my washing in. She had wrapped my washing neatly in brown packing paper tied with string. On the walls of the one room she had hung the three dresses she owned. One was a modern looking black-and-white dress with sequins patterning it. I commented on it.

'Mrs Pumpetiene gave it me,' she said in Russian. 'Lovely, isn't it?'

'Yes,' I agreed, trying to imagine where she might wear it.

I had known Svetlana for a number of years. Often when I dropped off clothes for her to wash, we sat and talked. She did not speak much about herself but she had once told me her father had been arrested when she was a child by the Communist authorities for propagating Christianity and producing samizdat books. Her parents had been moved to Vilnius from Russia under the Communist government's policy of mixing ethnic populations.

In the small annex, which served as kitchen-cum-porch, water boiled on the electric ring. Svetlana poured it into a small, old, blackened samovar. She poured me a sweet tea, and sat watching as I drank it. It was too hot to do anything but take the smallest of sips. Svetlana's cheek was, I noticed, slightly swollen near her left eye. She smelt of vodka.

'Your husband back?' I asked.

She touched her cheek self-consciously and nodded.

'Did you find out where he had been?'

She laughed and shook her head. She swore in Russian. 'Boozing some place, with some tart, I should think.'

'And Misha?'

I had met her son on a couple of occasions. He was about eighteen years old, with short, cropped hair. He looked like a thug but was unfailingly polite and spoke good Lithuanian, unlike his mother.

'He's working,' she said brightly. 'On the building site, five dollars for a ten-hour day. They pay him by the day, but there's plenty of work, he says. Should be able to keep going there just so long as no government sneak goes snooping around, checking on papers.'

I grunted.

'I don't know.' She shook her head. 'They keep thinking up these new laws. They want to force us to take exams in Lithuanian before they will let us become citizens. They are just trying to punish us.'

'They don't know what they're doing,' I said. I drained the last of the tea, scalding my throat. I didn't like talking politics; an old reflex tied my tongue.

'Thanks for the tea, Svetlana,' I said, taking my brown-paper package.

'Don't mind me,' she said, 'I had a bit of a drink earlier.'

I smiled. 'I'm going for mine now,' I said.

Her eyes lit up. 'You want one now? I've got half a bottle left.'

I shook my head and gently pulled away from the grip she had suddenly taken of the front of my clothing. 'Another time,' I said. She released me. I let myself out of the door into the dirty courtyard. The wooden walkway of the second floor sagged dangerously outside her doorway. Looking back, I saw in the dimness that she had already taken out the bottle and was pouring vodka into a glass. She stood with her back to me in front of an image of Christ crucified, askew on the dirty wall.

Closing the door of my apartment I flung the brown-paper package of clean shirts on to a chair in the small hallway. I opened the windows of the flat to let in some air. Then I started to work on my table. Carefully I replaced all the books in their places on the shelves. I took the many saucers and ashtrays, over-spilling their stale, grey ash on to my papers, and emptied them into the small bin in the kitchen. I gathered the scattered sheets of papers into random piles; they would have to be sorted at some other time. I pulled down the numerous photographs and prints that had been collecting on the walls and stowed them in a drawer. Taking a cloth, I wiped the spilt ash and the coffee rings from the table and placed my typewriter squarely in the centre, in front of my chair.

I sat down at my work desk and fed a clean, blank sheet of paper into the typewriter. For a moment I sat looking at the pristine blankness of the page. I pressed my fingers into my eyes. A shudder ran down my spine. With my eyes closed I was able to picture her. I did not see her figure, or the clothes that she wore. I did not see, either, the subtle flush on her cheeks, or the way her hair was tucked back behind her ears. I saw only her eyes. Those eyes that she shared with a woman fifty years ago.

I opened my eyes and typed out, 'Resurrection'. I scrolled down the page an inch and wrote, 'In the summer of 1938 I was living in a small village west of Vilnius.'

Chapter 8

We met the following day. I shaved carefully and pulled on a fragrant and stiff shirt, clipping the cuffs with a couple of simple links. I arrived at the American fast food restaurant ten minutes early. She was not there, of course. The weather was fine so I paced about outside wondering what it was she wanted my help with.

At twelve I heard the toll of the cathedral bell. I glanced at my watch, which was spot on. I gazed up and down the street but there was no sign of her. I wondered whether she had thought better of her strange request for my help. The idea that she might have forgotten all about our lunch was passing through my head when she stepped out of the bookshop close by and, seeing me, waved. I waved back, my heart lifting like a nervous schoolboy's.

'Sorry,' she mouthed.

Her face, I noticed, was flushed. She smiled broadly and touched my arm in a friendly manner.

'I'm sorry,' she said. 'I was browsing in the bookshop.'

'You found a book?' I asked.

She slipped a book from its wrapping and showed me. It was Conrad.

'You've read it?' she asked.

'Yes,' I said.

'Did you like it?'

'You know, I find it hard to get beyond the fact that it was a book by a Pole writing in his third language being read by me translated into yet another language.'

'But isn't that fascinating,' she said. 'To feel that you have to dig through all those layers of language to get to the heart of what it is about?' She had taken my arm gently and we walked up Gedimino to the crossing.

'Some things are better left buried,' I said, thinking of the paper that I had left in my typewriter with the one line typed across the top of it.

'Do you think so?' she said, her face alive, vivacious.

She slipped Conrad into the bag that she had slung over her shoulder. We waited for the cars to pass and then crossed the cobbled street. On the other side we turned up Jogailos Street.

'Do you really think that things should be left buried?' she asked again when I did not answer her.

'Why should we keep on exhuming things once they are dead?' I said. 'After all, we're not dogs that we need to keep on digging up bones.' I did not like the turn that the conversation had taken and wished I had not initiated it.

She was vigorous and animated when she looked at me. She reminded me of the students that I had at the university, lively in their desire for knowledge, before experience had taught them that it was better to bury than to dig up.

'Just because we dig things up doesn't mean that we are dogs,' she said. 'After all archaeologists dig things up. How would we understand our pasts if we did not dig things up?'

We understand and that is why we are so keen to bury, I thought, but I did not answer. Instead I rather crudely changed the subject. 'I thought that we could go to Lokys,' I said.

'Really?' she said. 'I'm not really dressed for it.'

I looked at her. She was wearing a black dress that reached down below her knees. Over the top of this she wore a rather plain jacket with its collar turned up. Around her neck she had tied an orange scarf carelessly. Her hair was swept back and held behind her head with a large clip.

'You look perfect,' I said, without a trace of flattery. She smiled and blushed a little, perhaps detecting how much I felt those words.

We made our way back into the ghetto by the narrow lanes, winding, crammed with parked cars. She did not seem to be in a hurry and I did not want to hurry her. The sun broke through the grey clouds and illuminated the spire of St John's Church, giving us a taste of brilliance in the dark shadows of the back streets. We chatted about Vilnius as we walked, commenting on the face-lift the city was enjoying. She was positive, not missing at all the dark crumbling buildings, or the spiked ribs of the fallen-in roofs of the houses. She approved of the modern shops and the new plaster and the bright colours that had transformed our city. I did not broach the subject that had got us together. She did not mention the help she had asked for either.

Lokys was quiet. One other couple were sat at a table, leaning close to each other. I pulled out a chair for Jolanta and she sat down. We scanned the menu in silence. After a few moments she tossed the menu aside and said, 'I'll just have a salad.'

'You're not hungry?' I asked.

'Just watching my figure,' she said.

When the waiter arrived I ordered her salad and cepelinai for myself. I ordered a bottle of wine too.

The waiter took the menus. Her young face was turned aside, she was casting her eyes about the room. Her fingers were on the table in front of her. They did not tap, just rested gracefully on the polished wood.

After a few moments of silence she turned her eyes on me.

I felt a thrill run up my spine. Nervously I cleared my throat. 'You said you wanted my help.'

She paused for a moment and then nodded.

'Yes.' She paused again and stared at me intently. 'You said that you were a writer.'

I nodded. 'Yes, that's right. I used to be. I find it hard now. The words don't seem to come any more. They have deserted me.' I smiled. 'I assume you haven't read my writing? You wouldn't have. It was quite popular once. Not enough to live off, but then who can write for a living in Lithuanian.'

'What did you write?'

'Historical fiction, mainly. *The Last Pagans. The Iron Wolf*? No?'

She shook her head, looking apologetic. She bent down and rummaged in the bag she had been carrying. For a moment I thought she was going to dig out the Conrad again. But she didn't. She pulled out a thick sheaf of papers and laid them carefully on the table. I looked at the paper questioningly. She smoothed the top sheet down and nudged them into order. She hesitated before speaking.

As she was about to speak the waiter emerged with the bottle of wine and she was forced to wait. He upturned two glasses on our table and proceeded to uncork the bottle. Carefully he poured a small amount of wine into my glass, taking care not to spill it, and waited for me to taste it. I nodded at him impatiently. He poured the two glasses with equal care, pedantically making sure they were level. Putting the bottle on the table he straightened up.

'Would there be anything else?'

I shook my head, irritated. 'No,' I said quite unpleasantly.

As he left Jolanta giggled. 'You shouldn't be impatient,' she said. 'He was trying very hard.' She took a sip of wine and then slowly pushed the papers towards me. I took them up and turned over the sheets. At the top of the second page I read 'Chapter One'. I looked at her inquisitively.

'It's my husband's, he's a writer,' she said quickly.

'Your husband is a writer?'

'Well, my husband is a student. He has almost finished his doctorate. But he has been working on this novel.'

I turned the pages slowly, casting my eyes across the lines. I was bemused. I had not imagined what help she had wanted from me, but still, this surprised me.

'Oh, don't read it now,' she said, leaning over the table slightly and placing her fingers onto the top of my hand. I let them rest there. She did not take them away. When I looked up she was smiling nervously. 'I'm sorry, I didn't mean to get you to read it now,' she explained.

'But you would like me to read it?' I asked.

She nodded. 'When you told me you were a writer, I got so excited,' she said. 'Kestutis hasn't shown it to anybody. He was working on it for over two years. Every night he would be sat up late in our room. I thought that he would drive me mad, typing away on an old typewriter, tap, tap, tap, all through the night.'

'Kestutis?' I interrupted her.

'My husband,' she said. 'He was obsessed. He wouldn't listen to me. He just sat there with a small light on, typing. But now he's finished he seems to have completely lost interest. He is a little ill, sometimes. I told him he should get it published, it might help, but he won't listen. He put it in a drawer. He won't speak about it. He says that it's no good.'

'Have you read it?' I asked.

She nodded again. 'When he was at the university I took it out and read it. I don't know.' She shook her head and pressed a palm to her forehead. 'To me it's really good,' she said after a pause. 'But he won't listen. He says I don't know anything about what's good and what isn't. Perhaps . . .' She hesitated. 'Perhaps if you could take some time to look over it?' She left the question hanging in the air.

The waiter re-emerged from behind the heavy wooden door carrying our dinners. I waited for him to serve us painfully correctly. Jolanta looked away from me, across the room at the other diners. She seemed tense. The muscles in her face were taut. I realised then that it had taken some courage for her to speak to me. That it was for this purpose that she had agreed to lunch with me. I softly stroked the page that rested on the top of the pile and smiled, remembering the feel of her delicate fingers on the back of my hand.

'Well, certainly I can read it,' I said. 'If you think that my comments will be of any value.'

'Well, you are a writer, you know what is good writing, what is publishable and what isn't?' she said.

She was looking at me beseechingly. I gazed into her eyes. Yes, this was what I had wanted. Ever since I had caught a glimpse of those eyes in the church I had been filled with the desire to see them turned on me as they had been before, so many years before. I had to pick up from that moment and carry on. I had to make the long journey back across the years, to find that moment and twist the course of our histories. I would not turn my back on those eyes once more. I would no longer feel them pleading to my back as they had done for the last five decades. I took her hand between my own and smiled.

'Of course I will look at it. I will see if this husband of yours is a genius or not. Whether we have here another Donelaitis, another Shakespeare. And I will tell you truthfully what I think. That is the least I can do. More than that,' I continued, 'I don't have that many contacts left in the publishing world, but there are still one or two. I'm not entirely forgotten,' I laughed. 'And I promise you that if I think it is worth while I will try my best to get it published. No, don't thank me,' I said, holding up my hand. 'It really is the least that I can do.'

The tension had disappeared from her face. She smiled at me, relieved.

'You must think it very odd a stranger coming to you with a request such as this,' she said.

'On the contrary,' I said. 'It feels quite natural. In fact you do not feel a bit like a stranger to me. It feels like I have known you for fifty years.'

She laughed brightly. 'I don't think so.'

'No,' I said then, ruefully. 'How old are you? Can an old man ask that question without it seeming ungallant?'

'Twenty-four,' she said.

I nodded my head. 'Well,' I said, 'perhaps we should eat?'

When she left I found a small café in the ghetto and drank glass after glass of vodka. I opened the manuscript she had given me, spreading the pages carefully across the surface of the table. My eyes flicked across the lines of text, but they jumped from word to word unable to take in the sense. And then a phrase caught me. The passage was about a young man serving in the Soviet army in Afghanistan. I read. 'Morality: In some other world – some other landscape – that word might yet resonate with meaning. But here there is only the need to survive. I hold your letter as though it will anchor me, but outside I can hear the crackle of flames and the sound of crying and know that I am lost.'

At that moment somebody stumbled against me, grabbing drunkenly at my sleeve as he slipped to the floor. I gathered the papers together and put them into a plastic bag; it was not the time to read it. I filled my glass and gazed out through the window into the darkness. His words echoed softly at the back of my mind. I drank quickly, refilling my glass as soon as it was drained. I fumbled over my cigarettes.

After the Great Patriotic War I had turned from poetry to write my first novel, struggling to bridge with narrative the fissure that had opened in our lives. I nudged the manuscript in its blue sheath. There was something haunting about the few phrases I had read, they traced their fingers through the silted backwaters of my mind, loosening earth. A light mist arose from the ground, clouding my eyes. A spasm of fear pinched my heart. I drank quickly, muffling the dull ache in my chest.

As I attempted to pull out a cigarette, the packet dropped to the floor, scattering its contents. I bent to collect them and lost my balance. The young waiter caught me. He lifted me carefully back into my seat.

'Bring me another bottle,' I said. He shook his head and refused to serve me more. He told me I had had enough. He was polite about it. I told him that I would tell him when I had had enough. Though he remained polite, I became belligerent.

I staggered home to my apartment. Grigalaviciene banged on the wall. I could hear her shouting shame on me. I took out the bottle of cranberry spirits and poured a large glass. I downed the first glass too quickly, so I poured a second. Her eyes danced in front of mine. Her large, dark eyes, like ripe figs, like almonds, like black cherries hanging from the tree about to burst from their skins.

Rachael, I shouted. Rachael, Rachael, Rachael. I opened the window and bellowed her name out into the night. I bellowed, hoping my voice would carry across the square, across the tops of the trees to Eliyahu, my friend Elijah, stony silent in his place at the top of Zydu Street. Rachael. Who else could I call that name to? Who else could I talk to but him?

I decided then to go and speak to him. But I was not able to get to the front door. I crumpled on the thin carpet. The empty bottle of spirits smashed on the wooden floor over the carpet's edge. I lay on the floor and listened to Grigalaviciene banging and cursing me. It was not till I awoke the following morning, stiff and ill, that I realised I had left the manuscript at the café the night before.

Chapter 9

When I woke I could not move. I lay in my bed shivering beneath the sheets, my head thumping, nauseous. Through the scattered thoughts that blew around in my head like scraps of newspaper in a derelict house, one fact assailed me with horrible clarity, the missing manuscript. When was it that I had let go of it? Where? My mind could not put together any logical sequence of events; it could only blow around that monument, the loss.

I watched the hours drag by on the clock by my bed. I counted them off, hoping that as they crawled on I would feel better, that the shaking would pass, the nausea would go, the thumping in my skull would soften. The sunlight rose and moved across the faded wallpaper. My neighbours stirred. The lorry came for the rubbish, its horn howling, sending my head beneath the sheets. Dusk came, resolved into darkness. I dozed, dreaming continually. Wild chaotic dreams that made my pulse race. Finally night settled onto the city once more. I managed some sleep, but by four I was awake again.

I dragged myself from my bed and sat in an easy chair close to the window to continue my watch. So it is with the old and lonely, we sit and watch ourselves through the night in our times of sickness. When light came at last, I shuffled into the small kitchen in my bathrobe and managed to eat a small slice of bread and cheese. The cheese was old and hard, and, on examination, mould was beginning to fur the bread crust. The food strengthened me a little, but still I was not fit to go out. I slumped once more into the chair by the window and stared out at the tops of the trees and the sky.

At eight o'clock there was a short rap on the door. I looked up. Irrationally I immediately supposed it was her. My heart thumped wildly. I sat petrified in my chair. After a few seconds the rapping was repeated. It could not have been her, she did not have my address. I shuffled over to the door.

'Who is it?' I shouted. My voice sounded strange to my ears, it had been so many hours since I had last heard it.

'It's me,' a voice replied. Grigalaviciene. I fumbled with the lock thankfully. She looked in at me through the doorway.

'You're still alive?' she said, looking like she had sniffed something foul.

'As you can see,' I said, quite jovially, attempting to indicate with a sweep of my hand how vigorous I still was. My hand hit the open door, bruising my knuckle.

Grigalaviciene pushed into the apartment, propelling me with her hand against the wall. I did not stop her. She nosed around like a suspicious dog.

'We were wondering,' she said caustically. 'What with all the fuss you were causing the other night.'

I did not answer. I closed the door and, cradling my knuckles in the palm of my other hand, followed her into the apartment. She picked up my waste bin, which was overflowing.

'You missed the rubbish van,' she reprimanded.

'I wasn't feeling too well,' I said.

'Shouldn't wonder,' she said without a smile.

Grigalaviciene was probably younger than me. She did not like me to think this though. She was perhaps seventy, but it was hard to place her, she could have been anything from sixty to eighty-five. She had lived in these apartments at least as long as I had. She was not married. Maybe she had been once, but that had been a long time ago. I studied her wrinkled, sour face. Her lips were puckered up, giving her the expression of continual prudish distaste. She was wearing a pink housecoat.

'When you didn't appear yesterday we thought you'd really gone and done it,' she said. She had made her way to the kitchen and put a small pan of water onto the stove. 'I was just saying to old Adamkiene, it looks like Daumantas really has overdone it this time. Did you hear him? she says to me. How could I not hear him? I said, shouting like that for everybody to hear. I don't know.' She shook her head. When the water boiled she spooned two generous heaps of Russian tea into a couple of cups and poured on the water. I stood in the doorway of the small kitchen watching her, a little amused, though her voice was not helping my headache.

'Here,' she said, turning with the steaming cup. 'Drink this. I bet you haven't any shopping in, have you?' She pulled open the cupboard doors and tutted over the crumbs and empty shelves.

'What do I want shopping for?' I said, taking the cup.

'You don't need to eat?' she spat at me.

'I buy what I need for the day. What's the point in getting more?' I wandered back to the front room and let myself down into my chair.

'And today you don't need anything?' Grigalaviciene said, following me, slurping her hot tea noisily.

'It's just after eight, I haven't had the chance to get out yet.'

She grunted derisively. I watched as she pottered around the room, tidying it. She picked up items of clothing and hung them neatly over the backs of chairs. She straightened the carpets and took a small dustpan and brush and collected the fragments of glass from the bottle I had broken two nights earlier. All this she did clicking her tongue angrily and muttering to herself. A little irritated I said, 'If you're talking to me, you'd better speak up because I can't hear you.'

She turned angrily, brandishing the dustpan full of glass. 'It's not enough that I have to clear up my own apartment, I have to come up and clear up after your drunken orgies.'

'I never asked you to,' I said belligerently, my head sore.

'I'm just supposed to watch you killing yourself, am I?' she shot back. 'That would be a good Christian attitude, wouldn't it!' She marched off into the kitchen and emptied the glass into some newspaper, which she folded carefully before putting it into a plastic bag. 'You're going to have to wait till tomorrow for the rubbish,' she called from the kitchen.

'I know when the rubbish van comes,' I said.

She wandered back out of the kitchen rubbing her hands. 'Well, it's a bit tidier now. That'll have to do for the moment. I'm busy, I can't go chasing round after you all day long. I'll pop down to the shops later to get a few groceries.'

'You don't need to,' I said.

She grunted derisively again, as though I was an imbecile. She poked about on my desk, rooting among the papers.

'What are you after there?' I asked.

'Where do you keep your money?'

'I'm not telling you where I keep my money.'

'Suit yourself, you can pay me when I come back.'

I sighed, irritated, and pulled out my wallet. I took a creased five Litas note out and tossed it to her. 'Here. Just buy some bread and milk.'

She picked up the note and poked it into her pocket. As she turned to leave she noticed the pictures of the women on the wall.

'What's all this then?' she asked, her voice alive with the expectation of gossip.

'Nothing for you,' I said angrily.

'Nuh!' she said, nose in the air, and shuffled off to the door not looking back.

'Grigalaviciene!' I called as she disappeared through the door.

'What is it?' she shouted back, not reappearing.

'Thank you,' I called testily. She grunted.

Chapter 10

As I sat in my chair by the window, watching the build-up of clouds, the hours passed slowly. The thought of the missing manuscript gnawed at me. I had arranged to meet Jolanta for lunch at the Filharmonija café on Thursday. That gave me two days.

Hour after hour I paced the floor of my apartment. I half thought about sending Grigaviciene out to the café, but in the end decided not to. By early evening I could stand it no longer. Despite the shaking of my hands I pulled on a thick coat, buttoned it up to my chin and left the apartment. The stairs seemed unusually steep and perilous and I had difficulty descending them. I clung tightly to the banister, my eyes straining at the steps in the dim light of the stairwell. Hearing my door, Grigaviciene poked her head out.

'Where are you going?' she asked.

'Mind your own business,' I told her.

'You trying to kill yourself or what?'

'I'm just going for a walk.'

'You're not in any fit state to go wandering around in the darkness,' she said. I noticed something akin to concern in her rough voice. I sighed and carried on down the stairs.

'Don't blame me if you kill yourself,' she shouted, slamming the door behind her.

The night was not cold but I could not stop shivering. My legs felt weak and my head ached. I pressed slowly on through the dark narrow streets of the ghetto towards the café at the corner of Pilies Street, where I had been drinking. The streets were quiet. The café, though, when I got there, was quite busy. Mainly young students drinking beer. The air was thick with smoke and the smell of coffee and cakes. I pushed through the chairs to the counter where a harassed young woman dashed from the coffee machine to the cake stand and back.

'Yes?' she said as I got to the front of the queue, displaying none of the new manners the West had brought. I hesitated a moment. Behind me the queue had grown longer, stretching back to the door. I felt a hand against my back.

'Two nights ago,' I began. 'I was drinking here.'

'What do you want?' the young woman cut in.

'I left something here,' I tried to continue. 'I left a bag here, a plastic bag. It had papers in it.'

'I'm sorry, I don't know anything about that,' she said annoyed. 'Do you want something or not?'

The hand against my back had become more persistent in its pressure. From farther back in the queue I heard a young male voice calling, 'Come on, granddad.'

'It's very important,' I said.

'I'm sorry,' the young woman said again. 'I don't know anything about it.' Her eyes had already started to wander to the customers behind me. Feeling helpless, I quickly ordered a coffee. As she stood at the machine making it, I continued, 'I think the bag was blue. It is very important, it didn't actually belong to me.' But she could not hear anyway above the explosive splutters of the coffee machine. She slopped the coffee down in front of me.

'Litas,' she said, and while I fumbled for my wallet she had already turned to the couple behind me with an apology. I laid the crumpled note on the counter and took my coffee. In the corner there was a seat and I made my way over there. A sweat had broken out on my face and I felt faint and sick. My hands shook so much, as I crossed the crowded room, that still more of the drink slopped over the side of the small cup into the saucer. At the table I slumped into the metal chair and rested my head in my hands. I closed my eyes and tried to stop my head swimming. After a couple of minutes the nausea began to subside. I felt exhausted.

It had been a mistake to come to the café at this hour; it was crowded. As one group left, another pushed in loudly through the doors. I glanced at my watch. It was eight o'clock. I sipped the coffee slowly, hoping that the crowd might thin out, taking some strain off the girl behind the counter.

By nine business in the café seemed no less hectic and I was beginning to despair. I knew that it would be sensible to go back home and come again in the morning, when things would be quieter. My eyes had been on the young woman behind the counter continually. She did not stop. Her long hair was tied back neatly, but as time wore on, strands came loose and flapped across her face. Perspiration shone on her forehead. Occasionally she forced a smile for a customer but otherwise her expression was strictly businesslike. It was a bit of a surprise therefore to see a real broad smile cross her face when the door pushed open just after nine, setting the small bell tinkling once more. Following her gaze my eyes jumped over to the doorway. A young man entered, his dark hair swept back, a scarf flung around his neck. He waved to the girl across the heads of the customers. It took me a few moments to recognise him.

He made his way to the back of the café and disappeared through a doorway. The girl called out to him as he disappeared and he shouted something back I could not hear above the noise of the chatter. My heart jumped with a spasm of joy and relief. I got up and pushed through the chairs and tables, excusing myself. Passing the counter I made for the door through which the young man had disappeared.

'Hey!' the girl called after me. 'You can't go in there.' She leapt out and grabbed me before I managed to push through the door. I tried to shrug myself free, but she held my sleeve tightly.

'Where do you want to go?' she asked. Recognition flickered across her face as she looked at me. A wearied, intolerant tone inflected her voice. 'That door is for staff only. If it's the toilet you want, it's out through there.' She indicated the direction with an impatient sweep of her hand. 'I'll get you the key.'

'It's not the toilet I want,' I said, equally impatiently. 'I need to speak to that young man.'

'What young man?' She frowned. The perspiration on her forehead glittered in the harsh light. She was so close I could feel the heat of her body.

'The young man that just walked through these doors,' I said. 'I must speak with him.'

'Gintas?'

At that moment Gintas appeared, looking clean and fresh in a white shirt. He stopped short seeing the two of us, there, in the small passageway. The young woman looked at him relieved.

'Everything OK?' Gintas asked.

'He says that he wants to speak to you,' the young woman said, rolling her eyes, not caring that I saw.

'Really?' he said, puzzled.

'You were working here two nights ago,' I told him. 'I was in here having a drink or two.' I recalled, as I said this, his politeness in the face of my abuse. I felt a blush of shame pass up across my face. I pressed on. There was no indication in his eyes that he remembered me. 'I left something very important here, in a bag. It was a blue bag, plastic. Inside there was a manuscript. You see, it wasn't mine. It's very important that I get it back. A young girl gave it to me to read.' I tailed off, seeing the confused look in his eyes.

'I'm sorry.' He shook his head. 'I don't recall there being anything left.'

I grabbed his arm desperately. He was a little taken aback by this but remained polite. He gently removed my arm. I let it drop.

'I'm sorry,' I said. 'Only this means so much to me.' Suddenly, feeling the hopelessness of it all, I turned to leave.

'Wait,' the young man stopped me. 'Last night, you said?'

'No,' I said. 'Two nights ago.' I paused. The young man obviously wanted to help and was searching around fruitlessly in his memory.

'I had too much to drink,' I said.

He laughed. 'A lot of people have too much to drink here.'

'You told me I had had enough. I told you that I would tell you when I had had enough. I was unpleasant. I'm sorry about that.'

The young man's face suddenly lit up. Then he frowned. 'I remember,' he said, clapping me on the shoulder. 'You're right, you were a bit unpleasant.' He laughed.

'And do you remember the bag?' I asked quickly.

He thought. But then he shook his head again. 'No, I'm sorry. I don't remember any bag.' But he caught my arm. 'Listen, I'm not really the person you should be speaking to. I don't really do any cleaning up here after hours. You should speak to the cleaning staff.'

'Are they here now?' I asked.

He shook his head. 'Jonas comes in the morning. Come here at about eight in the morning and you're bound to catch him. If anybody knows, he will.'

'Jonas? Do you have an address?'

The young man began to look a little impatient.

'Or just a telephone number?' I said, desperately. 'This is important.'

He thought for a moment, and then sighed. 'Fine, wait a moment, I will get his number for you.' He walked over to the counter. I saw the young woman address him, nodding her head in my direction. He pulled out a small book from under the counter and wrote a number down on a menu pad.

'Thank you,' I said as he pressed it into my hand.

Chapter 11

When I dialled the number, later that evening, from my apartment, nobody answered. I stared at the large black receiver, willing a response, but after listening to it ringing for minutes on end I finally dropped it back into its cradle. I went to bed early and tossed around before falling into a deep sleep. In the morning I awoke feeling much better.

At eight Grigalaviciene banged on the door again. I opened it and let her in. She had a parcel of goods in her hands that she bustled through to the kitchen.

'I was at the market this morning,' she explained. 'I thought I would get you one or two things to save you the bother.'

'It's no bother for me,' I said, but, feeling brighter, added, 'thank you.'

She clicked her tongue at this uncalled-for pleasantry. Not acknowledging my thanks, she turned and appraised me with her sharp old eyes. 'Well, you're certainly looking a bit better this morning.'

'I feel it,' I said, thumping my chest.

'*Nu*, well, you don't deserve it,' she said, making her way to the door.

'What do I owe you for the vegetables?' I asked.

'Ten,' she said.

I fished in my wallet and gave her a note.

'Oh,' she said as she left. 'You had a visitor last night, while you were out.'

'I did?'

'A woman,' she said pointedly.

My heart faltered. 'A woman?' I asked. Jolanta. Could it have been? How could it have been? I thought. My mind raced as Grigalaviciene stood there coyly holding back her information. What other woman would come to visit me? Was it so hard, after all, to find out where I lived? I was in the telephone book.

'A young woman?' I asked.

Grigalaviciene pursed her lips and narrowed her eyes. 'Young? You wanting young women to come visit, are you?' she said. 'Well, she was younger than me, but, *nu*, most are.'

'For goodness' sake,' I said impatiently.

'She wasn't so young you should be getting so excited about it,' Grigalaviciene said disdainfully. 'Svetlana, she said her name was.' She shook her head and wiped her hands against the faded apron she wore, as if wiping the dirt of my business from her.

'Svetlana?' For a moment I was startled.

'I don't know what you're up to and I don't want to know,' Grigalaviciene said, standing in the hallway outside my door, looking hungry for gossip.

'I'm not up to anything,' I said, irritated. 'What did she want?'

'As I said, I'm not a one for prying into your business.'

'Did she say what she wanted?'

'I've got better things to do with my time.'

'What did she want?' I shouted.

A look of fury crossed her old face then. The creases tightened and her mouth set in an angry straight line. 'She didn't say what she wanted and I didn't ask,' she spat out. 'And in future don't go loading all your dirty business on me. It's enough having to put up with your drinking and the fear of what violence you might do, without—'

A roar of rage sprang from my own throat and Grigalaviciene, frightened, scuttled away to her own apartment. I heard the two sets of doors slam and the sound of locks turning. I slammed my own door.

When I telephoned the number again that morning, a timid woman's voice answered. It was Jonas' daughter. Her father, she told me, was at work and would not be back till lunch. She did not know about a bag and said I would have to talk to her father about it. She agreed hesitantly to take a message. I left my name and telephone number with her.

Slipping on my jacket I made my way once more down the stairs and across the parking lot to Jewish Street. The sun was out and the sky was a brilliant cobalt. The spires of the churches shone. The oppressive weight that had been lying on my heart lifted slightly. But a hot flush passed over my face at the mere thought of telling Jolanta I had lost the manuscript when I met her for lunch the next day.

The café was closed and there seemed little sign of activity. The streets were busy. Tradesmen were setting out their stalls of amber trinkets to sell to the tourists, and students wandered to the university. I peered into the darkness of the café. The window was dirty and I could see little through it. The doors were locked and would not shift an inch when I tried them. I sighed and pressed my nose against them, banging as loudly as I could with my fist.

'There something you want?' A voice from behind startled me. I turned. A man with a heavily scarred face stood on the pavement holding a broom in his hand.

'I'm looking for the cleaner here,' I explained.

'Oh yes?' the man grunted. He cocked his head sideways as he spoke to me, as though he had difficulty hearing me through his left ear.

'Do you know him?' I asked. 'His name is Jonas.'

'Might do,' the man said, looking shifty. 'Depends.'

Not wanting to explain my business to a stranger I was a little annoyed at the man's obtuse approach.

'What does it depend on?' I asked sharply.

He shifted his broom from one hand to the other and wiped his brow with his sleeve. He leaned closer and I could smell his foul breath. I leaned away slightly. 'It depends on what you're wanting him for.'

One of his eyes strayed around a little loosely while the other pinned me suspiciously.

'When I was here a couple of nights ago,' I said, 'I left a bag behind. I asked the staff last night, but they said that this Jonas would be the one who picked it up.'

He nodded. 'Well, that'll be me you're wanting then.' He looked up into the sky, thoughtfully. 'A bag, you say.' He rubbed a thick finger along the heavy scar across his cheek. 'What kind of a bag might it have been?' His eye fixed me again.

'It was a plastic bag. Just an ordinary bag, one of these new supermarket ones. It had some papers inside. A whole lot of paper.'

The eye did not leave me now. He seemed to be considering whether I was joking. He breathed his foul breath over me, edging a little closer. 'You're telling me you're looking for a plastic bag full of paper?' he said. 'Paper?'

'It was important,' I said impatiently, not wanting to have to go into a full-scale explanation. 'They were documents,' I said, pronouncing the word with great gravity.

'Oh, ah,' he said, fingering the scar again. '*Nu*, well, if they were documents, then I understand,' he said. 'Documents,' he repeated to himself, savouring the word. '*Nu*, so they were documents that have gone missing, eh? Well!'

I waited, hoping his ruminations were leading somewhere. 'So?' I asked finally. 'Did you find them?'

He was startled by the aggression with which I spoke to

him. He stepped back, wiping his hands on his dirty jacket. 'Did I find your documents? Well, I don't know if I did. What night did you say it was?'

I told him.

'No, no,' he said, shaking his head. 'A plastic bag you say? No, I don't think so. But wait.' A thought struck him. He looked around to see that nobody was listening. He leaned forward, forcing me further back into the doorway. 'There was a bag the other day,' he whispered, conspiratorially. My heart leaped. Noticing my joy he seemed heartened. He nodded his head enthusiastically. 'Yes, yes, there was one,' he said, excited. He gripped my arm. 'Wait!' And he held up one of his spade-like fingers. He turned and disappeared around the side of the building. I followed him.

A short dark alley-way led around the side of the café. The alley-way gave out onto a small courtyard. On the left of the courtyard bins overflowed outside the back door of the café. Wooden walkways sagged around the second floor of the bare brick buildings. The courtyard was cobbled. Weeds and grass grew through the cobbles, pushing them up. Whilst the street had been smartly plastered and painted, these courtyards remained untouched. They lay in sad neglect, falling slowly to pieces as the whole city, only a few years before, had been.

Jonas ducked inside a doorway. I stood on the uneven cobbles, waiting, relieved. The next day opened rosily before me. We would lunch at the new café opposite the Filharmonija. I would be able to give her my opinion of her husband's writing. I would be able to watch her across the table. The way her dark hair fell over her shoulder when she let it loose. The way her elegant fingers rested on the table. And those eyes. I would feel the slight pressure of our feet under the table.

Jonas reappeared from the café doorway, grinning hideously. In his hand he held a large plastic bag with a semi-naked woman printed on the side. He held it up to me with a flourish, his good eye glinting in the dull light of the courtyard. 'There!' he declared.

'That's not it!' I cried, sagging with disappointment. The idiotic grin on his face made me angry. He regarded me nervously, noticing my anger and disappointment.

'No?' he said, crestfallen.

'No!' I shouted at him. I took the bag from him and emptied its contents with one fierce shake. A pair of old shoes bounced on the cobbles and lay among the weeds. Jonas looked at them stupidly.

In my disappointed fury I felt like beating him, and if I had been younger I might have given in to the impulse. He hobbled around in his old ripped shoes, red-faced. It took only moments for him to recover, however, and then he swore and shook his fist in my face. I demanded he tell me where he kept lost property. It soon became clear that it was dealt with according to its value. If it was something he felt to be useful he took it home, the rest was thrown away. I had little doubt as to the fate of my bag.

'No, no' He shook his head. 'Describe it again,' he said. 'A blue bag, the other morning.' He shook his head again. 'I certainly didn't throw it into the bin. I would have remembered.'

I left him scratching his scar ruminatively.

'If I come across it,' he shouted after me, 'who should I call?'

I stopped. There was little hope of it appearing. I turned, though, and taking a pencil from my jacket pocket wrote my telephone number on a scrap of paper. Holding it up in front of his good eye he examined it, then nodded.

'I'll look around today,' he assured me. 'You never know, it might turn up.' He tucked the scrap of paper into his shirt pocket. I turned then and left with no hope.

Be that as it may, for the rest of the day I did not go out. I hung around the apartment, my ear cocked for the telephone. The minutes dragged like hours and the hours were endless. The telephone sat like a squat, dark toad in the corner but failed to croak. By nine p.m. he had not rung. I kicked around the kitchen drinking brandy from the bottle, taking measured sips despite my desperation.

Had I really expected he would call? At nine thirty I approached the toad and grabbed it firmly. I dialled the number on the small menu sheet.

The receiver buzzed in my ear. On the third buzz it was snatched up. Distantly I heard the sound of shouting. A young woman's voice came on the line. It was the same girl I had spoken to earlier. I asked for her father. Dropping the receiver onto a hard surface, causing it to echo sharply in my ear, she shouted. Moments later Jonas grunted into the phone. I noted at once that he was drunk.

'Daumantas,' I said.

'Who?' he shouted down the line, aggressively.

'Daumantas,' I repeated, enunciating each syllable with pedantic care. 'We spoke this morning. The bag?'

'What?' Jonas shouted back, stupidly. 'What the hell are you talking about?' He turned his mouth only slightly from the mouthpiece to shout back into his own apartment. 'Turn that music down! *Blyad!*' The line clicked and then growled in my ear. I slammed my receiver back onto its squat body.

Chapter 12

Aware that it was almost twelve, the time we had arranged to meet, I trudged slowly up Castle Street. I could not force myself to walk faster. With each step I longed to turn back and make my way home; I could not face telling her I had lost the manuscript. Somewhere a church bell began to toll and the sound rolled across the rooftops. I glanced at my watch; it was twelve o'clock exactly. I hurried a little then, not wanting to be too late, but the streets were crowded and it took a good ten minutes to reach the Filharmonija. As I drew closer I glanced ahead gloomily to the restaurant where we were due to dine. Tables had been placed outside and the wind caught the edge of their cloths, lifting them, revealing legs suggestively. I braced myself and, like a man on the way to the gallows, forced my feet on.

The small restaurant was bustling with activity. I glanced around the diners, searching out her face; hoping, fearing, I would see her. I sat by the window, close to the door. Not studying the menu, I gazed out past the brightly blooming window boxes. It was quarter past twelve. I rehearsed my speech.

Late the previous evening, after my call to Jonas had convinced me there was no hope left, I realised I would have to tell her. I had half entertained the idea of pretending I still had the manuscript, explaining that I had not yet had the chance to read more than a few paragraphs of it, but that what I had read was good, that it had caught my imagination, the idea of the moral dislocation of war. It would be a good excuse to meet her again. But it would only delay the inevitable. The bag was not going to reappear. I could not doubt her response: disgust and fury at an old drunkard.

No waiter came to serve me. I watched for her. She had been late for our previous meeting, I remembered. Where was she? Another bookshop? I pictured her looking at her watch, suddenly noticing the time. Rushing out.

An unoccupied waiter strolled over. Not taking out a pad to write my order, he raised his eyebrows, questioningly, hands in his pockets. I glanced at my watch. Half past twelve. I hesitated.

'I'm waiting for somebody,' I said finally. 'I'll wait until she comes. She won't be long now.'

He turned away, unconcerned. The street looked dismal and cold. Thick clouds had rolled rapidly over the city; the wind whipped the skirts of the tables viciously. A rose toppled over. The couple sitting outside called for their bill and hurried off. I found a cigarette and lit it. The blue smoke curled away above me, caught on a warm stream of air coming from a heater close to my feet. There was no sign of her.

She had still not appeared by one o'clock. I worried. I hadn't for a moment considered that she would not meet me, my nervousness over the lost manuscript had erased any other worries from my mind. My eyes searched the street. Twice a minute I glanced at my watch. Where could she be? Not late. Not this late. I beckoned the waiter.

'There hasn't been a message left for me?'

He shook his head.

'Perhaps you could ask at the counter?' I said.

Irritation passed like a swift cloud across his face. He straightened up, however.

'What name?' he asked curtly.

'Daumantas,' I said. 'Steponas Daumantas. I was expecting to meet a lady called Jolanta.'

'Jolanta?' he asked.

'Yes, Jolanta,' I said flushing with embarrassment; I did not know her surname.

He smirked and traipsed away slowly. Leaning against the counter he joked with the girl. She shook her head. Not bothering to walk back across to where I sat he shook his head at me, then continued his conversation with the girl.

When I realised she would not be coming I ordered a drink. It had started to rain and the wind took the drops and threw them against the glass. The waiters ran outside and gathered up the tables and chairs. Emptiness replaced my fear. I wished she would come. Gladly now I would confess my carelessness; would have those beautiful eyes reproach me.

Gladly I would have seen her elegant fingers tremble on the tablecloth between us. I would take them between my own thick, clumsy fingers and beg her to forgive me. Allow her to think what she would of me, only to see those eyes. How were we to meet again? I did not know her address or telephone number and she did not know mine.

Leaving the restaurant I set out quickly in the direction of Gedimino. My first inclination was to get a trolley bus up to Karoliniškiu. I hesitated after a few steps though. Who was to say why she had not come. And what was I to do, go banging on all the doors in her block? How would I explain to her how I knew where she lived? No, it would not do. Tired and confused I stood in the road. I knew I should be sensible and make my way back to my apartment but the thought of sitting alone in the darkness filled me with horror. I wandered slowly along the gutter, knowing with a bleak sense of inevitability I would end up in a bar getting drunk.

As I wandered, however, I remembered that Svetlana had paid me a visit the previous evening while I had been out. I was puzzled as to what she had wanted. She knew where

I lived as on some occasions I had asked her to drop my clean shirts off at my apartment. She had never, though, been to my apartment for any other reason. It was possible, I thought, that she was in need of money. Not that she would have come begging. She was proud despite her difficulties. She might have come to see if I had need of her services.

The idea of going to see her restored a certain amount of purpose. I hurried back to my apartment to collect some shirts for Svetlana to clean. They were not really dirty and I could not afford to have them cleaned too frequently, but I needed someone to talk to. I threw the shirts into a plastic bag, making sure the bag was a good strong one with an attractive picture on it. I had to crumple one of the shirts to make it look as if it needed her work.

I hurried back through the old ghetto to Stepono Street, with its crumbling, decaying buildings and rutted cobbles. Plaster peeled from the walls and grass grew in the guttering. Ahead of me, turning out from Svetlana's courtyard, was a familiar figure. For a few moments I could not place who it was. The man crossed the street, limping slightly, his shoulders hunched. He had disappeared around the corner before I realised it was Jonas, the cleaner.

The cold, blustery weather made the buildings more dismal than ever. The wind drove the rain against the little glass panes in the windows, blowing back the rags and paper covering the gaps where the glass had broken. Plaster dropped in heaps onto the broken paving slabs. I bent beneath the sagging walkway and knocked on the door. Waiting, I tried to shield myself from the wind, which eddied around the courtyard. Behind the door I heard noises, but for some time nobody answered. I banged on the door again. It shook beneath my fist.

'Svetlana?' I called.

'What do you want?' a male voice answered irritably.

'I'm looking for Svetlana,' I called. There was further shuffling behind the door and then, finally, the sound of a key turning in the lock. The door scraped open and in the darkness I saw the face of a man, perhaps in his fifties. He was unshaven and his hair was matted and dirty. He wore a coat. His puffy face was a raw shade of red.

'She isn't here,' he said, leaning against the doorjamb. He looked me up and down reflectively.

'When will she be back?'

He coughed, a rasping cough that racked his thin frame. 'How do I know?' he growled.

'She didn't say?' I persisted.

He did not answer. He did not even look at me. He scuffed his ragged sports shoes against the doorjamb.

'I've got work for her,' I said, indicating the bag I was carrying. He looked up then.

'Where's the money?' he said.

'I pay her when they're done,' I said.

He pushed out a hand. 'Give me the money now and I'll give it her.'

'I don't know.'

'No money, no work!' His voice rose, setting him off into a paroxysm of coughs, doubling him up.

'You're her husband?' I asked, when he had managed to half straighten up.

He nodded his head. 'Yeah, I am. So, you can trust me and give me the money.'

I gave him the bag of washing and pulled out a few Litas.

'This is for you, if you give the washing to Svetlana. Tell her that Steponas Daumantas left it. If she brings it around to my apartment I will pay her a little extra,' I said.

'She'll do it,' he said, nodding his head. He had grabbed hold of the money and stuffed it into his pocket.

Before he closed the door, I asked, 'A man called Jonas didn't just call here, did he?'

For a long moment he looked at me without answering. Then he said, 'Yes he did, if it's got anything to do with you.' His voice was so threatening I did not ask anything further.

'The quicker she can get the shirts done the better,' I said. But he had closed the door and was locking it behind him. I trudged home.

As I pulled off my shirt, about to go to bed, the telephone rang. I answered it quickly.

'Daumantas?' a man's voice asked.

'Yes.'

'Jonas, here.'

'Yes, I recognised your voice.'

'I've got something that might interest you,' he said. His voice trembled slightly, excited. Or maybe drunk.

'Really?'

'Well, I say I . . .'

'What have you got?' I asked, impatient. 'Did you find it? Did you find the bag?'

'You were looking for some papers, yes?' he said. 'A kind of book that you had written?'

'Yes,' I said, my heart lifting with joy. 'You've found it? That's wonderful!'

'Hey, hey, hold on. Don't go jumping the gun. I didn't say I found nothing.'

'Well, have you or haven't you?' I asked angrily.

'You want to talk about it, I suggest we have a meeting,' he said. 'You know the Red and Black?'

'Yes,' I said, annoyed and bewildered by his opaqueness.

'Meet me there, tomorrow. Eleven thirty.'

'You'll bring . . .' I began, but the telephoned growled in my ear. I dialled his number. The telephone rang. It rang and rang but nobody answered. Excited and annoyed I went to bed.

Chapter 13

At eleven thirty I sat in the Red and Black cradling a brandy. The whole night I had tossed and turned, unable to sleep. When finally, just before dawn, I managed to drop off, I dreamt a series of very vivid dreams. The first was of Jolanta. We were sitting at a table in the restaurant opposite the Filharmonija. She was angry. 'How could you have lost it?' she said. Over and again she said this. I insisted, 'I have not lost it, Jonas has it.' But my words made little difference. After this I dreamt of Rachael. She did not speak but there was no anger in her eyes. She looked at me and I wanted to turn from her but I could not. Her eyes cut deep. By the time Jonas pushed open the door and limped into the bar I was tired and angry.

He nodded, seeing me, and limped over to the bar. He ordered himself a drink and came over with it. Sliding into the seat opposite me, he winked. His breath reeked of vodka; he had obviously been drinking already.

'Well?' I said, seeing that he carried no bag.

He raised his glass. 'Maybe we should toast to good business?' he said.

'I wasn't aware that a missing bag was business,' I said sharply.

'Ah, there you go, you see,' said Jonas, a lop-sided grin disfiguring his face. 'You have a need, the bag, I have a way of satisfying your need. That is business. That is what we have been learning from the West, isn't it? Capitalism!' He raised his small glass. 'To the West and capitalism,' he laughed.

I did not lift my glass. 'Are you telling me that you have the bag?' I asked.

'Yes,' he said. 'Let's get down to business, no time for chit chat. Here we are then. I know where your bag is.'

'You know where it is?'

'Yes!' he said, the same idiotic grin twisting his face.

'And where is it?'

'Ah!' He tapped his nose. 'I don't actually have the bag. If I did, of course I wouldn't be here bargaining with you.' He paused. 'However, the person that does have it says that if you want it so bad then you'll be happy to pay for it.' He shrugged his shoulders, as if such logic was alien to him.

'How much?' I sighed, reaching for my wallet.

'One hundred dollars,' he said without hesitation, fixing me with his eye. He downed his vodka and shuffled out of his seat. Indicating the empty glass he limped off to the bar. I leaned back in my chair. When he returned, he raised his glass to toast me once more, cheerfully, as if his bargain was the most reasonable that could have been expected.

'You are expecting me to pay one hundred dollars for a plastic bag and some paper?' I asked, incredulously.

He shrugged his shoulders again. 'I tried to argue him down, but that was his final price,' he said, reasonably.

'Who has it?' I demanded.

'Ah, well, I can't tell you that,' he said. 'Wish that I could, but he said absolutely not.'

'Tell me!' I said, my voice rising to a shout, blood rushing to my face. 'Tell me who has it, Jonas.'

He grinned. The barman glanced over, cleaning glasses, not too concerned.

'You don't need to shout,' he said. 'You don't want to go behaving like that.'

'I'll be doing more if you don't get me that manuscript back,' I hissed.

He shook his head, the sly grin slipping uncontrollably across his face. 'You should be careful getting so worked up at your age,' he smirked, 'it's no good for your heart.' He got up to leave. 'Call me if you're interested in getting the papers.'

Boarding the trolley bus on Gedimino, I sat down heavily. I ran a hand through my hair. My anger at Jonas was tempered only by my anxiety over Jolanta. My concern for the manuscript was not as strong as the fear that I would never see her again. The trolley bus crawled through the morning traffic. Rain patterned the windows and wind tussled the trees. Two women talked quietly, moaning about prices. Crossing the river, the trolley bus climbed the steep hill between the grass banks. At the Karoliniškiu stop I got off and trudged slowly to the bench outside her apartment block.

For an hour I sat in the light rain, until it began to soak through my jacket and I worried I might catch a cold. She did not appear. I travelled up the lift to the top floor and stood for a few minutes staring at the four blank doors that opened off the top landing. Not a sound came from behind any of them.

The trolley bus made its way back into the Old Town and I walked home slowly in the rain, head buried deep in my upturned collar. Cold, miserable and confused.

I kept two hundred Litas in a tin in the kitchen; that is about fifty dollars. In my wallet there was a little more. Carefully I laid all the money out on a table and sat down by the window. The rain had begun to fall harder. I poured a large brandy. The telephone did not ring and nobody knocked on the door. I went to bed at twelve, after finishing the bottle of brandy.

When I woke the next morning I hovered over the telephone, but my anger at Jonas prevented me from getting involved in negotiations with him. Jolanta I could not call.

I knocked on Grigalaviciene's door. When she called out through the doors, I told her that it was I. Locks and bolts slid open. One door after the other opened and she poked a sparrow-like head through the gap. She examined me for a few moments suspiciously, then, deciding I wasn't drunk, opened the door a little wider.

'*Nu?*' she said.

I shrugged my shoulders. I just needed some company, if only Grigalaviciene. She opened the door and let me in. Behind me I heard the bolts shooting. I made my way to her tidy kitchen and slid into the seat by the kitchen table. She filled a pan with water and lit the gas with a deft flick of a match. Pulling a packet of biscuits from a cupboard she neatly arranged them on a plate despite my protest. When the water boiled, she poured it into a thermos and put a cup and saucer in front of me with a teaspoon and a jar of tea. I helped myself. All the time she kept up a steady stream of chatter. I was glad of it and sat not listening to her, but rather to the sound of the rain against the window and the flame of gas licking another pan of water.

Chapter 14

The telephone was ringing as I put my key into the lock. I fumbled clumsily. Pushing open the door, I hurried quickly over and snatched the heavy receiver from its cradle.

'Yes?' I panted.

'Daumantas?' Jonas' voice asked.

'Yes.'

'Well? Have you given it some thought?'

I loosened my collar and clenched my jaw. Anger would accomplish nothing. I struggled to control the bitter edge to my voice.

'I've given it some thought,' I said.

'Good, good,' he said, sounding genuinely pleased. 'I knew we could come to some kind of a deal.'

'I didn't say that I had agreed to do a deal,' I cut in. 'I've done some thinking, as I said, and what I was thinking was that one hundred dollars was a ridiculous sum to demand.'

Jonas paused, masticating my comment. He came back cautiously. 'Well, it depends what it's worth to you.'

I sucked my teeth and held back a comment.

'Let's meet again, maybe we can fix a price that we're both happy with?' Jonas suggested.

'I want to see the manuscript,' I said. 'I want to know you've actually got it. I want to know you're not just stringing me along.'

Again Jonas paused. Finally he said, 'I'll have to see about that. The Red and Black, then, in an hour?'

I looked at my watch. 'Fine.'

*   *   *

The Red and Black was transformed by its early evening clientele. The bar hummed. Music pumped from the sound system, red lights flicked across the tables. Slick young men leaned against the bar chatting, arrogantly loud. They wore suits and flashed smart, fake designer watches at the girls. The men wore their hair cropped very short, as the girls wore their skirts. Small-time mafia types and girls looking for a good time. I felt out of place and wondered why Jonas had chosen this bar.

Arriving first again, I sat at a table in the corner, out of reach of the flash of red light. Sipping slowly at a brandy, I debated how best to deal with Jonas. I doubted threats would achieve much. If I wanted the manuscript it seemed inevitable that I would have to negotiate with him. I decided to offer him the fifty dollars and hope he would accept.

Jonas staggered in through the door and made straight for the bar. He ordered a vodka and downed it immediately. Ordering another he glanced around. He did not see me. He frowned and mopped at his brow with a handkerchief. For some more minutes I watched him before he saw me. A broad, crooked smile broke across his face. Lurching over from the bar he collapsed at my table.

'Didn't see you here,' he said jovially.

I was in no mood for chat. His face glistened in the blinking lights of the bar. I fixed him with a stare. 'Did you bring the manuscript?'

He stared at me for a few seconds, his eyes blank. Finally the thoughts seemed to arrange themselves into a vague order in his drink-befuddled mind. He scratched his crotch.

'Na, well, listen, Steponas,' he said. 'I asked Iv—' His hand flew to his mouth, covering the indiscretion. 'I've just got this,' he said. He pulled a crumpled piece of paper from his trouser pocket. With trembling hands he attempted to open it out and straighten it. As he did so, the paper tore. I snatched it from his hands and opened it myself. It was the front sheet of the manuscript. *Disease, a novel by Kestutis Rimkus*, was typed in small letters. I folded the sheet again and slipped it into my own pocket.

'Where's the rest of it?'

'Well, you'll get that when you've paid for it.'

The drink seemed to have made Jonas nervous. He was not as assured as he had been the previous morning. I felt that if I pressed him he would give more.

'Have you got it?' I asked. 'Where did you find it?'

'Well now . . .' Jonas laughed nervously. The sentence was left unfinished.

'What about another drink?' I asked.

His eye lit up. He nodded and lifted his empty glass. I clapped a hand on his shoulder and gave him a smile. He grinned.

'Well, a little drink and then we can do business,' I said.

His face shone with relief.

I took my time getting the drinks. I ordered a bottle and a couple of new glasses. Jonas sat at the table, his eye flicking nervously around the bar. He was smoking a cigarette when I got back. I lit one myself and poured two drinks. His I poured full, so that the vodka spilled slightly over the lip. My own was shorter.

'To business,' I said and raised my glass. He raised his. We downed the drinks and I poured another immediately. He was well ahead of me. If I paced myself he would be under the table before it had even begun to hit my system.

'You seen those girls at the bar?' I said, nodding my head in their direction. I filled his glass again. He laughed crudely. 'Bit expensive for the likes of me and you though,' I said.

'Oh, I don't know, they pay cleaners well these days,' he joked.

I laughed loudly and watched as he downed the vodka. I refilled as soon as his glass hit the table.

'Come on,' I said, taking my own glass, 'you're not keeping up.'

We downed the drinks.

'It wouldn't be bad though, would it?' I said, making a vulgar gesture with my hand. He laughed, his face glowing, bathed in sweat.

'The one in red isn't bad,' he said, smacking his lips. 'Look at that arse!'

His lips hung fat and loose, his eyes rolled and his head began to bob. He wiped his face with his hand, attempting to clear it. I could see he was having trouble focusing on the girls. I poured him one more drink and then began.

'So, now then, about the price?'

He turned to me, grinning stupidly. Spittle dripped from his lower lip. He nodded his head slowly, churning the words over, gradually making sense of them.

'The price?' I said slowly and clearly, worrying that he had gone too far.

'Hundred,' he lisped.

I shook my head definitely. 'No, too much. Not that I'm against paying, you see,' I clarified slowly, carefully, making sure he followed. 'I'll pay. It's only right I should give you something for finding it. Where did you find it?'

He shook his head. His lips worked, but he had difficulty getting his voice together. Tentatively the words emerged. 'It wasn't me.' He paused, grinning. 'I didn't find them.'

'Oh,' I said. 'Who did?'

'Ivan,' he said. 'Ivan had them.' He laughed as though this was hilarious.

'Ivan?'

Jonas' head slumped forward onto the table. I lifted him up. I slapped his face, but he was unable to control his eyelids.

They slid heavily over his eyes. I let his head drop. Leaving the dregs in the bottle, I slipped out into the cool darkness of the evening. Ivan, who was Ivan? I pondered who might have got hold of the manuscript and how they knew it would be important to me.

It was two hours later that I realised what, in fact, I had learnt from Jonas. I was in a small café in the ghetto, listening to a middle-aged woman picking out tunes on an old piano. The café was quiet. A couple of men sat with their drinks for company. I had taken a table by the window and smoked my cheap cigarettes, trawling my mind, searching for a clue to the identity of the mysterious Ivan. Fishing in my pocket for matches, I pulled out the front page of the manuscript. I opened it out and flattened it on the stained tablecloth. *Disease, a novel by Kestutis Rimkus.* It struck me then, suddenly. Rimkus. Could it possibly be? Had he used a pseudonym?

I jumped up from my seat, almost spilling my drink. The woman looked up from the piano. I stepped over to the counter where a small, thin young man was stacking cups. He did not look up as I approached.

'Do you have a directory?' I asked him, breathless with excitement.

He looked up, questioningly. His eyebrows rose and his forehead furrowed. He poked at his thin, wire-framed spectacles. 'What?'

'A directory? A telephone directory?' I asked.

He straightened and glanced over to the corner of the café, where in a dark doorway a telephone rested on a broken wooden shelf. Beneath the telephone was an old, dog-eared directory. Taking it I returned to my table and thumbed through it. Finding the R's I ran my finger down the page. There were only a few Rimkuses, no K. Rimkus.

Taking out my stub of a pencil I scribbled down the five telephone numbers that there were for Rimkus. It was quite possible that they were living with their parents, his or hers. It was possible to trace them. I slipped the front page of the manuscript into my pocket.

I finished one more cigarette, then pulled on my jacket and headed home. Passing the Gaon I gave him a slap and a grin. 'I'll find her,' I assured him. He looked on stonily. It was not yet ten o'clock when I got back to my apartment; I would have time to make some calls before I went to bed.

I pushed the light switch at the bottom of the stairs but nothing happened. I pushed it again, but the light did not come on. Slowly, in almost pitch darkness, I felt my way up the stairs. On each landing the faint light from the street lamps illuminated my path, but between floors I had to shuffle carefully, taking one step at a time. It took almost five minutes to reach my floor. I pulled the keys out of my pocket. As I put the key into the lock, I heard, behind me, a shuffle. I turned quickly to the darkness.

'Somebody there?' I called.

There was no answer, but a figure moved into the fringe of my sight. I caught a glimpse of the pale hem of a skirt.

'Grigalaviciene?' I asked, then hopefully, quickly, 'Svetlana, is that you?'

The figure stepped forward and her face swam into the faint light cast by the street lamps. Jolanta.

Chapter 15

'Jolanta?'

'Steponas,' she whispered, so quietly I could scarcely hear. She did not move forward. For a silent moment we stood in the darkness. I was bewildered by her sudden presence.

'Well,' I stammered, 'you didn't come.'

'No,' she said. Then after a moment she added, 'I'm sorry.'

'No, no,' I said, 'you don't need to be sorry. I was worried. I was just worried that I would not see you again.' I paused. 'I didn't know how to find you.'

'No,' she said simply.

I unlocked the door. Pushing it open, I held it for her. 'Come in,' I said, flicking on the light. She stepped back quickly. Puzzled, I waited. She moved forward slowly as though the light hurt her. As she moved into the thin arc of light spreading from my doorway, her face was illuminated. I gasped. Hearing the sharp intake of breath, she turned her face from me and squeezed by, looking down at the old wooden tiles on the floor. I closed the door behind her and locked it. She stood in the hallway, resting her head against the bricked-up doorway, her back to me.

'What happened, Jolanta?'

She did not answer. She allowed me to take her coat. I hung it up on a peg and showed her through to the front room. I put on the soft corner lamp and sat her in my chair by the window. Tears welled in her eyes. She held a handkerchief to her face and her shoulders shook but she did not make a sound. I stepped into the kitchen and boiled a pan of water.

Returning with coffee, I leant down beside her. Her eyes wore dark rings and her left cheek was swollen and yellow. A cut ran down the side of her face and another curved around her beautiful, delicate nostril. She turned her eyes away from me as I examined her, but she allowed me to look.

'Who did it?' I asked.

Not answering, she took the cup gratefully from me and wrapped her fingers around it, drawing it close to her, as though to comfort her. Taking my own coffee, I sat on the chair by the desk. I drank quietly, waiting for her to choose the time to talk. She sat in silence in the soft ring of light cast by the lamp, cradling her cup, occasionally putting it to her lips to feel its warmth, but drinking little. I was not to hear her story that night.

'I'm tired,' she said, after a while. She looked at me beseechingly. 'Could I . . .'

'Of course, of course,' I said. 'Stay here. I will change the sheets for you.'

'I don't want to cause you any trouble,' she said. 'You were the only person I could think to come to. I will sleep on the sofa, here.'

'Don't be silly,' I said, getting up.

'But how did you know where I lived?' I asked from the doorway.

'The telephone book,' she said.

'Of course.'

I pulled the old sheets off the bed and laid new ones that Svetlana had cleaned for me the previous week. They smelt clean and fresh. I touched the soft surface of the bed as I tucked the sheets in and was glad she would be sleeping there. She seemed almost to be sleeping when I returned to her. Her swollen eyes were closed in their dark sockets. I shook her shoulder gently. She opened her eyes and I saw that she had not been sleeping. A tear ran down her cheek. I wiped it away, feeling the softness of her skin.

'The bed is ready for you,' I told her. 'You should go and get some rest. Tomorrow you will feel better. Would you like me to call anybody for you? Or perhaps you would like to call yourself?' I indicated the telephone. She shook her head. 'The bathroom . . .' I said, but she had already started for the door. She half turned and I read the look of complete exhaustion in her eyes.

'I'll go straight to bed,' she said. 'Thank you.'

'There's no need to thank me.'

She stumbled into the bedroom and pushed the door closed behind her. The bedsprings squeaked as she sat down. The easy chair by the window was still warm from her body. I watched till the light disappeared from beneath the door and then sat on, thinking of her sleeping. Behind that door. I longed to offer her what comfort I could.

Much later I made a bed of the sofa, uncomfortable with its unfamiliar hardness. But I did not sleep. In the darkness I lay thinking of Rachael. When by two thirty sleep still had not come, I went to the bathroom. In a small cabinet was a box of sleeping pills. I took one with a glass of water. For a further half an hour I lay watching the shadows on the ceiling. Gradually the shadows thickened and I slept.

When I awoke my mouth was dry and my tongue felt swollen. Each time I moved a muscle, pains ran down my spine. I sat up slowly. Daylight flooded through the windows. The tops of the trees fretted in a fine breeze. I opened the window and let in some fresh air. Small white clouds scudded across the pale, blue sky. Down below, beneath the trees, Grigalaviciene was sitting on a bench talking to a neighbour. Both wore brightly patterned headscarves.

The door to the bedroom was closed and I could hear no sign of movement from behind it. Quietly I put my ear to the cheap, thin wood, but there was no sound. I dressed and went to the kitchen to make breakfast. On the table, propped up against the cup she had been drinking from the night before, was a note.

Steponas, *she wrote*. When I woke this morning you were still sleeping and I did not want to wake you. I want to thank you for your kindness. I'm sorry I could not explain to you all that has happened. I will, I promise you. I feel I have thrown myself on you, first with the novel and now this. I'm sorry. I do not wish to be a burden.

I need to sort out Rasa, my daughter. Last night she was with a friend, but I am taking her to my mother's in the village where she will be safe. I will stay there for a few days myself. My mother's telephone number is at the top of this page. Perhaps you could call?

Jolanta.

The telephone number was at the top of the page. I folded it carefully and slipped it into my pocket. She had not indicated which village her mother lived in, nor had she mentioned how she would be travelling there, so I had no way of knowing what time she might arrive. I would have to wait till evening.

I walked over to the Church of the Holy Mother of God where first I had seen her. Sitting in a pew near to the altar I silently offered my first prayer in many years. Though to whom, I don't know.

When I returned home, I telephoned Jonas. He was not in but his daughter answered, as timid as she had been during our previous conversation. I could only guess how Jonas treated her and, for a moment, felt guilty for having got him so drunk the previous evening. I was sure the young girl would not have enjoyed his hangover that morning. She offered to take a message, but I decided to catch him at work.

He was sitting on a bench in the small dirty courtyard when I found him. For a moment I thought perhaps he was sleeping, but when I touched his arm he jumped up. Seeing me he sat down again and clutched his head. He scowled.

'What do you want?' he grunted.

I laughed. 'Feeling delicate?'

He looked murderous but said nothing.

'I thought it was clear what I wanted,' I said.

'If you want it, pay up the money,' he said. 'If you don't then get lost.'

'Is that what Ivan says?' I said.

He looked up quickly and the faintest quiver of fear flickered in his eye. He examined me closely for a second before deciding I was bluffing. He sneered. 'Yeah, that's what Ivan says.'

I sighed and took the fifty dollars from my wallet. I waved them beneath his nose. He made to grab them, but the drink had slowed him and I pulled them away.

'No, no,' I said. 'You don't get these till I get the manuscript.'

He rubbed his face. I could see that thinking came with difficulty. Wiping his hands on his dirty trousers, he nodded.

'Fine,' he said. 'But you give me twenty-five now, or I won't go for it. Call it security.'

I gave him a ten-dollar note, seeing that nothing would get done without this little bit of oil. 'That's all you get until I have the manuscript,' I said.

'The Red and Black tonight then,' he said. 'I'll see Ivan this evening. Let's say ten?'

Reluctantly I agreed.

Chapter 16

I did not meet Jonas at the Red and Black that night. I sat in the crowded, noisy bar for an hour before finally giving up on him. It was raining when I wandered home. I cursed him, not knowing then that he was living his last hours. Or, perhaps, was already dead. Heavy-heartedly I dialled the number at the top of Jolanta's note.

Jolanta answered the telephone, sounding cheerful and relaxed. Her baby was shouting and the voice of another woman soothed it. 'Oh, hello,' she said, hearing my voice. 'I'm glad you called.'

The words eased my heart, as words have not for many years now.

'I wanted to thank you for last night,' she said.

'I was worried about you,' I told her. 'I am worried about you.'

'I'm fine now, you don't need to worry any more,' she assured me.

'What happened?'

'It's hard to talk now,' she said, her voice low, confidential.

Then she said brightly, 'Why don't you come out to see us? The country is lovely now. Get away from Vilnius for a day.'

I paused, taken aback. The desire to see her was so sharp I could not respond for a few moments. 'I don't even know where you are,' I said.

'Svencioneliai.'

'I have no car.'

'Nor do I,' she said. 'But I managed it! You can stay the night. Mama would like that.' She laughed.

'Are you serious?' I asked. A nervous old man.

'Of course,' she said, and her voice sounded bright with delight.

'Then I shall come.'

The next morning I caught the bus to Svencioneliai. The route took us out north, along the grass banks of the Neris, its water running fast and smooth. I sat back in my seat, closed my eyes and allowed the city to drop away behind me.

The fields shone under the clear blue sky. The sun rose above the trees, stealing the dew from the tips of grass on the verdant banks of the road. The small villages that we passed through were quiet; wizened ladies, scarves tied tightly around their balding skulls, hobbled out into their gardens, or met on dusty street corners to share a juicy morsel. Soviet era Žigulys rattled along the rutted, pockmarked streets. At midday the bus pulled into the centre of Svencioneliai. I walked out to the farm on the edge of the village, following the instructions Jolanta had given me on the telephone.

'Steponas!' Jolanta called, seeing me at the gate.

She was sitting on the back step of the cottage, peeling potatoes on to a sheet of newspaper. She dropped the potato and knife and jumped up to greet me, wiping her hands on the flowery apron she was wearing. Beneath the apron she was wearing a loose shirt and jeans. Her hair was tied back, behind her head, and on her forehead was a dark smudge from her dirty hands. Her eyes flashed in the sunlight. The dark rings around them were fading. Her skin shone. Her whole body spoke of the freshness of the country.

'Mama,' she called as she let me in through the gate into

the large yard. A handsome woman poked her head out of the yellow, wooden house.

'Steponas is here,' Jolanta called. Against my protest Jolanta took the small bag I had packed. 'Come and meet my mother,' she said, dancing along the path beside me. I was bewitched once more by her, by those eyes, her dark hair. A shiver ran down my spine, a shiver of pleasure and fear. This was a beautiful haunting.

Her mother stepped out to greet me. 'Egle,' she said and we shook hands. The middle-aged original of her daughter. And the impression was there too, the faint shadow of her in the eyes, the hair and the way she held her head. Older, though, older as I never saw her. Older as I could never see her, never gave her the chance to be. Rachael, I thought, and a pain stabbed my chest. The two women looked at me with concern as I clenched my fist against the pain.

'Are you all right?' Jolanta asked, gripping my arm, supporting me.

I gasped, feeling the pain dig deep into my chest. 'Tired,' I said. Her mother clucked sympathetically and, taking my other arm, led me into the cool darkness of the kitchen. Jolanta boiled some water and made me a herbal infusion. I sipped it gratefully.

'My father died some years ago in an accident in the fields,' Jolanta said, later, as we sat by the small river that ran along the foot of their land. 'He was the foreman of the collective farm. He was a big man. You look a little like him.'

'A little older, I would think,' I said.

'You don't look so old,' she said. 'Anyway, Mama has been on her own since then. It's not good,' she added. 'She should find somebody to keep her company. Did you see the way that she was looking at you?'

'Don't be silly.'

'She was,' Jolanta teased.

'You must tell me,' I said, changing the subject, 'what happened?'

Jolanta brushed her hands across her bruises and her face darkened. A thin breeze swept across the river and lifted her hair. 'Perhaps it's not such a bad thing to live on your own,' she said.

'It was your husband?'

'Kestutis is . . .' She paused. 'Since the army . . . I don't know . . . Sometimes moods take him and it's like he is somebody else. Usually he just rants and rages, he doesn't normally hit me.' She felt her bruises once more and I saw the tears start and glisten in her eyes. One swelled and rolled across her dark lashes. It dropped onto her cheek and sat there, fat, like a child's tear.

'Things have been strained just recently. He has been drinking more than usual. And then his medicine . . . It was getting late and I had gone to bed. Kestutis was in a fury earlier because the baby was crying when he was trying to work. He was drunk. I told him to go to sleep, that the baby would stop. He began swearing at me. I knew that I would have to sit and listen to him. There is no way to stop him once he has started. He can't be quietened or pacified, I just have to sit and listen.

'He began to shout and I was afraid. I tried to quieten him but that just made him angrier.' She stopped and looked out across the river. She shivered violently and clasped her arms around her body.

'I understand,' I said. 'You don't need to go on.'

'He hit me,' she said, looking out, far across the river. 'It seemed that once he started he could not stop. Like a dam had burst, a tap opened, something. He has never done that before. As bad as it has been, he has never done that before.' She fell then into silence. I was sorry that I had forced the subject and I told her so.

'No,' she said. 'It's better to talk about it. I had to get away. I needed to hide away. I knew that here, in the village, I would be safe. I feel safe here.'

I need to hide away. A molina. The village. The words took wing and flew across the years, black crows against the blue sky. I heard them as she had said them, her voice tight with fear, full of the horror that we did not know, yet knew. Yes, knew. After so many years of hiding, of covering up, those words were rising from the unsacred ground in which I had buried them. The ghosts were rising; they hovered in the twilight air, by the river, where it had begun to grow cold. I shivered.

Seeing me shiver roused Jolanta from her thoughts. She wiped her eyes and attempted a smile. 'You're getting cold,' she said. 'Let's go in and see what Mama has cooked for supper.'

She offered me her hand, and I took it. We walked slowly back to the house, her hand in mine. The light faded between the branches of the apple trees. The evening was still and pre-ternaturally quiet. Beyond the river, the hills rose steeply and their tips caught the last bloody light of the day. The ghosts followed through the trees, skimming above the dew-damp grass, closing the dandelions gently in upon themselves.

Egle had soup in the large oven. She pulled it out and set it in the centre of the table. The room was warm. The light came mainly from the oven where, through the open door, a fire burnt brightly. A pair of flies buzzed dozily around the unlit lamp. I sat heavily in a seat by the table, opposite the young, beautiful girl. Her eyes sparkled in the light of the fire and her hair shone. Egle fussed over us quietly. She ladled large bowls of soup and cut thick slices of dark bread. The smell of roast meat filled the room. As she served me, Egle came close so that I could smell the soap on her body. Her hair was cut shorter than her daughter's, but it was handsomely dark. She had a shapely, full body.

When it had grown quite dark Egle switched on a dim lamp in the corner. We drank beer and I listened to the women singing together. They sang about girls who met boys and lost them abroad, about boys wanting girls and having to pay the price. The boys rode white horses and the girls wore white dresses. Songs I had grown up with. Melodies to keep the ghosts outside the shuttered windows.

Later in the evening, when tiredness was pulling at my eyelids, they sang a new song, the lilt of which was not familiar. I listened quietly, recognising the strange non-Baltic harmonies.

Shluf Meine Kind, they sang, their dark heads together.
By dine veegel zitzt dine mame,
Zingt a leed un vaynt.

Sleep, my child,
My comfort, my pretty,
By your cradle sits your mama,
Sings a song and weeps.
You'll understand some day most likely,
What is in her mind.

'You're Jewish?' I said, astonished.

Egle nodded slowly. 'Yes, I am Jewish. My husband wasn't. I remember that song. My mother sang it to me when I was a child.'

Chapter 17

'My mother survived the war in a village,' Egle said. 'She was the only member of the family who did, as far as I know. The story is vague; I remember the details only from my childhood, long ago. I can tell them now, but who is interested to listen?'

Jolanta leaned against her in the dim light. Her eyes had closed and I could tell from the gentle and regular rise and fall of her chest that she was sleeping. Egle stroked her hair.

'Tell me,' I said simply, for it seemed that at last the ghost had risen and I must sit and listen.

'We lived in Vilnius before the war. When the Nazis came, my father went to join the Soviet forces, to fight against them. My mother was pregnant with me, though she did not know it. My father, you see, was not to know he had a daughter. My mother moved around. I was born in a village close to the Latvian border, where she had found refuge. It was not safe, but safer than in the city. A family there sheltered us. My mother pretended to be Polish. God was gracious, the Angel of Death passed over the small cottage we lived in.

'At the end of the war, who could believe that things were safe? My mother lived on in the village and married the son of the family who had sheltered us. They were poor farmers. She kept to her story of being Polish. She invented a whole life for herself. She was from Krakow, an educated family that had been destroyed by the Nazis for their patriotic behaviour. They changed my name to Egle. That was how I grew up, a proud Polish girl, the daughter of an impoverished farming home. Only at night, when I was small, she sang that song to me as I went to sleep.

'Vividly I recall her sitting by my small bed in the corner of the room, leaning over me, her long hair falling across her face. Tears misted her eyes as she sang, her voice sweet, low, full of longing and of loss. I didn't know the story then, of course, and I didn't understand why she cried. I did not understand the words of the song, but learnt them anyway, as a child will, from her singing.

'She died when I was ten. I grew up, then, with no one left who knew of my past. Anyone who could remember died or forgot as the years went by. Nobody cared, anyway, about the past of such a little girl. I was thin, a ragged waif.

'But by the age of ten, I knew. My mother, as she lay dying, told me it all, forcing me to swear to secrecy. And why would I tell? What kind of a thing was that to tell? I preferred the story of the Gentile life in Krakow, the stories of the brave resistance of my noble grandfather and invented father. That was a story of heroism and pride and I had no intention of giving it up in favour of the Jewish tale of poverty and persecution.

'But I was a lonely child. At night I cried myself to sleep, in the small cottage, singing that song. If ever my father heard me singing it he would curse and kick me and tell me to sing a good Lithuanian song. So I sang Lithuanian songs to him and that, alone, in my bed.

'I was a good student, and did well at school. But when I was sixteen, I met a young man. He was a good man. A real Soviet hero. He was tall and well built, blond with blue eyes. He would walk down the main street with a shovel tossed carelessly over his shoulder whistling communist working tunes. He would call the other young men out into the fields to work; the young women went too. We worked hard. For the revolution, he said. We girls worked for him. He was our idol, our god, and we followed him everywhere he went.

'We got married, but for many years we could have no children. Arunas was sad about this. He was a good husband; God could not have given me a better one. He did not drink and he didn't hang around with the women. He worked hard and built this house for us. And then we had a child, a daughter, a gift from God.'

She stroked her daughter again, sleeping gently beside her. A beautiful smile lit the soft curves of her face and her bobbed hair glistened in the dim light of the lamp.

'And I remembered the song. For many years I had forgotten it. It lay in some dusty drawer of my mind, locked away, during the happiness of my married life. I was afraid, at first, to sing it in front of my husband and would only sing it when he was out in the fields and the two of us, Jolanta and I, were alone. But one day he heard it. He told me to sing it to him. He knew, of course, but said nothing. A beautiful song was all he said. A beautiful song, and he looked at me with his pure blue eyes and looked at his dark daughter so like her mother and understood.

'One day he was out in the fields. They came home and told me. They stood by the door holding their caps in their hands not daring to lift their faces. I ran out to the fields but he was dead. We carried him back home. I did not get to say goodbye.'

The silence of the night descended on the cottage and I was too afraid to break it. We sat looking at each other. Jolanta stirred and half opened her eyes.

'Sing the song,' I asked her quietly.

She sang in a soft, low voice.

> *Sleep, my child, my comfort, my pretty,*
> *Sleep my darling*
> *Sleep my life, my only kaddish.*
> *Lu link lu lu*
> *Sleep my life, my only kaddish.*

Later Egle pulled a blanket over her daughter and we left her to sleep on the couch. She showed me my room and we said goodnight. As I lay waiting for sleep to take me, I sang the song to myself. Did she sing that song to her child? She too could have escaped to a village and her child would have grown up there, a skinny waif. She would have grown up beautiful.

The ghosts floated around my bed and I sang the song to lull them to sleep with me.

When I awoke in the morning, I was disorientated by the silence. I lay listening to the song of the birds and the absence of traffic. Of people. The sun shone through the net curtains, warming me. After a while I heard Jolanta's voice and then that of her mother. The baby shouted and burbled happily. It was good to lie there listening to their voices. Jolanta, smiling, brought me a cup of tea.

'Mama is happy this morning,' she said.

I simply smiled and thanked her for the drink. She left grinning, pleased with herself. I heard her taking the baby and then calling to her mother that she was going into the village. I got up, and dressed, and looked out of the windows across the green fields behind the house. Egle poked her head through the doorway and called me to breakfast.

I wandered around the village that day, hoping its peace would calm my taut nerves. Jolanta had said nothing about the manuscript, but I knew I was going to have to broach the subject. As the hours passed so grew my dread of shattering the calm composure that Jolanta had managed to achieve. That evening, before sunset, I asked her to walk down to the river with me. She lifted the baby and carried it with her. It wrestled in her arms. On the gentle slope of the river she allowed Rasa to wander around, keeping a close eye on her. The fear that had afflicted me a couple of days previously, when I had made my slow way to the restaurant, returned, constricting my chest so that my breath came in short, shallow gasps. Jolanta looked at me, concerned.

'We walked too quickly,' she said.

'No,' I said, 'I'm fine.'

I explained to her then what had happened to the manuscript. She listened carefully. I told her of how I had gone to meet her at the restaurant, so fearful, and then come away even more fearful when she had not arrived. I told her of Jonas and his deal over the manuscript.

'I will get it back, I assure you,' I said, my face flushing with shame that I had not just given Jonas the one hundred dollars. 'As soon as I get back to Vilnius I will get it from him.'

At first she did not respond. She watched her daughter playing with some sticks. Finally she turned to me. 'Well,' she said, and then she seemed at a loss what to say next.

Again I started to apologise and to reassure her that I would get it back, but she laid her hand on my arm.

'Don't,' she said. 'I am sure you will. It's my fault. I should never have imposed on you like that in the first place.' She pressed the palm of her hand to her forehead. 'I don't know, all this with Kestutis, it's been crazy. It's so good to come out here and forget about it.'

Rasa crawled up to her and she took the baby into her arms and clasped her tight against her breast. Her eyes screwed up and a tear slipped down across her cheek. Despite her words

I could see how concerned she was. Earlier in the evening I had heard her speaking on the telephone, her voice soft, pleading, as her husband's tirade drifted tinnily from the telephone receiver, audible across the room.

'It was the only copy of the manuscript?' I asked, hopelessly.

She nodded glumly.

'I will get it,' I said, her misery piercing my heart. I reached over and stroked her hair. She leaned back against me and I hugged her. 'The thing is, from what I read I was very impressed,' I said. 'I was moved by it.'

'Really?' she said.

'Absolutely. There was a passage about him gripping a letter, fearing he was lost. It was good writing.'

She smiled and wiped the tear from her cheek. The sun had set and shadows were creeping up from the river. The air had grown chill.

'We should get back,' she said.

Chapter 18

The next day I was in no rush to leave. I appreciated the quietness of the country and apart from wanting to get my hands on the manuscript found no other reason to want to hurry my return to Vilnius. I took a long walk in the forest then wandered to the village to buy a newspaper. The old woman who ran the shop, a wizened crone with barely a tooth in her head, quizzed me.

'Who are you?'

'Daumantas,' I told her.

'You're not from here.'

'No,' I told her, 'I live in Vilnius.'

'So for what are you here then?'

'Visiting.'

'Who?'

'Jolanta Rimkiene,' I told her.

'You mean Egle? *Nu*, a good girl.' And she looked at me critically. 'Her husband was a good man,' she told me. 'Oi, but life goes on.' She looked me up and down again, assessing whether I was good enough.

Walking down to the river I felt Rachael's presence. Her ghost followed me. It was as though she were happier, here, out of the city, away from the horror of those narrow streets. Here was where she should have been. Here she would have been happy and safe. She had entreated me, but I had turned my back. Fearful, I had not taken her. But now, at last, she was with me. She hovered beside me, raven-haired beauty, with the small child in her arms. As I walked through the forest, the slim branches bent softly against the weight of her delicate body.

Rachael.

I sat beside her on the stump of a log.

I'm sorry, Rachael.

Sorry does nothing, she told me. Sorry means nothing. Sorry heals nothing.

Still I'm sorry, I told her. I have no other words.

The words of Marcinkevicius came back to me.

> *I love*
> *with aching and shadows – oh, yes,*
> *I have not yet mentioned this,*
> *I love you with darkness and death,*
> *forgetfulness and light –*
> *with low grass on a sunken grave –*
> *I love*

Later I sat on the low wooden bench outside the cottage, thinking of her. The cherry-red, late evening sun shone on my face. Tears welled from my eyes and settled on the skin of my cheeks. Egle sat beside me and took my hand between hers. She wiped the tears from my cheeks, but said nothing.

Later she said, 'You came here to cheer Jolanta up and now you are the sad one.'

'I'm sorry,' was all that I could say.

'You don't need to say you're sorry,' she said. 'What is sorry for? Perhaps,' she said, 'you could tell me about it.'

I shook my head. 'For so many years I could not even tell myself about it,' I told her. 'For fifty years I have kept it locked up deep inside me, covered. I have buried it and I thought that it was lost, but now it's here again. First I must tell myself. I am only beginning, just now.'

She nodded. She stroked my cheek with her finger, softly and with care.

The next morning, Jolanta came to my room with a smile. 'Come,' she said.

'What is it?' I asked, but she would not tell. Egle stood in the doorway. They smiled like conspirators. Taking my hands they led me out into the garden. We walked across the grass to the old wooden outbuildings, the sauna and the disused work shed. Egle took a key from her pocket and opened the door. The room had been cleaned. A desk stood by the wall draped with a neat white cloth. On the table stood a sheaf of paper and a collection of pens. Light streamed from a high window.

'Jolanta told me you are a writer,' Egle said. 'I thought, perhaps, you should have somewhere to work while you are here.'

Looking at the table, I felt my stomach turn to ice. Not that I feared trying to write, on the contrary, I realised that the time had come. I knew the words would flow. I had to start peeling back the thick layers of my life; layers carefully piled one on top of another. Deliberately obscuring. For fifty years I had struggled to bury it, but it would remain buried no longer. The spirits were calling and at last I would confront them.

Still I procrastinated. After fifty years a few days, perhaps, would make little difference. I sat in the chair and looked at the blank sheets of paper. I weighed the pens carefully. I wandered the small wooden space examining the pine-clad walls, smelling its sweet fragrance. I listened to the quality of its silence. I did not think of her but I knew my mind was drifting across the years, slowly making its way back. Egle left me in peace, knowing, intuitively, that what I was to write had to be written and that it would need space and time and silence.

Two mornings later I awoke, having slept well, without dreams. She no longer burst out at me, I felt her presence always. I got up and washed carefully from a bucket of cold, fresh water, on the grass, by the well. Before going to the room I went for a short walk in the woods. The leaves rustled in a gentle breeze and, hearing a tap-tapping, I traced a woodpecker to the top of a gnarled old tree, digging for food in the dead wood.

Returning to the cottage I made my way straight to the writing room. Pulling the chair up to the table I took a clean sheet of paper. Carefully I selected a pen from the small pile. After pausing for only a moment, I wrote a sentence. 'In the summer of 1938,' I wrote, 'I was living in a small village west of Vilnius, or Wilno as it was called then.'

For the rest of the morning, I continued writing. When, at lunchtime, I paused, my hand was tired and my eyes ached from looking so closely and intently at the page. Egle had left a tray of food covered with a clean white cloth. I sat on the grass and ate the cheese and sausage and drank the beer. After, I returned quickly to the room to continue with my writing. Digging. Digging away at the layers of soil. Clearing the ground.

II

Svetlana

Lithuania
Mid 1990s

Chapter 19

Having spent the better part of the afternoon drinking hard, Svetlana went to the café late. As soon as she entered she noticed Daumantas. She was about to approach when she heard Jonas' voice. She shrank back into a quiet corner. There, steadily, slowly, she drank, pacing oblivion, watching the old man.

Daumantas was gaunt from too many cigarettes. His hair was silver, his blue eyes piercing. He was charming. Or could be when he wished. He sat draining a bottle of vodka. Glass after glass. Pausing only to draw hungrily on a cigarette. In front of him was a pile of papers, his head bent close to the page as he read. A man stumbled against him and he looked up, startled, dragged suddenly from another world. There was a haunted look in his eyes. Gathering the papers together he pushed them into a bag. He gazed out of the window into the night's darkness.

Svetlana brushed her hand across her face, poured another drink, her hand unsteady, the bottle chinking against the glass. She imagined walking over to him. A hand on his back. Hello. Drinking? We could drink together. Drown the darkness.

He fumbled over his cigarettes, clumsily attempting to extract one from the packet, all thumbs. It dropped to the floor. Cursing, he bent for it, but overbalanced, knocking the plastic bag onto the floor. She almost rose to steady him.

The waiter helped him back into his seat. Daumantas shook him off angrily.

'Maybe you've had enough,' the waiter said.

Daumantas shook his head. He extracted a cigarette and tried to straighten it. It snapped between his fingers, the cheap tobacco scattering across the gummy tabletop.

'Come on.'

'Leave me be,' Daumantas growled.

'You've had enough.'

Daumantas slammed his fist on to the table. The vodka bottle jumped and swayed, nearly toppling.

'I'll tell you when I've had enough,' Daumantas said. His voice shook and his tongue stumbled on the words. The waiter remained patient. He glanced over to the counter.

'Get him out, Gintas,' the girl called.

Gintas nodded, smiling still. Taking Daumantas firmly under the arm he pulled him to his feet. He was taller than Daumantas. Daumantas struggled to free himself but the waiter propelled him to the door.

Daumantas protested.

He attempted to swing round to face the waiter but could not. They disappeared into the darkness. Svetlana pulled on her coat. She was drunk too, but controlled. She glanced over to where Daumantas had been sitting. The plastic bag lay on the floor confettied with tobacco. She hesitated. Jonas' beetroot face glowed crudely as he leant over the table, close to his companion.

Slipping through the tables she picked up the bag. Turning, she felt a hand catch her.

'Svyeta!' Jonas said.

She pulled her arm free and glared at him. He grunted. She hurried to the door. The dark-haired waiter, Gintas, entering, held it open for her, smiling politely. She slipped out into the street. It was not well lit and she stumbled on the cobbles. Gripping Daumantas' bag, she hurried towards the area of the ghetto where he lived. There was no sign of him.

He had been too drunk to move so fast. She stopped a moment to consider where he might have gone. In the darkness she heard the sound of retching. Her eyes searched the entrance to a courtyard. Nothing was visible but, distinctly, she heard feet shuffling. She edged into the darkness, placing each foot carefully, straining her eyes.

A man was supine on the cold cobbles. Instinctively she cried out. Bending to examine him, she pulled him up, cradled his body upon her lap. Turning him over, she pulled his face into a sliver of light falling weakly from a window. A raw, bloated face stared up at her. Repulsed, she pushed him away. The body rolled on the cobbles. She stood quickly, steadying herself against the crumbling plaster wall.

Footsteps clattered on the cobbles behind her.

'Daumantas? Steponas?'

A twisted grin flittered across the weak beam of light and disappeared. Before she could move fingers had grabbed her, thrusting her back against the wall. She grunted, the breath forced out of her. Jonas pushed his face into hers. Saliva speckled his lips.

'How about it, Svyeta?' he stammered, breathless.

She tried to push him back, but he was all thrusting hands and legs. He groped at her clothes, his red and fleshy tongue protruding from between his lips.

'Don't you want it, Svyeta?'

'Get lost, Jonas,' she breathed.

'But you like it, don't you?' he said, his hand slipping up into her blouse. The thin cloth tore. She pushed him hard with her knee and spat in his face. His grip loosened and she shoved him backwards into the darkness.

'What's the matter with you?' he shouted.

She grabbed the bag and ran for the street.

'Svyeta,' he called. 'I'll pay.'

She did not turn.

Jonas was on his feet, stumbling after her.

'Whore! Since when did you get so picky?'

His voice echoed in the dark emptiness of the street. Svetlana hurried away.

'Ivan is back,' she shouted into the darkness. 'Watch it, Jonas. I'll tell him.'

When she was sure Jonas was not following, she slowed her pace. She chuckled darkly at the idea of using Ivan's name to defend herself. He had been back three days and already she had a black eye to show for it. Reaching behind her, she found the tear in her blouse.

Museum Square was quiet. She walked slowly, listening to the sound of her heels on the paving. The buildings were springing to life. New plaster and coats of bright paint. Spruced up for the tourists after years of neglect. Stepono Street, half a kilometre away, crumbled still. The roofs sagged, the wood was rotting, the windows broken. Tourists did not go there.

In her room on Stepono she found her two sons sleeping side by side on the floor. Misha with his arm around his young brother. A thin blanket covered them. For a few moments she stood gazing at the gentle rise and fall of their bodies, illuminated by the thin light seeping through the window. Misha's body had filled out. His arms were thick with muscles. Soft stubble furred his chin. Bending, she stroked his cropped hair tenderly.

Undressing in the darkness she hung her blouse carefully on a wire hanger. Taking it to the window she examined the rip in the dim light; she would be able to fix it in the morning, she decided. She studied her body in the cracked mirror on the wall. Holding back her hair, she pulled the skin tight on her face. Not so old. Still attractive.

She would take the package back to Daumantas. The writer. She knew he was, he had told her once.

Pulling on some thicker clothes, she collapsed wearily onto the sagging bed. Ivan was not there. She pulled herself up close against the wall to leave him space.

Chapter 20

Svetlana woke with a start. Sitting up, she wiped the perspiration from her forehead. The sound of fists pounding on the door rang in her ears. A steady, forceful thud. The wind was howling through the treetops and somewhere a dog was barking. She put her hands to her ears. She could hear their voices still, calling. Male voices. Edged with anger, sharp with malice.

She shook her head and opened her eyes wide. She swung her legs off the bed and staggered over to the small sink. The water in the bucket was icily cold. She splashed it over her face, cooling her burning cheeks. Slowly the voices subsided. The pounding faded. She stood in the darkness listening to the sounds of the city. The occasional car, uncertain footsteps that drew slowly closer, passed the window and then faded into the distance.

When she lay back on the bed, she was shivering. She wrapped her arms tightly around her. She did not sleep. In sleep, she feared, they might return. The thump on the door, the men's voices. She lay watching her sons sleep on the floor. Gradually the darkness faded. A grimy light flushed the walls. Her eyelids relaxed and she felt the fear ebb and her muscles loosen.

The door rattled and shook as somebody struck it hard. Svetlana sat up. Her head ached. Nikolai was in the corner reading a comic; Misha was gone. Ivan snored loudly beside her. She glanced at the clock on the wall.

'Who is it?' she called, angrily, as the door rattled once more on its hinges. She pulled a coat over her rumpled clothes and staggered across to the door. Jonas' face leered at her when she opened it.

'What do you want?' she hissed, attempting to close the door on him. He jammed his foot into the space.

'I've come to see Ivan,' he said.

'What do you want with him?' Behind her she heard her husband stir.

'What's going on?' he demanded, his voice thick with sleep.

'Jonas. He wants you.'

Ivan sat up and groped for his cigarettes. Jonas kicked the door hard so that it sprang open, hitting Svetlana. He pushed past her.

'Get me a coffee, Svyeta,' he said.

Ivan, lighting a cigarette with a grimace, muttered, 'You heard him, get us a coffee.'

Jonas strolled over to the window. Ivan pulled deeply on the cigarette, frowning. He said nothing.

'Svyeta told me you were back,' Jonas said.

Ivan watched as Svetlana poured water from the bucket into a pan on the small hob. She placed the bucket back beneath the dripping tap, collecting unmetered water.

'So?'

'Just thought I'd come to say hello.' Jonas grinned.

'What do you want?'

Jonas sat on the end of the bed and took out a packet of cigarettes. He lit one slowly; he seemed in no hurry to get to the point. Blowing the thin, blue smoke out in wispy rings, he said finally, 'I was wondering if you wanted some work?'

Ivan laughed.

From the doorway Svetlana gazed outside. The sun rarely

reached into the courtyard and mould grew up the walls. The wooden walkway providing access to the upstairs rooms was rotting and threatened to fall.

Ivan stood up and pulled on some trousers. 'What kind of job?'

Again Jonas hesitated. He glanced at Svetlana in the doorway and indicated slightly with his head. 'Maybe we should go for a drink?'

When they had gone, Svetlana tugged a large tub into the room and dropped it on the floor. Taking a bucket she put it under the old radiator in the corner. With a metal key she had shaped, she opened the radiator valve and poured hot water into the bucket, which was cheaper than running it out of the tap and boiling it on the stove.

Taking an armful of the soiled clothes, dumped by the door, she dropped them into the hot water. For a while she let them soak. Taking a bottle of vodka from inside the broken jug where she kept it hidden, she gazed up at the image of Christ aslant on the dirty wall before her. She did not cross herself, but half reached out to touch the crucified body gently with her fingertips. Before they touched she withdrew them.

She sat on the bed, absently stroking the sheet, remembering how Daumantas had sat there just two days before.

The thought of Daumantas jerked her memory. Rummaging in the corner she pulled out the plastic bag. Setting down her vodka, she opened it. Gingerly she pulled out the papers. The writing meant nothing to her. She had only a vague knowledge of Lithuanian lettering, enough to get around. She turned the sheets. She held them up, smelled them. Carefully, then, she put them back into the bag.

On her knees she pounded the washing in the tub, hair falling over her face. Perspiration gleamed on her forehead. Her arms ached. Soapsuds soaked her blouse. She beat the clothes distractedly. Christ looked down on her from his discoloured cross but it was Daumantas she was thinking of.

Chapter 21

'One thousand dollars?'

Svetlana looked at Misha. The washing was drying in the sharp gusts that swirled around the courtyard. The tub was leant against the wall. Misha sat before her silently, his head bowed as though he was ashamed. His hands were grimy, his young face weary. It was quiet and in the courtyard she could hear Nikolai kicking a ball against the wall. The figure dazed her. For some moments she could not think. Misha picked at his short, broken nails. She felt her breathing constricted. She got up and went over to the door. For some moments she stood staring out blankly at her younger son.

One thousand dollars.

Tears welled up in her eyes. She wrapped her arms around her body, holding in the pain. Behind her she heard Misha get up. Coming to her, he put his arms around her. She felt his rough stubble against her neck.

'Mama,' he said. She could smell the sweat on his body, the dirt from his work on the building site.

She turned, wiping the tears away with the back of her hand.

'He said he could do it?'

Misha nodded. When he spoke she could tell that he was trying to keep the eagerness from his voice.

'He will get me into England and will organise a job for me. There will be somewhere to stay and he will arrange all the papers I need.'

'You trust him?'

'He's done it before, for others. He says he can introduce me to others he has helped over.'

'He's English.'

'Yes.'

Svetlana let her breath out slowly. One thousand dollars. She ran a hand through her hair. On a good day she earned ten dollars. She closed her eyes and leant back against the doorpost. Where would she be able to find one thousand dollars? Not taking in washing, that was for sure. The money that she made was barely enough to feed the family.

'I have some,' Misha said. 'Some I have saved over the year.'

Svetlana watched as he crossed the room and carefully lifted aside a sack of junk. From under a brick in the corner he pulled an envelope. He brought it over to her and placed it in her hand.

'I've been trying to save,' he said, 'a bit at a time. But it's hard. For almost a month now they've paid us almost nothing. The investors have lost money. They might have to stop building.'

Svetlana slid the notes out of the envelope. She counted them carefully. One hundred dollars. She looked at her son. Tall, muscular, he worked ten hours a day and didn't drink as far as she knew. His face was hard and his short, cropped hair made him look like a thug. She reached out and stroked his cheek.

'We'll see,' she said.

He nodded. He took back the notes and carefully put them into the envelope. To hide her tears she turned into the courtyard. The shirts and sheets flapped in the sudden furious gusts of wind. She felt them; they were cool, almost dry. She pulled a shirt into her arms. Felt its stiff cleanness on her skin. England. Work. Dreams. From where could she get such an amount of money? Not from this washing. From

Mindaugas. She shuddered, remembering her old pimp. She pulled another clean shirt from the washing line. A sheet, voluminous, fresh. She sank her face into it. Not Mindaugas. There had to be other ways.

She folded the washing neatly, dividing it into piles. Misha sat by the window, in the easy chair.

'I'll help,' he said.

She looked at his large, soiled hands and laughed.

'You want me to have to do them all again?'

He looked at his hands helplessly. As if they had betrayed him.

'Where did you meet this English man?' she asked to distract him.

'Through Anton. There are all types of jobs you can do there. Labouring. Thousands of jobs on building sites, he says. They haven't got enough people to do the work.'

Svetlana watched her son as she folded the washing, tying each lot neatly in brown wrapping paper. His face was animated and she saw a look she had not seen in his eyes since he had been too young to understand. Hope. Her heart contracted. Work. Dreams. Just not Mindaugas, she thought. Not back to that.

After delivering the washing, she walked up towards the last remaining part of the old city wall, the Gates of Dawn. There, on a bridge spanning the narrow lane, the Virgin Mother held court. The street was busy. Pensioners manned stalls selling trinkets. Crosses and beads, amber icons; photographs of the Pope stood at the open window above, on his visit in 1993. Svetlana climbed the stairs to the upper room. The air was heavy with incense. The room was crowded. Her ears were assaulted by the babble of excited prayers. Prayers in Polish. In Lithuanian. Latvian. Russian. Byelorussian. She found a space for herself, close to the window. Getting down to her knees she lifted her eyes to the flickering candles, the thick, curling plumes of incense. On the wall was the icon. Maria the Mother of God. The Queen of Heaven. The Black Madonna.

The Virgin's black skin shone. Her golden gown glittered in the light of the candles and the late afternoon sun, which reached over the tops of the city's rooftops and spires and filtered in through the window. Maria's hands were folded across her chest and she inclined her head as if to listen to the prayers of those who came to kneel before her. Soviet pensioners. Farmers' wives, smelling of chickens and garlic and sweat.

Svetlana knelt before her, silent, no prayer on her lips. She could no longer remember them. Once she had known them. She had delighted in them. But she did not want to go back to where they lay, deep in the shadowy corners of her mind. Better this silence. Wordless supplication.

'Find a way,' she managed to say, finally, when her knees had started to hurt. 'Another way. Not Mindaugas. Please. For Misha's sake.'

And here there was no shame in crying, for all the women cried, their wrinkled faces wrapped tight in black scarves. The men too. Silent tears slipped from their rheumy eyes.

Chapter 22

On the occasions Svetlana had delivered Daumantas' washing to him, she had handed it through the door, staying only long enough to receive her money. With the bag and the papers, she felt she would perhaps get beyond that door. She imagined so, anyway, as she dressed.

She was nervous. She did not want to confess to having watched him get drunk. Watched him closely enough to notice the bag he had left. In the end, with the washed clothes blowing in the sharp gusts that swirled around the courtyard, she tucked the package beneath her arm and left.

In the ghetto she stopped at a bar to have a drink. She drank slowly, making it last. Pumpetiene had called earlier with clothes and given her ten Litas, up front, to keep her going. Five had gone immediately on food; a quarter loaf of coarse dark bread and a little milk, a handful of potatoes and a small paper bag of flour. That would not last long, she had to be careful. Sipping the beer, she imagined conversations with Daumantas. Half an hour later she bought another small beer. She clutched the blue plastic bag close to her, afraid to lose it.

In the toilet of the café there was no mirror. The dirty hole in the floor stank. Svetlana walked down to the Three Friends. The waiters, knowing her, frowned. In the toilets she leaned close to the mirror and examined her face. Fine wrinkles spread from her eyes and worked around her cheeks. The bruise had almost disappeared, little more than a faint darkness beneath her eye. She applied the cheap lipstick she had bought at the market, working carefully, trying to calm the shaking of her hand. She examined the job. A slight sweat had formed in the thin hair above her lip, threatening to ruin the sharp edge she had managed to achieve. She smiled at herself; it was a tight, nervous smile, more a grimace.

Hello, she said.

She straightened the dress. It was the black-and-white dress decorated with sequins that Pumpetiene had given her. He had commented on it. The sequins ran across and beneath her breasts, accentuating them. She smoothed the glittering slivers over her breasts.

Nice dress, he had said.

I found this bag.

The dark roots of her hair were showing. Her hair grew faster than she could earn money for dye. She scrunched it, slightly, to hide the unsightly, dirty roots.

I think you lost this bag.

The door opened and a uniformed girl came in, a waitress. She looked at Svetlana, stony faced, keeping the door open behind her.

'What are you doing?' she asked sharply, in Lithuanian.

'Pissing,' Svetlana said in Russian.

'Piss somewhere else.'

Svetlana pushed past, deliberately catching the girl's shapely shoulder, knocking her back against the door. The girl's pretty face creased with anger.

'Whore.'

Walking across Ghetto Square and into the narrow lanes, Svetlana paused to gaze into the window of a new boutique. The clasps on the Gucci bags sparkled under the brilliant display lights. Leather Italian shoes shone like mirrors. Neat, petite price tags dangled like decorations. She drew the plastic bag close to her body, cradling it, like a baby. Passing the new café on Zydu Street, she emerged into the car park, shrouded already in early evening gloom. Pigeons had settled on the branches of the trees, cooing softly.

Entering Daumantas' block, she climbed the stairs slowly to his floor. At each landing she paused, reworking her dialogue. Outside Daumantas' apartment she breathed in deeply, held her breath for a moment then pressed the bell.

Hello.

I found this; I think it is yours. You left it in the café . . .

Nice dress.

She pressed the bell again.

I think this is your bag. I found it. I was drinking in the café . . .

The light in the stairwell clicked off, leaving her in sudden darkness. She groped about the wall to find the switch. She pressed the bell a third time, her heart sinking, knowing that if he had been in, he would have opened the door by now. Yet she felt she could stand there for the whole evening, pressing the bell, simply for the slight feeling of hope each press gave her.

A shoe scuffed on the stairs behind her. She turned, but it was not him. An old woman appeared, face stern, hair caught up in a net. As she approached, the time ran out and the stairs were plunged once more into darkness. Svetlana hesitated a moment, then hit the switch.

'You won't find him,' the old woman said. 'He's out.'

'Will he be back soon?'

The woman shrugged and arched her pencilled eyebrows, ironically. 'God only knows. I told him he shouldn't be going out, the state he was in. He listens? I told him it's his fault if he drops down dead.' She shook her head and sucked her teeth. 'Nah, a right carry-on.'

'What is wrong with him?'

The old woman stood still, some steps below her. She lifted an imaginary bottle to her lips and gulped it back. 'Just about drank enough to kill him,' she added. 'What a fuss he caused and then we all thought he'd gone and done himself in at last. Didn't appear the whole day. Grey as anything this morning, when I saw him. I went to get him a few things from the market.' She stared at the sequins, glistening across Svetlana's breasts. 'What did you want him for?'

Svetlana hesitated. She saw the beady old eyes moving from her glistening breasts to the parcel under her arm. She saw her take in the dark roots in her hair, the cheap lipstick, the wrinkles.

'Could you tell him I called,' she said at last.

The old woman clicked her tongue. 'I'm not chasing around after him,' she said.

Then, 'What's your name?'

'Svetlana.'

'And you have a message you want passing on?' Grigala-viciene's eyes gleamed.

'No, just Svetlana called.'

'Phuhh!' Grigalaviciene exclaimed angrily. 'I'm not running messages for him. Enough that I have to go looking after him, like I do.' Seeing that she would get no more from Svetlana, she turned and stalked back down the stairs. Svetlana followed. She saw the old woman's door close as she passed, then creak open, a crack, as she descended.

The wind had cleared away the clouds. The moon clung to the roof-tiles. The pigeons were quiet. Svetlana stood beneath the trees staring up at the darkened windows of Daumantas' apartment. She could leave the bag, of course, leave it with the old woman, leave it by the door for Daumantas to find. She hugged the papers to her.

One thousand dollars. The price of a clutch of leather handbags and Italian shoes. The price of work, of freedom.

Chapter 23

Svetlana stumbled through the nocturnal ghetto streets, clutching the parcel to her. She placed one foot in front of the other with carefully thoughtless deliberation. Letting them find their own way. Not thinking, yet knowing where they were headed. Where there were no streetlights the narrow, winding lanes were sunk in pitch darkness. A car passed, slowed, then moved on. She hugged the bag tighter. Clasping it to her chest, feeling its papery warmth. She imagined Daumantas bent over the typewriter, illumined by a single reading lamp, the click of her heels echoing the rhythm of his fingertips.

On the brow of the hill was the train station, busy with evening traffic. Taxis and trolley buses. Men in groups. Svetlana stood on the corner. She shivered. The wind was cool and she wore only the sequinned dress. She could have turned then and made her way back to Stepono. But Misha would be there, silent, helpful, smeared with the dust of his labour.

She walked down to a small bar on Kauno Street. She paused again outside the door. The windows had steamed up. She could hear the music, the jangle of laughter. Just calling in, she said to herself. Nothing more, she encouraged herself. Nothing more. Her hand shook as she pushed open the door.

The bar was busy. Young girls glittered under the red lights' glare. At the bar was the face she recognised. The face she knew she would see there. She walked across confidently, allowing the bag to drop from in front of her. Letting the red lights catch the sequins across her breasts and cascade off, dazzling. Steeled to the glances, territorial and predatory. She caught his elbow.

'Mindaugas.'

The man turned, hearing his name. For a split second he paused, then grinned. 'Svyeta!' And gave her a kiss. The gold rings shone on his fleshy fingers. The cuffs of a dark shirt protruded from the sleeves of his jacket far enough to display his jewelled cufflinks. His face was thicker, rounder than it had been last time she saw him. His hair a little thinner. She saw his eyes appraising her. Noticing the yellow shadow beneath her eye. The thin, meandering creases, pushing down towards her cheeks. The roots of her hair. Seeing too her body, as she eased herself onto a stool, still shapely. He pushed a glass in her direction and poured a drink.

'Nice dress,' he said.

She nodded and smiled.

He clicked her glass with his own and raised it. She raised hers and drank.

'It's good to see you again,' Mindaugas said. He patted her thigh with one of his fleshy hands. 'It's been a long time.'

'Yes,' Svetlana said. 'It's been a while.'

'Are you . . . ?' Mindaugas asked.

She shook her head quickly. 'No,' she said. 'No, I just dropped by to say hello.'

'Fine, good,' Mindaugas said. He smiled again. 'Good.'

She sat with him, watching the girls, skirts riding high up their thighs, taking a break. These girls were professionals, with tough smiles and bright make-up. Their laughter pierced the rhythmic thump of the dance music.

'Look,' she said, nudging Mindaugas' elbow as a young girl pushed into the bar. 'She can't even be sixteen.'

'Ruta?' Mindaugas said, sipping his vodka. 'Thirteen, or so.'

Svetlana shook her head. 'Not one of yours?'

'No,' he said. 'Don't you go worrying about that one, she'd cut your throat if you looked at her the wrong way. Feisty little bitch. She's been on the game since she was ten.'

'Whose girl is she?'

'Viktor's.'

'Bastard.'

'There's worse. Some American moved in a couple of months ago. Thinks he can do what he wants. I'm telling you, things are going to get a bit rough soon.'

Svetlana watched the girl as she strode over to the bar, high heels clicking on the tiles. She ordered a drink and remained standing, on her own, not glancing around. Her face was tightly professional. A working girl. Hiding her fear in aggression.

Feeling her heart contract, Svetlana looked away. The memories bubbled up. Thirteen. Preferring loneliness to the sharp bitterness of life at home, she had escaped from her mother. Emotions curdled in their apartment, where loss hung as heavily on the air as had the aromatic smoke of her father's cigarettes. She had a sudden vision of men approaching her, an open window and fear in the pit of her stomach.

Mindaugas finished his vodka. He wiped his lips, carefully, on a neat, white handkerchief. 'Ivan's back, I hear.'

'You heard?'

'Kasimov hired him on some job.'

Svetlana shrugged. She picked up the bag from the counter. 'I have to be going.'

'Good seeing you, Svyeta.' Mindaugas smiled. He held her arm as she slipped down off the stool.

'If you should need . . . There is work.'

Svetlana shook her head. She forced a smile.

The night was cool. She leant back against the wall and it washed over her. Pounding, rolling waves, drowning her.

She gasped for breath. Her sob was choked off by nausea. She bent over and vomited.

When she reached Stepono, the building was in darkness. The thin light of a candle flickered in a neighbour's dirty window. Her washing flapped, glimmering ghostly white. She gathered it into her arms and buried her face into the fresh clean shirts, savouring the smell for a moment.

The air in the room was fetid. Nikolai was asleep in his clothes in the corner. She bent over him and kissed the stubble on his fragile skull. Finding a thin sheet she pulled it over him. She sat on the edge of the bed, laying the bag beside her.

Chapter 24

She was sitting on the edge of her bed, the sheet wrapped tight in her small, white fist. There was whispering. Low, urgent voices. The wind whistled through the treetops. From somewhere, out in the darkness, she heard the sound of a dog howling. A fearful chill ran down her spine. She drew the sheet up to her lips. There were footsteps, the sound of bare feet slapping on the cold, wooden floorboards. And then a thump on the door. The sound echoed through the quiet house. Dying away slowly in the furthest, darkest corners. The feet were still. The whispering staunched.

The fist pounded on the door again, steady in its furious insistence. A man called, his voice muffled. Open the door. Voices were whispering in her parents' room. Get dressed, her father said. She could hear her mother whispering, whispering. Get dressed, said her father again. His voice shaking, but loud, determined. The apartment rang to the sound of the pounding fists. She covered her ears. Men were calling. Angry orders. Open the door. Open the door.

Svetlana woke. The room was quiet. Nikolai was sleeping in the corner, tucked in the thin sheet. Beside her lay Ivan. She wiped the droplet of perspiration from her forehead. Waited for her pulse to slow. She eased herself out of bed slowly. Quietly she walked across to the door and opened it. The courtyard was illuminated faintly by moonlight. She leaned against the doorframe and lit a cigarette, inhaling deeply the raw, scorching smoke.

*   *   *

Fine, her father said, moving down the corridor to the door. They moved into the apartment quickly, pushing him before them. She heard their boots on the floorboards. A grunt as her father tried to protest. A small cry from her mother. Somebody said her father's name. Yes, he said, that's me. Again the sound of scuffling. It's fine, it's fine, her father said, breathless, scared, I'm not fighting. Svetlana curled into her bed. Her heart thudded. She pulled the covers over her head, hiding in the darkness.

The books, she heard a voice demand. We know that you have samizdat literature. The papers, get them out.

Give them, show them. Her mother's voice was tight with fear.

The darkness was hot, airless. She hugged her legs tight against her chest. Pressed her forehead against her sharp knees. She whispered the prayer her father had taught her. Over and over she said the words.

For God's sake, just give them the books, it's what they want. Her mother's voice was faint as though she was in the apartment below. Her father said nothing.

Beneath the sheets she whispered her prayers. Their secret. If she told anybody he had been teaching her the prayers he would be in trouble, he had said to her. She did not tell, it was their secret.

Her mother was crying. Svetlana waited until the echo of the boots had faded, the voices gone. Peeling back the sheet she peered out into the still darkness. She slipped out of the bed and stood in the doorway. Her mother was on the bed, a dressing gown pulled with careless haste around her. Her face was pressed into the sheets. Her body heaved as the sobs tore her. The apartment door was closed. Her father's suitcase was beside the bed, clothes falling from it. Her mother sobbed. Her father was gone. His shoes had gone but his umbrella was still there, by the door. And his scarf hung on the coat hook. But he was gone. She looked at her mother sobbing on the bed. A sharp pain cut her heart. She felt bile rising in her throat. Her small fists tightened. A cry escaped her. The squawk of a frightened, angry crow. She flew across the room and lashed at her mother with her small clenched fists. Her mother looked up, startled.

Svetlana flicked the butt of the cigarette out into the courtyard. The night was quiet. A car drove slowly down Pylimo, the soft snarl growing then fading away.

Chapter 25

Ivan was whistling. Svetlana watched him potter cheerfully around the room. He brought a cup of coffee and a pair of scissors over to the bed.

'Clip my hair round the back.'

Slowly Svetlana sat up, attempting to unglue her eyes. She took a large gulp of the bitter coffee and took the scissors from him.

'Wait,' she said. 'I can't open my eyes.'

'You'd better be straight.'

He sat on the edge of the bed, an old towel wrapped around his shoulders. Carefully she clipped an inch of hair, straight, across the back of his neck. He moved his head from side to side as she cut, making her job difficult. The blades of the scissors glinted in the sunshine falling through the window. She slid the blunt edge across the skin of the back of his neck. Each time footsteps clattered past the window, he bent forward to catch a glimpse.

'You expecting someone?'

Ivan did not answer. He lit a cigarette. Holding up a small mirror he directed which parts of his hair she should be cutting.

Testily he said, 'Shorter round the ears, I look like a tramp.'

She hardly dared interpret his good mood as meaning he had picked up some girl, had found somebody who might engross his interest and keep him away for a longer stretch of time. She noticed she had the scissors open wide, testing their sharp edge against her thumb. His throat was pink and freshly shaved.

'Come on, get on with it,' Ivan snapped. 'I haven't got all day.'

When he left, she got up. The cupboards were empty. She sat on the floor holding her head in cupped hands. The vodka bottle was empty.

Pulling the tin tub from the corner she laid it on the rug. The bucket under the tap was almost full; she hoisted it onto the stove and lit it. While the water was warming, she pulled washing from the pile and dumped it into the tub. Pouring the warm water onto the clothes, she began to pound them. The tendons in her arms felt as if they had been ripped. She washed slowly, wearily. The blue plastic bag lay on the end of the bed and she could see it from where she knelt, over the tub. She thought of Misha. Of the one thousand dollars and of the hundred he had carefully managed to save.

When the washing had dried, she wrapped it carefully in paper and tied it with a piece of string. Putting it under her arm she walked down the road towards the old ghetto. She was hungry and felt faint by the time she got to the apartment block where Pumpetiene lived. Sitting on the lower steps, in the darkness of the stairwell, she rested her head against the wall.

'My goodness, you look terrible,' Pumpetiene said. She opened her door wide and grasped Svetlana to prevent her from falling. Taking her beneath the arm, she helped her into the apartment.

'What has happened to you? Have you eaten? You've not been drinking, have you? You're not drunk?'

The thought held Pumpetiene a moment and they stopped in the darkness of the hallway. Pumpetiene sniffed her.

'No,' she said. 'You're just tired. Come on in.'

She led Svetlana through to the living room and settled

her on the neat settee. Svetlana murmured softly, but found she was not able to say anything. The blood seemed to have withdrawn from her face and a cold sweat broke out on her forehead. Her lips were grey. Pumpetiene put the parcel of washing on the table and disappeared into the kitchen.

A key clicked in the door lock and it opened. A man cleared his throat in the hallway. A few moments later his head appeared in the living room. Seeing her, his pale blue eyes widened. He gasped and was about to say something, but disappeared instead. Svetlana heard Pumpetiene greet her husband in the kitchen. Her voice was timid and edged with fear.

'What is she doing here?' His voice was an angry whisper.

Pumpetiene answered him, her voice low and urgent.

'She's a whore,' he said. 'I'm not having a whore sitting on my sofa.'

Again Svetlana heard the sound of Pumpetiene's voice, twittering like a frightened bird.

'Get that whore out of my chair.' Her husband's voice rose so that it was perfectly audible in the neat living room. Svetlana was already standing when Pumpetiene returned. Pumpetiene's small face was wrinkled with embarrassment. She looped her arm under Svetlana's and helped her back through the dark hallway in silence. As she pushed her through the door, she grabbed Svetlana's hand and pressed a twenty-Litas note into it.

Pumpetiene had closed the door before Svetlana could protest. She rested her head against the wooden door. Through it she could hear Pumpetiene's voice.

'She's gone,' she said. 'Little whore,' her voice pleaded nervously. Her husband grunted. Svetlana clutched the money tightly in her hand.

Chapter 26

'Ah, there you are,' Ivan said, seeing Svetlana in the doorway. 'What's there to eat? I'm starving!'

He was slouched on the bed watching TV. Svetlana shrugged. Her faint spell had passed but she felt weary. She bent over the small cupboard and gathered the last of the potatoes, sprouting in the dark corners.

In the courtyard she peeled the potatoes, letting the wrinkled skins drop into the muddy grass. She sliced them and fried them in an old pan on the stove.

'Smells good,' Ivan said, not taking his eyes from the blurred picture on the black-and-white screen.

The door opened behind Svetlana as she stirred the potatoes in the spitting fat. Misha squeezed in, his face dirty and tired. Svetlana hugged him.

'Trust him to turn up just in time,' Ivan moaned.

'There's enough,' Svetlana said quietly.

'Don't worry, you old bastard,' Misha said. 'Nobody's going to be taking the food from your mouth. I've eaten.'

He put his arm around his mother's shoulders.

'There's enough for everyone,' she insisted. 'We can all eat.'

'There's never enough for that greedy bastard,' Misha said bitterly.

Ivan rose from the bed, angry. 'You watch your lip.'

'Misha,' Svetlana pleaded.

Misha pulled off his jacket and hung it on a nail by the door. He said no more. Walking across to his brother he ruffled his hair. Nikolai smiled. Svetlana heaped the potatoes onto plates. Ivan sighed heartily. Taking the plate he fell upon the fried potatoes greedily.

'Where's the salt?' he complained, his mouth full.

'Mama, I've eaten.'

Misha pushed the plate away.

'Take it, don't be silly,' Svetlana insisted. 'You've been working hard. You need the food.'

'Oi, oi!' Ivan complained. 'How can I eat these fucking potatoes without any salt on them?'

'So don't eat them,' Misha said, turning on him.

Ivan eyed him, considering. He forked the potatoes into his mouth and glared at his stepson.

'You'd better watch how you talk to me. You should learn a little respect.'

'I've learned respect, but not for lazy bastards like you.'

Ivan leapt up, furious. Veins stood out on his neck. Misha jumped up too, his blue eyes blazing, unafraid.

'Watch your tongue!' Ivan shouted, his fists rising to strike, his face pushed close to the youth's. He shook with rage. Spittle flecked his unshaven chin and sweat jumped out on his forehead. Misha glared. He stood inches taller than Ivan. His skin, though dirty, was healthy and his arms were thick with muscles.

Svetlana moved between the two. 'Stop,' she pleaded.

Misha moved away. He pulled his jacket from the nail and slipped it on. From the corner, Nikolai watched quietly. Svetlana grabbed Misha's arm.

'It's fine, Mama,' he said. 'I'm going for a walk.'

He glanced back at Ivan, his lip curling with disgust. Stepping into the courtyard he spat loudly. Ivan collapsed onto the bed. He drew a cigarette from a crumpled pack. His hands shook as he lit it. He waited until Misha's shadow had passed the window before turning on Svetlana.

'You see how you bring them up! Where's the respect?' He threw the remaining potatoes aside. 'I can't eat these, they're disgusting.'

Svetlana picked up the plate. 'Why do you have to be such a bastard?'

Ivan looked up, incredulous. 'Me? What did I do?' He exhaled wispy clouds of cigarette smoke.

'Why do you hate him so much?'

'It isn't me. He hates me. And why? Because you're always complaining, that's why.'

Ivan stared at the fuzzy images on the television screen. He smoked the cigarette with quick nervous puffs. Stubbing the cigarette out, he lit another immediately and smoked that slowly. Svetlana watched him for a few moments. His shirt was wrinkled and dirty. It was unbuttoned, displaying the thick hair on his chest. His hair was greasy, making it look darker than it actually was.

Rubbing his face he shifted on the bed, glancing at the clock on the wall. Svetlana realised he was waiting for something. She rinsed the plates in a small pan of cold water in the sink.

At six o'clock there was a knock at the door. Ivan sat up. Jonas stood in the courtyard, looking sour and beaten. He slouched past Svetlana without a word and settled heavily in the chair.

'Well?' Ivan said, coughing.

Jonas's face was red and puffy. He gazed dismally out through the small window into the street. Wind blew in through the broken panes, fluttering the plastic bags Svetlana had used to cover them.

'Well what?' he said evasively.

'Did you go to Zirmunai or not?'

'Of course I went,' Jonas said shortly.

'So?'

'So what?'

Ivan jumped up from the bed irritated. He grabbed Jonas and clouted him around the head.

'Don't mess me around, you little prick!' he yelled. The exertion caused him to cough violently. Jonas shrank further back into the chair. 'Did you see the guy or not?' Ivan said once he had recovered from his coughing. 'I give you fifty dollars of Kasimov's money and you can't do the simplest of jobs!'

Jonas scratched his head. He winced when Ivan raised his voice. 'Of course I saw him. Just like Kasimov said, he was drinking at the bar in Zirmunai. You heard him, he drinks there all the time. Every night. What you getting so worked up about?'

Ivan frowned. 'So tell me! I want to picture it. We got to do the job this week, Kasimov is on my back. I need to get it right. I need to go through the whole thing in my head, so that it'll be natural.'

Svetlana took a cigarette and stood in the doorway. She watched the two men but tried not to listen; she did not want to know what job Kasimov was paying them to do. Ivan stood up, pulled the blanket from the bed and wrapped it around him. The blue plastic bag that had been on the end of the bed slipped off, the sheets cascading out across the floor. Jonas leaned forward, suddenly animated. His eyes fixed on the scattered pages and the blue bag.

'That's it!' he exclaimed.

Svetlana started. She flicked the cigarette out into the courtyard and stepped forward to pick up the papers.

'That's what?' said Ivan.

Jonas leapt quickly from his seat and scrabbled on the floor, gathering the sheets, grabbing hold of the plastic bag before Svetlana could reach it.

'What's the matter with you?' Ivan said.

'I've had this crazy old guy on at me. He left a bag in the café the other night. A blue plastic bag, he says, full of paper. It's some book he wrote or something. He's pretty desperate to get it back.'

Svetlana pulled the bag from his hands and bundled the sheets into a pile. 'Give them me,' she said. 'Keep your hands off.'

Ivan stared down at the two arguing on the floor at his feet. He kicked out at Svetlana and grabbed Jonas by his collar, yanking him to his feet with the front page of the manuscript still in his hand. Svetlana stumbled back, holding the rest of the papers tight to her chest.

Ivan shook Jonas hard. 'I don't give a fuck about any old men, I've got a job that needs planning.' He threw the blanket back onto the bed and pulled on a jacket. 'Let's go for a drink.'

Reluctantly Jonas followed him out into the courtyard. Svetlana watched them go, not letting up her grasp on Daumantas' package. Once they had gone she sprang across to the bed, where the last of the papers lay scattered. She gathered them together carefully. As she was sliding them back into the bag, Jonas entered. He looked at her, then at the bag in her hands. She stood up slowly. Jonas pointed at the bag, but she stopped him.

'Forget it.'

Jonas seemed about to say something. He shuffled forward. Svetlana glared at him fiercely.

'Come one step closer,' she said, 'and see what I do.'

For a few moments longer he lingered, his eyes on the bag in her hand, judging whether he could take it by force.

'I'll be back,' he said, licking his lips, nervously. He folded the sheet he held in his hand and slipped it into his pocket. 'I'll be back for it, Svyeta.'

Chapter 27

When Jonas left, Svetlana's eyes flicked quickly about the room. In the corner, by the wall, was the bed and by that the one armchair. Against the opposite wall was a small table, with the television perched on it. In the corner by the door, a sink, a small cooker with two hobs. On the floor, laid over the twisted, old wooden floorboards, a threadbare rug.

She held the bag in her arms, tightly. She feared that at any moment Jonas might return with Ivan. Her eyes searched for some space where it might be hidden. Somewhere she could be sure he would not look. For a moment her eyes rested on the pile of junk in the darkest corner where, she now knew, Misha kept his savings hidden. Not there. If Ivan searched the room it would not take him long to discover. She worried then that if Ivan did search the room he would find Misha's money.

Down on her knees, she peered beneath the bed. Bags of clothing, thin and ragged sheets, broken toys. The floorboards creaked under her knees as she shifted. The floorboards. The thought struck her. She examined them. The wood was old, worn, but it was nailed down firmly. She ran her fingers along the edge of the boards, finding their ends, examining the rusty nails, prising at them with her fingertips.

In the courtyard she heard the sound of voices. She paused and sat up. She listened, tense and still, straining to hear. Her fingers tightened around the plastic bag. Male voices, low, hard to distinguish. She rose and stepped stealthily across to the door. Peeping out into the courtyard, she saw two men sat in the sun, beer bottles in hands. Neighbours.

She hurried back across the room. Lifting the rug she ran her fingers over the wooden boards. The tip of her finger clipped a loose nail. It cut her. The blood oozed up quickly and she pushed the finger into her mouth and sucked it. She examined the board. It appeared moveable. Taking a spoon from the sink, she prised it up. With a little resistance it shifted. The nail squeaked as it moved in the wood. And then it was out. She lifted the board away. There was a space beneath it, quite wide enough to slip in the plastic bag. Carefully she did so. She pushed it through the gap and away from the hole.

As Svetlana withdrew her fingers, her nails brushed against something. It was cold, smooth. She hesitated. She knelt down and tried to peer into the gap, but it was too dark. Cautiously she slipped her arm back into the space and felt around in the darkness. Her fingers touched it. It moved. A metal box. A small metal box. She clutched at it and drew it to the gap.

It slipped out easily. She laid it on the bed. Replacing the floorboard she pushed the old rusted nail back into the hole, pressing it down with the palm of her hand until it lay flush with the others. Rolling back the rug she smoothed it out. Nothing showed. She rinsed her fingers in the bucket of cold water under the slow-dripping tap. Only then did she turn her attention back to the metal box that lay on the rumpled sheets.

It was old and coated with dust. The corners had rusted. Taking a cloth, she wiped it carefully, revealing the decoration on its side and the writing. The writing was odd. The first thing that struck her was that it was not Lithuanian, as she might have imagined. Nor was it Polish. The distinctive script was not Cyrillic either. The box was red and the writing yellow. Faded and dirty now. Hard to imagine that once it must have shone, have reflected the sun. The lid that sealed the top of the box had rusted closed. It would not budge when she tried it. She fetched a knife and slid it inside, moving it along to loosen the corroded metal. When she levered it, the metal bent. Finally she had to bend the metal back on all sides before it gave way and dropped off.

What had she been expecting to find? Treasure? Gold coins? It had rattled when she shook it gently. There was something metal inside. But she had not opened it in the hope of finding money. It was curiosity that made her fingers fumble, as she scooped out the contents.

There were three objects inside the box. She laid them one beside the other on the bed. A handkerchief, a ring and a medal. Nothing more. She looked inside the tin. The corners were brown with rust. The metal glistened still, a little.

The ring was gold. A thin band. A wedding ring. She lifted it carefully. It had fitted a slim finger. She tried it on her own and found that it would only slip over the knuckle of her smallest. She pulled it off quickly. It accentuated the thick, red knuckled roughness of her hands. She examined it closely. There was no inscription engraved on it.

The handkerchief had been white. It was grey now, with large growing lakes of brown where the rust had spilt out over it. In the corner, carefully embroidered, were the initials of the owner. It puzzled Svetlana that somebody had taken the trouble to hide a handkerchief. The ring and medal had not been wrapped in it; it was not there for functional purposes. It had meant something to the person.

The last object was a small metal disk with a hole punched into it. The Lithuanian emblem was printed on the disk, crudely. It was a cheap medallion and it too had been infected with the rust. Svetlana rubbed the brown crust between her fingers, revealing more of the knight astride his horse, sword flourishing in the air above him.

Who, Svetlana wondered, had hidden these humble treasures? Three personal relics, dull with age. She gathered them into her hands and pressed them to her. There was something pitiful about them. She placed the mementoes back into the rusted box, but did not replace the lid.

She held the box on her lap and gazed down into it. At the flotsam of life, hidden, cherished. Hidden memories. She had not seen her father again. That night was the last. He had kissed her earlier, when she had gone to bed. She knelt and said her prayers. She crawled in between the cool sheets. He came in and leaned over her. She did not open her eyes. She sensed his presence above her. His beard. His large face. She pulled her face down under the sheet.

Later – after – she opened the door. It was dark outside, a freezing wind blew in and lifted the curtains. Her mother stood in the door of the bedroom and told her to close it. She turned and stared at her. Her mother withdrew.

Svetlana closed her eyes. She leaned back against the wall. The two men were still talking in the courtyard, their voices a murmur, a quiet, drunken argument. She felt weary. Not tired, a deep weariness that suffused her whole body. She lay on the bed, cradling the metal box against her breast.

The sound of voices. A forest. A low hymn rising from the cone-strewn hollow, lifting on the pine-scented breeze. The birds were singing. The trees whispered. Svetlana's hand was in his. Her small white fist screwed up inside that large leather pouch. The singing was low, tentative, as though it was the very earth itself, fumbling to find its voice. They crept over the ridge and saw them. Gathered in the clearing, they stood in a group not far from the wooden cottage. Svetlana looked up as her father raised his hand in greeting. His large face was flushed with a smile.

Always when he spoke his voice was quiet. That was how she remembered it. They slid down the ridge into the clearing. Sunlight cut through the tops of the trees and fell in thick beams through the tall trunks. The ground was soft beneath their feet and she slipped on the pine needles as she descended from the ridge.

'You must not take her,' her mother had said, before they went. She looked at her mother. A small, creased woman. Her father said nothing. He had his back to her and did not turn.

'It's dangerous. You mustn't. If the police find out . . . God knows what they will do.'

'God knows,' her father said, his voice calm and low. 'And we must trust in Him.'

Svetlana slipped into sleep, clasping the metal tin to her tightly. The rust rubbed against her skin, colouring it.

He had taken her. How she had gloated. A warm flush of victory blushed her cheeks as she turned her back on her mother and put her hand into her father's. She looked round briefly as they left. Her mother stood in the corridor, lips pursed tightly, arms folded. Svetlana smiled.

The singing grew louder as they drew closer, their footsteps silent on the thick carpet of needles. Behind the group the cottage door was open and faintly she could hear the click and hum of a machine. The printing press, operated by an old man covered in ink, who came and stood in the doorway as they approached, wiping his hands on a dirty cloth. Her father began singing, his voice rose like that of a deep-throated bird, winging its way across the clearing, joining the voices of the group, who had turned to greet them.

When they knelt, the needles bit into the soft flesh on her knees. She pressed close to her father, her eyes shut tight. Screwed up. Her nose wrinkling. She did not listen to the melodic chant of the priest's prayer. Her father had slipped his arm around her. Opening her eyes suddenly, she saw the last rays of the sinking sun as they broke through the branches. The air was pink and, close to the earth, blue.

In their arms they took the newly printed books from the cottage. They smelled sharp and fresh. They loaded them into the back of the car and as he closed the door, in the gloom, her father raised his finger to his lips. Our secret, he said. You must say nothing, not even to your mother. Two nights later he was taken.

Chapter 28

The weather in the morning was blustery. Dark clouds scudded across the rooftops and the wind blew the rain hard against the windows. Svetlana had one small bag of washing to do and she did it early. She wrapped the clean shirts carefully and slid the paper parcel into a plastic bag so that it would not get wet when she delivered it. As she stepped out into the squall, Jonas ducked into the courtyard, his collar turned up against the weather. Svetlana was glad of the excuse to avoid him.

Jonas rapped on the door and entered. Ivan was stretched out on the bed, an eye lazily on the television. Jonas slumped into the armchair.

'That bag,' he said after a few moments, as though the thought had just struck him. 'What did she do with it?'

For a moment Ivan looked at him, blankly.

'Those papers,' Jonas reminded him. 'The blue plastic bag.'

Ivan shook his head. 'No idea.'

'He called again last night.'

Ivan sat up and pulled a cigarette from the packet. He did not seem to be listening, absorbed as he was in the fuzzy image of the South American soap opera. Jonas glanced around the room. There was no sign of it. He bent over and glanced beneath the bed.

'He seems pretty desperate to get it back,' he said.

Ivan did not reply.

'I thought he might offer some money for it,' Jonas added

cautiously. Ivan's eyes flicked away from the screen. They studied Jonas' face. He lit the cigarette that had been dangling from his lips. After a few moments his eyes drifted back to the screen.

'How much?' he said.

'Not much, not much,' Jonas said. He tried to think of a sum. He couldn't say much or Ivan would want the business for himself. If he said too little Ivan would not be interested. 'Twenty dollars.'

Ivan sat up. He walked over to the television and turned it off. Placing the cigarette on the edge of the sink, he rinsed his face in the water collected in the bucket.

'If he offers some money, I'll find where she's put it,' he said, drying his face on a cloth.

Jonas nodded. 'Right,' he said. His eyes continued to search the room, but there was no sign of it.

Not five minutes after Jonas had left, as Ivan was pulling on his coat, there was a rap at the door. Ivan ignored it. Finding Svetlana's jacket he searched through the pockets, looking for some cash. There was another bang on the door. It shook beneath the blow.

'Svetlana?' a voice called.

'What do you want?' Ivan called angrily.

'I'm looking for Svetlana,' the man called back through the door.

Ivan threw the jacket onto the bed. He swore. He needed a drink. He stepped over to the door and opened it. Pressed in against the wall, trying to avoid the flurries of rain, was an elderly man. His silver hair had been blown by the wind, but he was dressed smartly, as if he had been out for dinner. Though obviously in his seventies, he looked fit and his eyes were lively and bright. Ivan could see the man was appraising him critically.

'She's not here,' he said sourly, leaning against the door-jamb.

'Oh,' said the man and then paused. 'She'll be back soon, will she?'

Ivan pulled the coat around him. A raw wind sprayed the rain into the doorway. He coughed. 'How would I know?' Ivan said, irritated at the man's persistence. Beneath his arm he carried a small parcel.

'She didn't say? I've got work for her,' the man said, indicating the bag he was carrying.

'What about the money?' Ivan said, not reaching out his hand to take the package.

'I pay her when they're done,' he said.

Ivan stared at him. For a few moments they stood eyeing each other, then the elderly man held out the bag and pulled a few Litas from his pocket.

'Here,' he said. 'Tell Svetlana that Steponas Daumantas left it. If she brings it to my apartment I'll pay her a little extra.'

Ivan nodded, his fingers closing around the money. He stuffed it into his pocket. The name seemed familiar to Ivan and for a moment he paused.

'A man called Jonas didn't just call here, did he?' Daumantas asked.

Ivan looked at him for an instant without answering. The name clicked. For a moment he considered whether he should say something about the papers. He could perhaps get some more money, he considered. But he needed a drink. He needed one badly.

'Yes,' he said then. 'Yes he did, if it's got anything to do with you.'

Daumantas turned away into the squall. He turned before he had taken a few paces and said something more, but Ivan had already closed the door.

When Svetlana returned in the late afternoon, Ivan was gone. On the bed lay the package of clothes Daumantas had left.

She examined it. His name was written neatly in a left-hand corner. She sat on the bed and held it on her lap. He had been and she had missed him. She examined the rug. It did not seem to have been moved. Laying the package aside, she got to her knees and rolled it back. The floorboard was in place. Taking a knife she lifted it carefully and slipped her hand into the dark space. It was there. She pulled it out. She laid the blue bag on the bed beside the package of shirts. The shirts were barely dirty. One seemed deliberately crumpled.

She drew a bucket of water from the radiator. She would wash them immediately, she thought, and return them with the bag of papers that evening. Pouring the steaming water into the tub she dropped in Daumantas' shirts. She held one close to her face, inhaling the sharp scent of his skin, and caressed the soft cloth against her cheek.

Chapter 29

Svetlana was hanging Daumantas' shirts on the string, strung out across the courtyard, when Misha appeared. Seeing her he ducked away, head drawn down in to the collar of his jacket as he dodged in through the doorway. Svetlana secured the last shirt with the wooden peg and followed him inside. Misha was sitting on the bed, his jacket still on, head in hands.

'Misha?'

He did not answer. Svetlana crouched beside him, taking his arms in her hands. He strained against her, not allowing her to pull his hands away from his face.

'What is it, Misha?'

'Nothing,' he said, his voice furious, belligerent, as it had been as a child. Then he sighed. 'Nothing,' he repeated, his voice drained now.

He sat back. Svetlana started. Around his eye the flesh was swollen and discoloured. A deep cut split open the skin on his cheek. Small beads of coagulated blood clung to his lower lip. Instinctively her hand reached out to him, but he jerked back, away from her.

'Don't,' he said.

'What happened?'

He stood up and paced across to the window.

'Nothing,' he said.

Standing with his back to her, he stared out into the street, through the plastic sheeting and the small square of grimy window. Svetlana did not approach him. She sat on the edge of the bed. For some moments he said no more, then he turned his head slightly.

'The job has finished.'

'Finished?'

He stuffed his hands into the pockets of his trousers. Still he did not turn. The anger had disappeared from his voice and when he spoke it was with resignation.

'I lost the job.' He paused again. 'The builder was having trouble with money. It was understandable, it wasn't his fault. He lost money when the bank collapsed. Nobody was buying; everybody wanted paying immediately. Matulis came down himself to the site. He promised he would pay us, that he would keep the jobs. We just had to be patient.

'He was here again this morning.' Misha paused. He gazed out of the window, rubbing dust from the glass with his fingers. 'Then some of Kasimov's men came. Matulis had borrowed money from Kasimov to keep things going. They wanted him off the site. They said that Kasimov was calling in the loan. Matulis tried to reason with them, but they weren't going to listen.'

He fingered his cheek, absently. 'A fight broke out.'

'Kasimov?' Svetlana said.

Misha turned away from the window and faced her. He shrugged. Svetlana gazed at her son. He was eighteen. For four years he had been working on building sites. He looked ten years older than he was. His arms bulged, his face was dirty and lined and his eyes sullen. Her heart contracted with pain. She longed to take him in her arms and hug him as she had when he was a child.

'There'll be other work,' he said, leaning back against the windowsill. He chuckled darkly. 'There's plenty of work. Perhaps Kasimov will hire us.'

The daylight had begun to fade and the room was grimly shadowed.

'We'll get the money, Misha,' she said. 'We'll get enough.'

'One thousand dollars? Some hope.' Misha scratched his scalp with one of his thick fingers. 'Without a job? Where would we get that kind of money?'

'We'll get it,' Svetlana said. Her fingers sought out the plastic bag that lay near her on the bed. She caressed it. 'We'll find a way.'

'I could try going to England myself,' Misha said, thoughtfully.

'With no papers? They wouldn't let you in. They would send you straight back. You would just waste your money.'

'There's nothing here.'

'We'll get the money. We will.'

Outside, she felt the shirts that were dancing a slow polka in the breeze. They were still damp. She walked down Stepono to the shop on the corner and bought some bread and a small bag of milk with the last of the money Pumpetiene had given her. Returning she spotted Nikolai playing quietly in the rubble of the old Jewish school.

The building sagged. Its roof had fallen in, and each floor had given way. Thick joists hung like broken ribs. Windows gaped. The walls stood, still, stooped like old soldiers remembering the dead on the ninth of May.

Svetlana crossed the road and paused at the cavity, which had once been a doorway, before the war. She called out to her son. Hearing her voice, Nikolai crooked his head. He was squatted on the heap of fallen floors, sifting through the broken bricks and dust. He scuttled away, into the darkness of a room left standing. Svetlana, fearing for him, stepped through the doorway and clambered across the rubble.

The centre of the building opened out into a large room, sheltered now only by dark clouds. On the walls, the Hebrew script was clearly discernible. In all the years she had lived across the street she had never been inside the shell of the building. She had never associated it with its past. Seeing the writing on the wall, faded but clear, it struck her now. She thought of the metal box in her room. The pitiful treasures.

'Nikolai,' she called.

In the darkness she heard scuttling, a small cascade of rubble, the rattle of an old tin can. Silence. She peered in. There was no sign of him. She edged towards the dark doorway, straining her eyes in the growing gloom.

'Nikolai,' she whispered.

'Svyeta!' a voice called from the street.

Svetlana jumped. She turned, stumbling on the loose building scree. In the gaping doorway, which gave out onto the street, stood Jonas. He grinned. The streetlight above him flickered on, casting a sickly light upon his deformed face. A cold flush of revulsion and fear surged over Svetlana. She stooped and took in her hand a half brick.

'Stay away from me, Jonas,' she called, her voice low and threatening.

'Just saying hello,' he said, grinning still. He waved, then turned back into the street. She could hear him chuckle as he made his way towards Pylimo. She waited until his footsteps had faded before she stumbled out of the building.

Before gathering the clean shirts into her arms, she washed her hands carefully in a small bowl of water. She brought the shirts into the room. Misha had gone. Moving the television, she carefully laid a clean sheet across the table and ironed the shirts. Folding them precisely, she wrapped them in paper and tied the package with string.

It was only then that she glanced at the bed and realised it had gone. For a moment she could not believe it. Rooted to the spot she stared at the rumpled sheets. At their emptiness. The freezing dread rolled back over her, a vicious wave that nearly toppled her. She stooped and peered into the blackness beneath the bed. She turned on the small lamp and scanned the room. Every surface. She opened cupboards, upended piles of clothes. Stupidly, irrationally, she bent down and rolled back the threadbare rug. Taking a knife, she levered up the floorboard, prising out the rusted nails. She lay on her belly and thrust her hand into the gap beneath the boards. Further, her arm extending into the vacant opening. It was not there. It had gone. She had known the moment she glanced at the bed and saw its absence. She had known then where it was. Who had taken it.

She pressed her forehead onto the rough wooden floorboards and cried. That was how Nikolai found her, when he slid in from the darkness fifteen minutes later.

Chapter 30

A medal, a ring, a handkerchief. Svetlana spread them out around her. Someone's memories. In her right hand she cradled the bottle of vodka. She lifted it to her lips. Nuzzled it. Drank. Nikolai, in the corner, gazed out into the darkness, vacantly. The bottle fell away from her lips. Empty. She dropped it over the side of the bed onto the floor. The sudden clatter startled Nikolai. He looked up. For a moment he gazed at the bottle spinning on the floorboards. Then his eyes shifted, back to the shadows.

He had been taken. When she woke the next morning her father was not there. She made believe it had been a dream. She could do that then. Under the sheets she lay listening to the silence of the apartment, imagining the hour was early yet. That her father was still sleeping. Elaborately she planned her day, and he was there, in his place. She did not allow the silence to undo her. The absence of his voice, the slop of his slippers, the rubber breaking loose of its stitching again, slapping on the parqueted floor in the corridor. She took only shallow breaths and so did not notice the absence of his morning cigarette, the aroma of his coffee.

When finally she slipped back the sheets, acknowledging the time the clock displayed, and washed and dressed in the unnatural silence and went to the kitchen, still she allowed herself to believe it had been a dream. Her mother sat at the table, eyes rimmed scarlet, lips white and her hair dishevelled. Svetlana said nothing. They avoided each other's eyes. Carefully she stepped around her mother, breakfasted. A sandwich like her father made her. She packed her books into her school bag and left the apartment, closing the door behind her quietly.

The class was subdued. Eyes flicked up from their books and studied her. She wrote carefully, forming each word with pedantic neatness. Sofia Petrova, the teacher, stood behind her. She felt the teacher's presence but did not look up. It was only when Sofia Petrova placed a hand upon her shoulder that she felt the bubble of tears rise to the surface and she woke from the dream. The pen shook in her hand and the neat word that she had just written disappeared under a thin blue pool of ink. Her eyes blurred and a pain stabbed at her heart so violently she bent forward. The sob caught in her throat and for a moment she could not breathe. It came out then, a howl, which sent a shiver down the spine of her teacher.

Sofia Petrova took her by the arm and led her from the classroom. In the small office, used by the teachers, she sat that morning, gazing out across the rooftops to the forest. The tips of the pines trembled in the breeze. Blonde insubstantial clouds were pulled apart and dissolved against the chilly blue celestial canvas. When Sofia Petrova returned at the lunch hour, she carried a small package. She sat down on one of the low stools beside Svetlana.

'This is for you,' she said, and handed her the package, wrapped in brown paper.

Svetlana took it. She folded back the crisp, thick paper and pulled a picture from the package. It was an icon of Christ crucified.

'You must not say anything to anybody,' Sofia Petrova said. Svetlana saw the anxious look in her eyes. She understood the trouble her teacher would be in if the Communist authorities discovered she was giving religious icons to her students.

'I won't, Sofia Petrova,' she said.

The teacher stroked her hair. Svetlana gazed down at the image in her hands. The colours were bright and new, the sky blue, Christ glistering gold. It was vivid, cheerful, despite the bloody crimson tears of the pierced Saviour.

'Svetlana – your name means light,' Sofia Petrova told her.

Svetlana nodded.

'You should try to be a light to others, to your mother in these difficult times.'

Svetlana frowned, but she nodded again, out of respect for her teacher. She slipped the image of Christ back into its paper wrapping and hid it in her school bag.

She concealed the glittering icon beneath the neatly folded pile of clothes in the drawer beside her bed. When she knelt beside her bed that night, to pray as her father had taught her, she took it out and placed it before her. Hearing her mother's footsteps, she tucked it quickly beneath her sheets, interrupting her prayer for her father.

Her mother stood in the doorway.

'It won't be long,' she said. 'They won't keep him for long. It will just be a for a few weeks, a month or two at the most.'

Her mother's voice was brittle with emotion. Svetlana leaned her forehead against the bed. She heard her mother approach behind her. A hand reached out to her nervously, the fingers trembled as they rested on her shoulder. They felt cold through her nightdress. Svetlana stood up quickly, moved away. She slipped in between the sheets, and turned her back on her mother. For some moments her mother lingered, silently, and then she went, turning off the light before she closed the door. By her feet Svetlana could feel the cold hard frame of the icon. She pulled it up and hugged it to her breast.

He did not return. Not after a few weeks, nor after a couple of months. In late October a letter arrived. He had died due to complications arising from undiagnosed ulceration of the stomach. This her mother explained to her, sat at the table in the kitchen where he had breakfasted each morning, and smoked his first cigarette of the day from behind *Izvestiya*.

She did not look at her mother. Nor did she say anything when her mother's words had dried up, finally, on her thin lips.

'Svyeta,' her mother said. She extended her hand across the table. 'Svyeta.'

'It was you,' she said to her mother, as calmly as she could. 'It was your fault.' She looked her mother in the eye. Took pleasure in the pain she saw registering in those little eyes. Drew strength from the knowledge that she could hurt as well as be hurt.

'You killed him,' she said. And turned and left the room.

In the woods, the shabby copse of willow and birch and maple that shrank back from the apartment blocks, she wept. Her heart was torn with the pain of her loss and the pleasure of her assault on her mother. Her mother had told. Don't say a word, her father had told her, and she had not, it was their secret. But her mother had told, twisted with fear, blackmailed by the Party representative at the school, as Svetlana was later to learn.

Svetlana gathered the ring, the medal and the handkerchief together and dropped them back into the tin. She glanced inside the jug beneath the grubby Christ but there was no bottle there.

'Nikolai,' she said. She rummaged about, grubbing together some small coins. 'Go get me a bottle.'

He took the coins in his slim little hand and sloped off into the darkness.

Chapter 31

The vodka saw her through the night. She was sleeping when Ivan returned. In the morning he was tense. He paced back and forth around the room, glancing at the clock. Svetlana watched him from the bed. Her head felt thick and her body ached.

'Listen,' Ivan said finally. 'Jonas was supposed to come. You tell him when he arrives to meet me tonight.'

She nodded. When he had gone she dragged herself up. A pile of washing was piled by the door and she knew it must be done, but could not bring herself to pull the large tin tub in from the courtyard. She boiled some water for tea, then found the unfinished bottle of vodka. She turned off the gas and fell back onto the bed.

They walked around each other, Svetlana and her mother. Wary. Distrustful. At first her mother had reached out a tentative hand, a thin, claw-like hand unused to caresses – to caressing. Svetlana shied away, her lip curling. She never attacked so openly again. But the hostility grew. Her mother, unable to continue her work as a teacher, despite the letter she had been forced to write to the local newspaper denouncing her husband, managed to gain work in a shop.

'You don't know,' her mother sobbed, one evening, worn down by the brutal silence. 'What do you know? What could you know? You are a child, what do you understand about these things?'

She stood in the centre of the kitchen, her red eyes puckered.

Her face was worn, prematurely aged. Deep wrinkles cut away at her pale flesh. The tears distorted her face. Svetlana got up from the table and turned from her. She went out to the door and opened it. The cool breeze blew in her hair. Her mother moaned. A dog barked and she heard the wind surge through the tops of the trees, tossing them violently.

When the vodka was finished she dozed. When she woke again her head thumped and her tongue was swollen and dry. She needed a drink. She eased herself from the bed. Her pockets were empty and when she checked beneath the cracked jug, where sometimes she hid cash, there was none.

The pain pulsed behind her eyes. Head in hands she tried to think. Cautiously, she got up and knelt by the pile of junk in the corner. She hesitated. She lifted the tangle of clothes, the broken toys and the split box, the brick. The envelope was there. Again she hesitated. Pressing her fingers onto her eyes she squeezed back the pain. Fumbling with the envelope, she opened it. She licked her lips, attempting to moisten them, and pulled out a ten-dollar note. She glanced around. Gloom was settling on the room. The corners were lost in shadow. Creasing the note into her hand, she replaced the envelope, pushed back the rubble. She slipped the note into her pocket.

She struggled into an old coat, stepped out into the court-yard and pulled the door closed behind her. For a moment she lingered, back against the door, resting on it. In her pocket, she clasped the crisp note tight. She made her way down Stepono and crossed Pylimo into the centre of the Old Town.

The Three Friends was bustling with early evening trade. Svetlana noted the sidelong contemptuous glance of a wait-ress, as she squeezed in through the doors. The waitress, the same she had previously met in the toilets, elbowed a security guard and pointed her out. The guard nodded but did nothing. Svetlana found an unoccupied table in the corner.

She did not notice Jonas until he stood over her.

'Svyeta!' he greeted her expansively. He was drunk. He rested his fingers on the edge of the table to steady himself.

Svetlana stiffened. Beneath the table her fists clenched tight, her nails biting into the palms of her hands.

'What do you want, Jonas?'

'Want? Nothing. I have a little bit of business.' He grinned a lop-sided, unpleasant grin and tapped the side of his nose. 'Feeling lucky?' he chuckled, pushing her shoulder with his spatula fingers. He winked, throwing his whole face into a grimace. 'Buy you a drink? Pay me later?'

Svetlana knocked his hand off her shoulder. She clenched her teeth, containing her growing fury.

'Hey, Svyeta, don't be like that,' he said, not in the least deterred. He shifted the blue bag he had been holding from one hand to the other. Svetlana recognised it immediately.

'You bastard,' she breathed. 'You took it.'

He grinned.

'I want it back, Jonas,' she said, her voice low, trembling with anger.

He shook his head.

'You stole it.' Her voice rose. 'Give it me.'

Jonas chuckled. He held the package behind his back. Svetlana rose to her feet. She stood at the same height as Jonas. Her face was flushed with anger.

'It's mine, Jonas,' she shouted. 'I want it.'

A hand grabbed her. She turned to the security guard. With a swift, smooth movement he propelled her towards the door, before she could say a word. At the door stood the waitress, face smeared with contempt.

Outside he let her go. Svetlana turned to kick him. Placing one of his large hands on her chest he held her off. Behind him she saw Jonas slope out of the bar, a twisted grin on his face. She pulled away from the guard and advanced on him. He hurried away across the grass.

'Give it me, you bastard,' she shouted.

He waved it in the air. 'What, this?' he mocked. 'You want this?'

Breathless, she caught up with him. She reached forward to take the bag, but he hit her clumsily. He had been drinking and had not intended to hit her so hard. He was quite pleased to see her fall to her knees before him, gasping.

'Tell you what,' he said, cheerfully, 'I'll let you have it.'

Svetlana looked up from her kneeling position.

'For a price, a small price,' he said.

'I haven't got any money,' she said. 'And why should I pay for something you stole from me?'

'I don't want money, Svyeta,' he said.

She observed the excitement in his eyes. The nervous rise and fall of his chest. She considered. For a few minutes' work she could have it back. With it she could go to Daumantas. And Daumantas . . . maybe, just maybe, could help.

Jonas stroked her cheek roughly. 'You can have it, if you want it. Just pay me right.'

She nodded and dragged herself to her feet.

Chapter 32

Jonas leaned heavily against her, causing her to stagger. Drink had slowed him. Keen to be rid of him, Svetlana looped her arm beneath his and half carried him through the dark streets. When he stumbled and fell in the courtyard, he dragged her down, scraping the skin from her knees. He kept the blue bag well away from her, atavistic greed checking his drunken carelessness.

Inside the small room it was mournfully dark. The air was stale and cold. Svetlana did not switch on the light, preferring the darkness to its frail glow.

'What about a drink?' Jonas grumbled, settling on the bed.

'There isn't any.'

Svetlana went to him immediately, but Jonas pushed her away. 'I want a drink,' he insisted. 'My mouth feels like an ashtray.'

Svetlana dipped a chipped cup into the bucket of water and passed it to him. He grimaced in the darkness, tasting it.

'Trying to poison me?'

Svetlana chuckled darkly. 'If I had any poison, I would.'

On her knees, by the bed, she leant forward, taking his zip. He stopped her, shaking a thick finger at her. In the poor light she could not see his eyes.

'What?' she said, impatiently.

'Do you know how much I was going to sell this for?' he asked. Svetlana, in no mood for negotiation, did not answer.

'One hundred dollars,' Jonas bragged. 'Daumantas is desperate for it. He promised to pay me a hundred. For one hundred dollars I'm thinking I should be getting the full deal.'

Svetlana shook her head. 'No way, Jonas,' she said, her voice barely more than a whisper. 'No way.'

He stood up quickly, balancing himself with a hand on her head, the blue plastic bag tight beneath his arm, clasping it as he might a bottle of vodka. She grabbed hold of his jacket. He pushed her back and she stumbled and fell to the floor. In a moment he was on her, his weight pressing her against the leg of a chair.

'Come on, Svyeta,' he said. 'It's worth a bit of fun, don't you think?'

His clumsy hand ripped at her clothing, trying, only half successfully, to pull it away.

Svetlana groaned. His weight hurt her and the chair leg bit into her flesh. 'Let me get up,' she said. 'Get comfortable.'

He loosened his grip and she lifted herself from the floor. She rinsed her face in the cold water in the bucket. She controlled her breathing. The bed springs creaked as Jonas lowered himself onto it. She closed her eyes, pressed her forehead against the wall. She listened to the buzz of traffic on the main road. The faint sound of a muttered conversation, barely audible through the thick damp brickwork. Resigned, she turned to him on the bed.

It became clear within a few moments that he had drunk too much. Frustrated, he complained, but there was nothing she could do. Tired, she stood up, leaving him fiddling with himself. She lit a cigarette and peered out of the small dirty window into the street. Jonas struggled off the bed and pulled up his trousers.

'Ugly bitch,' he muttered.

Svetlana turned and reached for the plastic bag on the end of the bed. Seeing her movement, Jonas grabbed it quickly.

'Hey!' Svetlana protested.

'What are you expecting?' Jonas shouted angrily.

'Give me the bag.'

'Fuck off.'

'You said . . .'

'I said you had to pay for it.'

'It's not my fault you can't get it up.'

Angrily she grabbed Jonas' jacket, pulling him round. He struggled, swearing. A thin shaft of streetlight fell through the broken windowpanes onto his face. Her grasp tightened and the knuckles on her hand grew white. The muscle and bone stretched beneath her bruised skin, giving her hands the appearance of the claws of a wild bird. He pulled free, ripping the cloth of his jacket. She grabbed for him again, but he moved quickly across the room towards the door.

'Did you think I was going to give it you anyway, you crazy bitch? Why would I give it to you? Do you think you're such a good lay? You were only good for one thing and now you're not even any good for that.'

She called after him, her voice carrying loudly in the darkness though she did not shout. She saw him dimly outlined in the doorway and heard the sound of his laughter. His feet scuffed on the cobbles in the dark courtyard.

By the sink lay a kitchen knife. Its blade glimmered in the dim light. She clutched it as she slipped out into the darkness behind him. For some moments she could not see him. He was close against the wall shrouded by the deep shadow. Pissing. She heard the heavy splash on the cobblestones. He started when he turned to find her behind him. Seeing the look on her face, the flicker of light as a streetlamp caught the long blade of the knife, the grin slipped from his face. Slowly she brought the tip of the blade up to his neck. Her hand trembled. She saw the fear flush his cheeks, fill his eyes. She pressed the point against his skin. Jonas stepped back, his foot splashing in the pool of urine.

He was breathing hard. She noticed the quick rise and fall of his chest. The rapid dance of his Adam's apple. She knew she should thrust, now, that it would only take a determined jab. She faltered. He moved swiftly, knocking the knife from her grasp. It clattered on the cobbles. She bent for it as he ran. Her fingers scraped through the warm urine and she plucked them back, disgusted. When she stood he was at the entrance to the courtyard, framed in the faint light. He looked back, once, swiftly, over his shoulder and saw her following. He stepped out.

A shower of gravel sprinkled the wall of the building. Car tyres squealed. There was a dull thud and a small surprised cry. For a few moments there was silence, then the car engine roared into life and skidded away down the narrow street. She stopped in the shadows. Still. Slowly she turned and walked under the sagging walkway, through her door.

She did not go to look through the small windowpanes, which gave out onto the street. She stood with her back to the door, her hands to her face. She vomited in the sink. Wiping the bile from around her mouth she fell onto the bed.

Chapter 33

The Gates of Dawn was busy. Svetlana pushed past a large party of Poles and mounted the stairs. A cold wind was blowing in the street and the upper room was warm and thickly scented with incense. She bent before the Madonna, not raising her eyes to the beautiful image. She was bustled from either side as more worshippers attempted to push into the confined space.

'*Przepraszam.*'

Excuse me.

'Move up, there's no space.'

A sweat broke out on her forehead. She closed her eyes. She clasped her hands. It was too crowded for her to get to her knees.

The bodies and languages swirled around her. Banter, prayers, entreaties. We should have come later. The bus is leaving at five. I prayed last year. The Holy Father was here, I saw him. A miracle. At the window. My son, his leg. It's so busy. A remarkable experience. He was cured, praise God and the blessed Holy Mother. *Przepraszam. Przepraszam.*

She steadied herself against the wall. She worked her way through the crowd to the window. Opening the window, she breathed in the cool air deeply. Her head cleared a little. Her breath came easier. She rested her elbows on the sill, holding her head in her hands.

It had been an hour before she had gone out into the street the previous evening. She lay on her bed and listened. Heard the passers-by, the ambulance, the police. The low voices, and then the return of the night's silence, broken only by the hum of the trolley buses, an occasional car, the shout of a drunk. The papers were scattered across the street. She gathered them carefully. They were ripped and creased and soiled. Some lifted on the wind and danced away, out of her reach. She bundled them up and brought them inside.

'Are you all right?'

A priest stood behind her. She nodded and turned away from the window. The busload of Poles had left. A few old women remained, on their knees, crossing themselves fervently, muttering beneath their breath, their toothless gums working without pause. She glanced up at the Madonna. Her gown shone in the light of the candles, her crown glittered. She inclined over her folded hands, listening.

'Forgive me,' Svetlana whispered. 'Forgive me. It's for him. For Misha. You know what it is to give yourself for your son . . .'

Chapter 34

It was dark when Svetlana alighted from the bus in front of the train station. Taxi drivers milled around in small groups and a few girls paced the street, hugging their shoulders to keep warm. She stopped briefly in the small café inside the station. She paid fifty cents to the old woman seated at the door of the toilets, and a further fifty for some coarse gray tissue. In front of the polished surface of the tin mirror she wiped her face with the dampened tissue. She straightened her hair with her fingers and tried to smooth some of the lines from her face, massaging it gently with the tips of her fingers. Carefully she applied her lipstick.

The tin mirror was misshapen and the figure reflected back was indistinct and distorted. She was wearing the dress Pumpetiene had given her. She stroked smooth the glittering sequins across her chest. Her arms, she noticed, were bruised. She pulled the sleeves down to hide the yellow-brown marks.

Throwing the damp ball of tissue into the wastebasket she examined herself once more, delaying the moment rather than nervous of her appearance. And then she left. Down the hill towards Kauno Street, to the café where she knew she would find him, ignoring the stares of the taxi drivers, the cool appraisal of the young girl she passed on the corner. And then there was Ruta, in a doorway, sheltering from the wind. Svetlana hesitated. The thirteen-year-old stared out from the darkness. A hundred paces down the road was the red glow of the bar. Her gaze moved from the bar to the girl huddled in the shadows. Ruta raised a finger in a coarsely aggressive gesture. 'Fuck off.'

Svetlana had been thirteen when she danced that last bitter, silent waltz with her mother. She ran away. She was caught and taken home. And ran away. Thirteen. In an apartment where she had taken refuge with a girl she met, men approached. They laughed. Silver teeth and vodka on their breath. The window was open. She hunched up on the sofa, wrapping her arms around her thin legs. Knowing nothing of sex, except that they wanted it. Outside it was dark. She did not know how far it was to the floor. When the man unbuckled his belt, when she heard the tone of their laughter and saw the look in their eyes, she ran for the window. She landed on her side. The pain shuddered through her, paralysed her. She looked up and saw their faces at the window. They laughed down at her as she cried into the grass.

'Fuck off,' Ruta said again.

Svetlana turned away. She walked slowly down towards the bar. She heard the steady thump of the music. Faintly, the sound of laughter. The door opened and the noise spilled out into the street.

Mindaugas was at the bar. She slid onto the stool beside him. He half turned. She did not greet him. He bought her a drink. A glass of Alytus champagne, Saldus – sweet.

'I need some money,' she said.

He nodded.

'It's not like the old days,' he said, with a small grin. 'No more of the Americans and Germans at Hotel Lietuva, at the Gintaras.'

Svetlana nodded. 'I know.'

She tasted the champagne. It made her feel neither good nor nauseous. She drank it quickly. No dark wave enveloped her. In the mirror, behind the bar, behind the bottles of vodka and cranberry spirits and English gin and Grant's whisky, she could see herself. She looked better than she had in the station toilet. She attempted a smile, a small one, and was half pleased with the result. When she replaced the glass on the bar her hand shook and it nearly overbalanced.

III

Rachael
Poland
1938

Chapter 35

In the summer of 1938 I was living in a small village west of Vilnius, or Wilno as it was called then. The farm on which we lived lay on the edge of the village. Rolling pasture fell down from the house to a small river where we fished for trout. Across the river the forest started. The dark green leaves cloaked the rising hill and wound around the village protecting it, cutting it off. One road wandered through the forest's depths, grey and dusty in the summer, and in the winter, rutted and dark and treacherous. Its meandering route cut south-east towards the Polish capital, whilst fifty kilometres to the north the road took you to the ancient capital of the Lithuanian people, to Vilnius.

June was hot. The sun rose early. It peaked the forest and seeped through the dirty windows of the small room, at the top of the house, in which I slept. It woke me and for some moments I lay without moving, feeling its fingers caress my face like a grandmother, with hands smooth and leathery with age.

'*Sunus*,' my mother called. 'Son.'

I pulled back the sheets and stretched. Choosing some warm clothes, I hurried outside. The early morning was fresh and dew clung to the grass, glittering like strewn diamonds in the low sunlight. The sun, which had been so warm behind the glass in my room, was freshened by a nip in the air, left by the clear, cold night. The scent of the pine forest was pungent and lively. I breathed it in deeply. In the distance I could hear the cattle. Setting off down the path to where the cows were tethered, my feet sprang on the wet grass and the dew quickly soaked my shoes. I hummed a melody I had heard on the wireless the evening before. It was a Polish tune. Since the war our village had found itself within Poland's borders, though most of the village's inhabitants were Lithuanian or Jews, with only a scattering of Poles.

The udders of the cows were full and they lowed irritably. I stroked the smooth warm flanks of Ramune and reassured her. The frothy milk splashed into the cold metal bucket. Having eased the udders of the cows, I wandered back up the path to the house, the bucket sloshing and steaming. The small meadow flowers had begun to open up to the sun and a heron poked around by the river. By the door of the house, on the brim of the hill, my grandmother, seeing me ambling up the path, stood and smiled her gap-toothed smile. As always she was dressed in black. Having lost her husband in the war, she had worn black ever since.

I lowered the bucket to the ground and rubbed the palm of my hand. Standing with my grandmother, I took in the morning scene with the delight of a boy who knows that soon he will leave it. It was all the world I had known. A peaceful world. Idyllic.

My father, though a farmer, was a cultured man. Before the war, during the Russian occupation, he read the underground papers and built up a library of illegally published Lithuanian books. The Polish occupation of the region had been a blow to him as a nationalist. But he was a businessman too, a realist, and though, still, he harboured hopes of a larger, united Lithuania, he threw his energy into his Polish farm and educated me, his son, as best he could in the hope of my becoming a doctor or a lawyer. I tried hard not to disappoint him. I worked stubbornly and gained entry into the university in Wilno.

My last months in the village were sweet with the nostalgia of expected departure. I worked on my father's farm, enjoying feeling my strained muscles, enjoying hearing the sound of the birds and, in the afternoons, wandering in the dark silences of the ancient forests. In the evenings I went down to the river, where the young people from the village gathered, and sat fishing and talking, and singing as the moon rose above the forest.

After delivering the warm, fresh milk to my mother, I scooped out a cup for my breakfast. I sat at the scarred old table that stood in the kitchen and hurriedly ate some heavy brown bread and cheese. The day would be a fine one and I did not wish to lose a moment of it. I slipped out, once more, into the sunshine and headed for the dusty road where I had arranged to meet a couple of my school friends.

Jan, I saw, was there waiting, on the edge of the road, casting stones into the stagnant millpond. Seeing me, he raised his hand in greeting. I threw myself down onto the grass beside him and rolled onto my back to gaze up into the high blue sky. For a moment we lay there in silence.

'Nah! And what are we going to do then?' Jan asked, casting another stone into the pond. The stone made a thick plop as it broke the moribund surface. A bullfrog croaked, lustfully. There was barely a breeze to stir the tips of the tall trees further down the road and the early morning chill had evaporated. The sun was strong and the dust road quivered under its heat.

'Mendle has some work going. He said to come over.'

'Working for the Yid?'

'What does it matter that he's a Yid?'

'*Blyad!*' Jan swore in Russian. He spat into the grass contemptuously.

'Ach!' I muttered and turned over, irritated.

Old man Mendle had a farm on the edge of the village, a couple of miles from our own. He was a pros-
perous old man in his sixties. His son, Young Mendle as
he was known, worked as a blacksmith. His shop was in
the centre of the village but he still lived in his father's
large farmhouse with his own child. Young Mendle's daughter was dark haired and thin and, to me, mysterious. Sitting in the corner of the village schoolroom, she stared
out of the large, dusty windows, across the fields, to the
forest. My gaze followed hers, losing itself in the darkness
of the trees.

'Christ killer,' Jan said. He ran a hand through his short,
blond, Polish hair.

When school finished Rachael tucked her books under her
arm and wandered slowly down the dusty lane to the village.
My way home took me past her father's shop, where I would
see her leaning up against the wooden door. Her father had
a fierce, black beard that jutted out aggressively before him.
He was a communist and agitated in the village. When my
father first took me to the workshop with one of our horses,
I cowered in the corner. The furnace cast hellish shadows
around the room. Young Mendle stood in the centre of the
workshop with a large mallet in his blackened hand, beard
bristling. Sweat glistened on his furrowed forehead as he
brought the mallet down with furious blows onto a shining
horseshoe.

'Young Mendle's a good man,' my father said on the way
home. 'He does a good job for a good price. Better than
Polish shit.'

After leaving her father's shop, Rachael cut across the
fields. She liked to skirt the edge of the forest on her way
home and I would follow her.

'It has a power all of its own,' she said one day, as we sat in the shadow of a birch tree. Our schoolbooks lay scattered on the thick green grass. I read to her from Baranauskas' long, rambling poem, inspired by the deep primeval forests of Lithuania.

'Sometimes the forest scares me,' she said. 'And sometimes it seems to be the safest of places.'

I nodded. Many times when I was with her I was not sure how to respond to her comments. I would nod, only, and gaze at her. Her hair was dark and played on her narrow shoulders. Her eyes always wore a far-away look.

'Where's Povilas?' I asked Jan.

Jan nodded down the road. In the dip, where the wooden bridge crossed the brook, I saw Povilas. He walked slowly up the road to meet us, kicking the dust as he came. He flopped onto the grass, a lop-sided grin on his face.

'How's life?' he asked in his heavily accented Polish. Jan spoke no Lithuanian.

Jan threw another stone into the millpond. I smiled, and shook Povilas' hand.

'What's up with him?' Povilas asked, inclining his head in the direction of Jan, who lay silent on his stomach. I shrugged.

'Nothing is up with me,' Jan said, turning over. His eyes flicked in my direction and I could see that he was angry. For a moment he seemed about to comment on something, but held back.

'So what about going down to the beach?' Povilas grinned. 'Glorious day for a swim!'

'Nah, and why not!' Jan said. 'Better than some suggestions I've heard today.'

Povilas raised his eyebrows and I could only shrug again. Jan got up and stretched. He kicked my leg. 'You coming?' he asked. I shook my head. I watched as they walked down the deep rutted road towards the river. Jan limped, his leg lame from polio.

When they had crossed the wooden bridge I got up myself and trudged towards Old Mendle's farm.

Chapter 36

Old Mendle was in the large old farmhouse eating breakfast when I arrived. The old manor had once been home to the *grafas*, the local nobility, Lithuanian gentry who knew not a word of Lithuanian. Lithuanian was the language of the peasants. They had lost the house at the end of the war. Count Matulevicz, the last of the family, had squandered the dwindled inheritance in St Petersburg on champagne and gambling debts. Matulevicz's son, a man who physically and temperamentally mirrored his scarlet-faced father, died at Tannenburg, face down in the mud, his carefully pressed Russian officer's uniform trampled in a chaotic retreat. Old Mendle bought the property from the old count's humbled wife, who returned to her family in Krakow.

'Steponushka!' Old Mendle called from the end of the table. A long, grey beard straggled over his large chest. He wiped his mouth with a white handkerchief. 'Come sit with me.'

Daiva, his Lithuanian maid, pulled out a chair for me and fetched a rich, honey-sweetened tea. Old Mendle's eyes were quick still, and quite blue. Though he was an observant Jew, he favoured the ideas of the enlightenment, the Haskala. He was fluent in Russian, Polish, Hebrew and Yiddish and spoke passable Lithuanian; to talk to his workers, he said, and better still to listen. Young Mendle revered the works of Marx and Lenin rather than the Talmud and Torah and his father did not complain. For all that, Old Mendle looked every bit the Yiddish patriarch.

'Rachael tells me you'll be going to Vilnius.' He used the Lithuanian name rather than the Polish or Yiddish. I nodded, wondering that she had spoken of me to him.

'Yes, sir.'

'And what will you be studying?' he asked.

'Law.'

He clicked his tongue. '*Nu!* A lawyer. A blessing to the family.' He grinned, revealing a prominent golden tooth. 'Your mother and father will be able to enjoy their latter years.'

'The farm is profitable enough,' I said, 'for them to feel safe.'

He nodded his head, peeling an egg with his long, delicate fingers. 'That is the truth. A good bit of land they have there.' He paused a moment. Thoughtfully he sprinkled salt onto the egg and bit it with his golden tooth. 'Hmm,' he said and his eyes fixed me, strong blue eyes. 'I've been looking for a bit more land myself.' He paused again, not taking his eyes from me.

'Oh,' I said, in his pause.

'Perhaps,' he said. But he did not finish the sentence. At that moment the door opened and Rachael appeared. Her usually melancholic eyes shone brightly. Seeing me, a small smile crept across her lips, but she affected not to have noticed my presence. She wandered over to her grandfather, who opened his arms to greet her.

'*Liebchin,*' he said.

Seeing her, I felt my heart pound. I felt a hot flush in my cheeks and hoped that neither she nor Old Mendle noticed. Old Mendle slipped his strong arm around the waist of his granddaughter. His eyes flicked back across the table, considering me beadily.

'I was just going to ask young Steponas if he knew of any land in the village that might be for sale,' Old Mendle said, addressing Rachael.

'Why would Steponas know?' Rachael asked. Her voice was soft and quiet. Each word seemed to have been considered carefully before it was uttered.

I flushed again and this time I knew Old Mendle had noticed. The truth was my father's farm was not as profitable as I had intimated. A fact Old Mendle was aware of. The old man knew, too, that my father could perhaps have been persuaded to sell some pastureland by the river. The land brought my father little profit and the cash would have enabled him to invest in a tractor of the kind Old Mendle used on his farm.

'*Nu!* You're right,' Old Mendle said, pushing the young girl away and getting up. He shook the crumbs from his dark waistcoat and the white fringes of his undershirt danced.

Old Mendle had already approached my father about the land. I heard my father speaking of it over the kitchen table.

'He's offering a good price.'

'To Mendle? The Jew? Our good pastureland?' My mother was quietly outraged.

My mother was born in Zematija, the ancient, obstinate inheritors of the Samogitian spirit. She was a stubborn down-to-earth woman. When my father married her she was a handsome woman and, while the years of labour showed, she remained attractive with the deep, engrained common sense of the ancient peasant stock she was raised from. Often her thinking was circumscribed by folk wisdom, and more often still by fear of what the neighbours thought.

'Justas, think,' she told him, her voice fearful with concern. 'The village, what will they think of you selling up to the old Jew? And how much land does he want anyway? Has he not already got enough?'

'What do I care about the village?'

I heard the clink of the bottle of samogonas, spirits brewed in the forest, against my father's glass.

'What do you care for the village? *Durnas!* Blockhead,' she scolded. 'And who buys the milk from your cows? Who buys your cheeses and your vegetables?'

'Me a blockhead?' My father was heated by the spirits. 'They're the blockheads. Tomasz Bozek is a blockhead. Pawel Polmanski is a bullshitter. *Durnius! Idiotas!*'

'Oi, oi!' my mother gasped, hands over her ears. 'What do you want to do to us?'

My father growled. Tomasz Bozek and Pawel Polmanski were local councillors and agitators, who believed the right-wing dictatorship was too restrained. I feared to pass them in the street, when walking with my father, in case he lashed out at them. Their frequent, Nazi-inspired diatribes roused my father to fits of rage.

For all that, and for all his learning, my father was wise enough to listen to my mother's peasant wisdom. She left him alone at the table, with his bottle.

'*Nu*, and as you wish.' She shrugged. 'I'm your wife and I'm not so proud that I won't wear rags.'

She skipped away as my father roared and slammed his glass down upon the scarred surface of the old kitchen table.

Old Mendle let the subject drop. He adjusted his yarmulka and stepped, sprightly, across the room to the door.

'Well, Steponas, you've come to give me a hand today.'

I followed him through to the hallway. Rachael called me back. We stood in the doorway, nervous. Her eyes were both mournful and playful, in a way, perhaps, only a young girl could manage.

'Steponas, will you take a walk with me later?'

I nodded, mutely.

*   *   *

In the field Old Mendle was waiting. We walked around to his large barns, where a group of workers stood assembled around a large tractor. He introduced me. The older man I recognised, he had worked for my father some years before. He nodded slightly. He wore a flat cap perched jauntily on the side of his greying head. His moustache bushed out across his cheeks, quite white against his dark, leathery skin. Over his shirt he wore a dark, stained waistcoat, and his trousers fell down onto the peasant's clogs on his feet. His hand rested proudly on the tractor by which he stood. I ran my hand along the smooth metal flank of the machine. It stood almost as high as a horse. Its engine thrust out before it and the enormous metal wheels rose up around the driver.

'Fine, *ne*?' Old Mendle said.

'Fine,' I said. 'Really fine.' But whilst my hand caressed the metal, hot already from the sun, my mind was on Rachael.

She was waiting for me at the corner of the road, out of sight of the farmyard, wearing a long red dress with a black shawl thrown over her shoulders. Under her arm she held Adam Mickiewicz's *Ancestors*, a book we had been studying in class. We ducked under the trees and for a while walked in silence. The maples offered a cool shade. The sun dappled the grass; there was not even a breeze to stir the leaves above us. It was not unusual to walk in silence with Rachael and I felt no compunction to make conversation. There were few sounds; our breath, the rustle of clothing, a man's voice somewhere back in the fields, faintly shouting.

'What do you think about when you are so quiet?' I asked her later.

'I don't know,' she said, 'maybe I'm not thinking at all.'

'You must be,' I insisted. 'Tell me.'

She was quiet again then, thinking. A small crease appeared

across her clear forehead. 'Sometimes I feel sad and I don't know why,' she said. 'Do you know what I mean?' Her eyes searched my own, but I didn't know what she meant, I could only look back at her blankly.

'Sometimes it just comes over me, I feel this wave of sorrow rolling through me so that I feel like crying, only there doesn't seem to be a reason for it.'

We sat with our backs against the solid, elegant trunks of the maples. Only now, perhaps, can I be thankful that I did not know how to answer her and was silent; that I could find no words to cheer her. Silence is a mercy. A small but precious one. These long years it has been the greatest I have been able to enjoy.

'Sometimes I dream that I am in the forest,' Rachael continued. 'In the dream it is nighttime and we are all there, my father, grandfather, Mama, Rivka from the village and her little Yosef. We are running through the forest, deeper and deeper. It feels so scary in the forest at night, but I dare not leave it. The fields and the village fill me with dread.'

She stopped. We sat listening to the rustle of birds picking through the leaves, searching for insects.

Later, on the way back to the farm, we ran down the slope to the brook. Rachael laughed as I chased her and then she snagged her dress on the brambles of a blackberry bush. Carefully I unhooked the red fabric, trying to avoid it unravelling. When she was free, she rewarded me with a blackberry, which she pushed through my lips. Its juice ran down her fingers, bloodying them. She beamed gleefully, immobilising me. I grinned back stupidly.

I went to bed that night thinking of her smile, grinning myself, still, in the darkness of my room.

Chapter 37

At the beginning of August my cousin was married. My father and I harnessed the horses early and I drove my mother in the gig to my uncle's farm on the other side of the village. Whilst our farm was situated on a rise, with pastureland falling away from it down to the river, Uncle Stanislovas' was nestled in the crook of the river valley as it meandered sharply out of the village. The farm was smaller and less profitable. The cottage, however, shaded as it was by a copse of birch and poplars, with the river running fast and loud across the dirt track, had always been a romantic spot for me. Doubtless this impression was not discouraged by the fact that my cousin was a beautiful girl. Asta was two years older than I.

When we arrived we were surprised to hear shouts coming from the cottage. My mother rushed in through the open door and, as I was tying up the horses, I heard her voice join those of her sister-in-law and niece. I hurried after her. Uncle Stanislovas, the cause of the fury, was slumped in his worn armchair, seemingly oblivious to the commotion going on around him and the insults that were being hurled at him by the women. My mother turned, hearing me enter.

'Get him outside, Steponas,' she ordered.

She lifted Stanislovas' left arm while I took him by the right, managing to prise the bottle from his hands as I did so. He looked surprised and annoyed at this assault and tried to fight his way back into the seat.

'What's the matter with you?' he complained. 'Can't a man celebrate when his daughter's to be married?'

'You're a disgrace,' my mother railed.

'Today, of all days,' his wife moaned.

'*Tetis!*' cried Asta.

I dragged him out into the yard and sat him down in the grass by the well. He leaned back against the wall of the well and closed his eyes, enjoying the early rays of sunlight that filtered through the dense covering of verdant leaves. I pulled up the bucket and was about to discharge the contents over his head when he opened an eye.

'You just try it,' he said.

Nervously I lowered the bucket and placed it on the grass by his feet. He sighed and hauled himself up. Bending over the bucket, he cupped some of the cool water into his hands and splashed it onto his face, wringing his beard dry. If he had really been drunk he had achieved a remarkable degree of sobriety by the time my father arrived.

The cottage rattled with activity. Neighbours and relatives arrived and while the women took voluble control, the men gathered by the barn to smoke and drink. At eleven o'clock a gang of four young men arrived on the back of an old cart. They reined in the horses at the gate and stood up to shout into the house. The men broke away from the barn, calling back through the trees at the bridegroom's brothers and friends.

'We've come for the dowry,' a young man shouted, leaping down from the cart, a grin on his face.

'Get away with you,' my uncle shouted, 'how do we know you're not just scoundrels and thieves?'

'Come on, you old skinflint,' the young man called back. 'You know who I am, hand over the goods.'

'Who are you calling a skinflint?' Stanislovas shouted, pulling his jacket off and rolling up his sleeves.

The men laughed. Three of the dowry carriers vaulted the gate while the fourth kept hold of the reins. They broke through the crowd, which jostled and jeered at them, and banged their fists on the cottage door.

'Open up!' the young man shouted.

When the door opened my mother stood in the entrance, hands on her wide hips, an indomitable expression on her stern Zematijan face. For one moment I thought she intimidated the young man. He hesitated. Then he grinned and pulled off his hat, bowing low.

'*Ponia*,' he addressed her respectfully. 'We have come to claim the dowry.'

The three men were jostled from behind by the crowd, and fell through the doorway, shouldering my mother aside. A scream went up from the women in the cottage.

There was the sound of a scuffle then a voice. 'Sit on it, sit on the chest.'

A young woman squealed and laughed as the men tried to dislodge her from the dowry chest.

'Hey, now, no getting fresh!'

'Oi! She bit me!'

'Serves you right, thug!'

The young men emerged, moments later, dragging the chest between them, their clothing dishevelled. They hauled the wooden chest, with its decorative carvings of stork-filled trees, onto the back of the waiting cart and then, with much shouting and insults and vulgarity, trundled back down the road to the bridegroom's farm.

We drove to the village church for the service, the gig bedecked with flowers. Passing through the village, I drove by Young Mendle's blacksmith shop. Rachael was seated beneath a tree reading a book, while the regular ring of a mallet on metal reverberated from the gloomy interior where her father was working. Looking up, she saw me and waved. Soberly I lifted the whip, aware of my mother's disapproving glance.

On the way back to the farm young men had hung flower-entwined ropes across the lane, delaying the bride and groom on their return from the service. At each stop the matchmaker and principal dowry carrier bargained the couple's passage through with sweets and bottles of whisky. At one rope the cheering gang of men pushed forward a blushing young girl from a nearby village, demanding a kiss from the matchmaker.

It was at one of these ambushes, perhaps, that the damage was done to the wheel of the wedding cart. By the time the bride and groom had arrived back at the cottage, the cart bobbed and creaked and one of the horses had developed a limp. Stanislovas clicked his tongue, assessing the damage done to the wheel and lifting the hoof of his horse.

'We're going to have to get somebody out from the village,' he said.

'What about Mendle?' my father said. 'He'll get the two sorted quick enough.'

'I'll go for him,' I volunteered.

My mother frowned, but Father nodded. We hitched up the horses and I took the gig back into town, hurrying it along the lane so that the dust billowed up from the wheels and the hooves of the horses, covering me in a fine layer of dirt.

When I got to Mendle's shop it was quiet. Rachael was nowhere to be seen. Disheartened I ducked into the entrance of the workshop. The day was warm and with the furnace blazing fiercely in the dark workshop it was intensely hot inside. One small window, high up in the wall, lit the room. It took my eyes some moments to adjust.

From the shadows a large figure stepped forwards. A hefty hammer swung in his hand. His thick, black hair stuck angrily from his head, forming an alarming silhouette against the light of the furnace. I stepped back.

'Sir,' I addressed him politely in Polish, trying to suppress the nervous tremble in my voice. 'My father sent me to ask you to come out to Stanislovas' farm urgently.'

He squinted at me. 'Stanislovas'?'

At that moment Rachael appeared by his side. 'Steponas!' she said brightly.

'You're Daumantas' son,' Mendle said, placing me.

I nodded.

'*Nu*, in that case I'll come. Your father's a good man. What is it then? A horse in need of a shoe?'

'That and a cartwheel.'

'You're looking very smart,' Rachael said, eyeing my wedding suit.

'A wedding,' I said.

'*Tatinka*,' Rachael said to her father. 'Can I come?'

Mendle nodded. 'Why not?'

'I have space for you,' I offered.

I let the horses find their own pace on the road back to the cottage. Mendle soon passed us. When we got back to the Stanislovas farm, the sound of singing drifted from the cottage. The guests were seated around the long table. 'The food is bitter, bitter,' they were singing, banging their spoons on the wooden table, 'when the bridegroom kisses the bride it will be sweeter.'

While Mendle went to work on the cartwheel, Rachael and I wandered across the lane. A small wooden bridge spanned the river, where the banks drew in close between two low hills. It was old and little used and we had to cross with care, picking out the planks that did not look as if they would give way.

'Who is getting married?' Rachael asked when we were sitting on the crest of the knoll, on the far bank of the river.

'My cousin, Asta. Stanislovas' daughter.'

For some moments we sat in silence, gazing back across the river through the trees to the cottage and barns and work sheds. The sound of singing and shouts was just audible above the rush of the river through the narrow banks.

'I have something to give you,' I said.

'Oh?'

I pulled a small metal disk from my pocket. There was a hole punched into it, through which ran a thin chain. On the disk was the engraving of a knight seated on a rearing horse, his sword swinging above his head. I gave it to her. She examined it closely.

'It's a Vytis,' I told her. 'The emblem of Lithuania. This insignia was on coins minted in the times of Vytautas the Great, one of the early Grand Dukes of Lithuania.'

She looked up at me. Her eyes were dark, almond shaped, shaded with thick, curled lashes.

'Thank you,' she said softly, and touched my hand.

'Vytautas was one of Lithuania's greatest Grand Dukes,' my father told me, one evening, sat at the table, drinking, after supper. Often he taught me the history of Lithuania in the evenings. At school we were taught only what the Poles wanted us to learn about the history of our united countries. 'It was he,' my father continued, 'who defeated the Teutonic knights in the battle of Tannenburg. For years the German Orders had been trying to invade our country, interested more in snatching land and riches rather than spreading the gospel. Latvia and Estonia were already theirs, and they were bleeding them dry. They never fully recovered from the defeat at Tannenburg.'

More and more often my father returned to this tale. The contemporary resonance of the story of that struggle between the German knights and the Lithuanian people was growing more pronounced each day. The Nazis were agitating in Klaipeda, laying claim to the region, which had been part of the empire taken from them by the Versailles

Treaty. There were daily demonstrations organised by local Nazi party members, protesting against the ill-treatment of German citizens.

The German government had initiated a trade embargo against Lithuania, in protest at the country's abuse of its German minority. This was a heavy blow to Lithuania, as Germany was its main trading partner. The Nazi party in the Klaipeda region of Lithuania was demanding that the Nuremberg Laws be applied to what they called Memelland. Many of the region's Jews were retreating into safer areas of Lithuania.

It was for his treatment of the Jews that I held Vytautas in esteem. He drew up a charter that gave the Jews in his empire legal autonomy, safeguarded their business interests and outlawed the blood libel, attempting to put a stop to the accusations of Jews murdering Christian children for their Passover preparations. He initiated an era of religious tolerance the like of which Western Europe would not enjoy for hundreds of years.

'I will keep it with me,' she said. 'It'll be my good luck charm.'

She wrapped it carefully in her handkerchief and slipped it into the pocket of her dress. When we returned to the cottage, the wedding guests were spilling out onto the grass. Mendle had finished and Rachael joined him on his gig. I stood in the road and waved as they drove down the lane towards the village. When I turned back to the cottage, I noticed my mother was watching me.

Chapter 38

The kitchen was the heart of my home; it was the place I loved to be. In the evenings, by the light of a candle, I worked at the scrubbed table. A large stone held the door open, in the summer, and the fragrance of the night hung on the air. In the winter the kitchen was the warmest of the rooms in the house. The large oven glowed in the corner and all day the house was filled with the smell of bread baking. At nights, in the winter, there was the delicious smell of pork as my mother slow-cooked *kugelis* through the night. For breakfast we ate the grated potatoes soaked through with the fat of the pork.

When my schoolwork was finished I worked on my poems. They were filled with tales of the Grand Dukes, heroes of the old empire battling the German knights, or of woods and valleys and clear lakes, of the Nemunas and simple peasants, the country that existed in literature, more than in reality. I was very much under the influence of the romantic Lithuanian poets, Mickiewicz and Baranauskas, and the father of Lithuanian poetry, Donelaitis. My father was exceptionally proud of these poems I wrote; they were to his taste. I wrote in both Lithuanian and Polish. Whilst my Lithuanian poems flew with exuberant metaphors, my Polish poems were more tempered, precise and often gloomy.

In the late summer of that year the annual poetry reading festival was held in the village hall. I entered myself with a couple of poems I was proud of and had worked at intensely. The poems, in Polish, were nationalistic in tone. One, called simply Hymn, took as its starting point the village itself, its humble wooden buildings, dusty roads, its hard working folk, the fields and forests that surrounded it. Its gaze widened further out to the rolling hills, the cities and then finally the whole nation, from the Baltic Sea to the Carpathians, from Poznan to Wilno, Krakow to Gdansk. My father grunted when I read it to him. Wojciech Rudnicka, my schoolmaster, was enthusiastic. He clapped energetically when I read it out to the class. 'Bravo,' he called, and 'Good poem'. As I left he clapped his friendly hand on my shoulder, and whispered in my ear, 'You'll be entering the tournament, I hope, Steponas.' He spoke of it always as if it was a medieval jousting rather than a poetry reading contest.

I took extraordinary care when I dressed for the competition. I hurried home from the fields where I had been working and carelessly rushed my tasks, apologising to the chickens that I stepped on in my hurry. A large bowl of steaming water was waiting for me in my room and I peeled off my clothes and washed the dust and sweat from my body. My mother had laid out my best clothes, neatly pressed. They smelt clean and were stiff against my body.

'Oi,' my mother said, 'what a son I have! He is a man already.'

'He's been a man a long time,' my father grunted, forking potato pancakes into his mouth. 'Works like a real man,' he added proudly.

'*Nu*, but of course,' my mother said, beaming. Grandmother, in black, hovered in the doorway, a gentle smile on her face.

I met Jan and Povilas on the road into the village. They were going to the village hall though they had not entered the competition. They were boisterous and tried to lift me onto their shoulders. I pushed them off, worried they would mess up my appearance. The village was busy and in carnival mood. There was music and in front of the village hall girls from the school in traditional dress were dancing. A small crowd milled around, mainly students and teachers from the schools in the neighbouring villages. As I pushed through the crowd my excitement grew. It was not so much the sight of Jurczyk, editor of the local paper, that made my hands tremble nervously, it was the knowledge that in the crowd of spectators Rachael would be sat listening. I very much wanted to impress her.

At the doors of the large, wooden village hall I met Itzikl, a cousin of Rachael. He was a thin boy with yellow skin. He was tough enough, though. If he was provoked he did not hesitate to settle the argument with his fists at the edge of the wood, by the millpond, where all school disputes were settled. He grinned, seeing me. His teeth were all out of place and one of them was black and dead. I smiled.

'I see you entered the competition,' I said.

'You bet.'

'What's your poem?'

'It's satirical.' He grinned his mash-toothed grin.

Itzikl's father was a communist, a member of the Bund. He was a big, good-looking, blond-haired man. He played the guitar well and sang communist songs. Itzikl was so unlike him that there were many who laughed at the 'bastard'. Itzikl worshipped his father though, and enthusiastically embraced his communist ideals. So passionately did he spread the ideas that he had heard among the students at school that even mild mannered Wojciech Rudnicka was forced to give him a warning.

'Good luck,' I said and shook his bony hand.

The hall filled. The competitors sat on a row of wooden chairs on the low stage. I sat stiffly, scanning the sea of heads for her dark hair. I could not find it. To my right sat Itzikl, grinning confidently. He would follow me. I took a deep breath and closed my eyes. My mind flicked over the lines of the poem I had learnt by heart, rehearsing it as I worked in the fields.

'We are very pleased to have a real live poet among us today,' Wojciech Rudnicka said, rubbing his soft, scholar's hands together. Being Master of Ceremonies he had dressed up for the occasion in a dinner suit. He flicked his lank, dark hair back from his forehead and half turned from his position at the front of the stage to indicate a round, red-faced, seedy man seated at the back of the stage by the purple curtain. The real live poet bowed his head slightly in acknowledgement of the polite applause that rippled around the village hall. His shoulders were white with flakes from his scalp. His lips were large and moist. He surveyed the audience suspiciously and did not seem to notice the nervous line of young poets beside him.

'As you can see we have ten talented young folk entered for the competition this year, and I can guarantee you that each one stands a strong chance of winning. A fine talented bunch that give us faith in the future of our noble Polish language and its strong tradition of poetry.' Wojciech Rudnicka flicked back his hair and jutted out his weak chin. 'Maybe one of these young folk here,' he said with a florid sweep of his pink hand, 'will one day be as admired as our esteemed guest. Who knows?'

Again the audience rippled with applause. Wojciech Rudnicka smiled. 'It only remains, then, for me to introduce the first of our young poets this evening.' The first competitor was a boy called Karol. He stepped forward, confidently, to the edge of the stage, closed his eyes, lifted his head and shouted his poem to the wooden beams that held up the roof. I noticed the fleshy, wet-lipped poet cringe by the curtain. He closed his eyes too, a crease scarring his pink forehead, and looked as though he wished he were anywhere else. Karol's poem ricocheted around the rafters and fell dead at the back of the hall. He stopped suddenly as though he had forgotten his last line. For a moment the audience held its breath, but then he opened his eyes and bowed deeply. The audience clapped enthusiastically. Wojciech Rudnicka jumped back onto the stage nodding and clapping. He smiled enthusiastically at the cringing poet, who managed to raise a weak smile in return.

Each poet stood in turn and took their place at the edge of the stage. Somebody opened the window and above the sound of the audience fidgeting it was possible to hear the sound of the men standing outside the door, with the horses, waiting, smoking, drinking and laughing.

As my turn approached I grew more confident that the poem I had written was far superior to those of the other competitors. I did not, however, get much satisfaction from this confidence. And then I noticed Rachael. She slid through the doors stealthily and sat on a wooden bench by the back wall, among a group of women.

The competitor to my left stood up and edged towards the front of the stage. I did not hear her words but willed her only to be finished quickly so that I might get my chance. There was a spattering of applause from the bored audience as the girl bowed shyly and retreated to her seat. The greasy poet seemed to have fallen asleep. His head was sunk low against his chest and his eyes were closed. I took that as a challenge. I stepped confidently to the edge of the stage and looked out across the faces. I paused before I began and sought out her eyes. She smiled.

Turning to the sleeping poet, I addressed him, loudly, in Polish, '*Proszae Pana!* Sir! With respect I would like to dedicate this poem to our nation. Ladies and gentlemen, my poem is titled Hymn.'

The poet awoke with a start and regarded me with a spark of malice in his liquid eyes. Sure of his attention I began.

I imbued each line with as much pride and longing as I could. The words seemed to spin out from me like smooth pebbles across a clear cold lake. They dropped like fresh dew into the laps of the audience. A silence fell upon the room. I felt my words become pregnant with meaning, each one swollen with love for our country. The images of the nation from its tiny villages to its ancient cities, its forests and lakes and mountains, its heroes and heroines, kings and queens, resounded in the silence.

As my voice rose to the last stanza I heard a noise growing in the audience. They had become blurred before my eyes. I sensed them shifting, the sound of feet and voices. I drew the last word from my heart and tossed it to them, and then felt it explode like a bomb. I opened my eyes to the audience on its feet cheering. A wave of heat coursed through my veins. A sense of sweet exultation lifted me from the boards of the stage. The damp poet was beside me, his arm around my shoulder, shaking my hand. Wojciech Rudnicka was beaming and clapping vigorously at the edge of the stage.

'A young poet for the nation,' the lank-haired poet said to my teacher. 'Moving. Most moving. God in heaven, a poem to rouse the soul of our nation.'

I bowed, trying to pull back the smile from my lips. I edged back to my seat, aware that still the audience was clapping. My cheeks burned red. Rachael had seen my moment of triumph. My joy was without bounds.

Itzikl clapped a hand on my knee and smiled at me wanly. He pulled himself to his feet and stepped slowly forward to the edge of the stage. The audience was still on its feet. At the front, I noticed, stood Tomasz Bozek and Pawel Polmanski, the councillors. Shouts resounded in the small wooden hall. The doors opened and the men who had been waiting outside pushed through, cheap cigarettes between their thin lips and vodka bottles, half empty, still clutched in their hands. Itzikl stood motionless at the front of the stage. Wojciech Rudnicka moved forward to the edge of the stage but then hesitated, drew back. A word was thrown forwards from the audience. It seemed to hit Itzikl like a physical blow for he staggered back a step. It was thrown once more, and this time it came from more than one mouth.

'*Ty Zydzie!*'

'*Swinia!*'

'*Ty Zydzie!*'

Jew. Pig. *Blyad*. Jew-pig. *Zydzie! Zydzie!* The words hailed down upon the stage. They roared in my ears. I felt the blood draining from my face. Itzikl stood still on the edge of the stage, colourless, his poem arrested on his lips.

'Give us the national poet!' somebody shouted. 'Get rid of this fucking Yid!'

To my horror I heard my name on the lips of the drunken men. Tomasz Bozek was grinning at me, his bald head glistening in the late light that slanted through the windows. 'Give us the Polish boy,' they shouted. 'Let's hear the Polish boy again.'

Itzikl crept back to his seat beside me, cringing away from me. I turned to him, but he backed away as if I was about to hit him. Fear lit his eyes.

Wojciech Rudnicka spoke into the ear of the guest poet. He hustled him forward to the edge of the stage. The poet cleared his throat and held his hands out like Moses about to part the waters before him. Slowly the noise began to drain from the room. Wojciech Rudnicka crept across the stage behind the poet-prophet and pulled Itzikl up by the arm.

He pushed him through a door behind the stage and closed it behind them. I sat silent, rooted to my wooden chair, hot and cold flushes washing through my body. Painful waves. Rachael, I noticed, had left.

Chapter 39

Wilno. Its church spires rose above the winding streets. Gediminas' tower stood on the ancient hill, the birth-site of the ancient city. On this hill the greatest of the Grand Dukes had fallen asleep one night, on a hunting trip in the deep old forests. As he slept he dreamt of an iron wolf howling at the moon from the hilltop. In the morning he summoned a wise old man to him and told him the dream. The bearded pagan priest interpreted it. On this hill the Grand Duke was to found a city. It would be a powerful city. The howling of the iron wolf signified how the fame of the city would spread out around the world.

I climbed the hill on the morning of my first day in Wilno and looked out across the city. The early autumn mist clung, still, to the hollows of the valley, shrouding the town. Below me the two rivers joined, the rivers where the first Christian missionaries met their watery end, martyred by the fierce natives, the last of Europe's pagan tribes. Below me, too, stood the cathedral, which even as I watched began to glisten under the rays of the sun that had climbed above the hills and cut through the milky sheets of mist. The pope had won in the end and set his church in the place of the temple of the ancient gods.

My mother said nothing as she stood by the old cart that was to take me to the city. She cried silently into her handkerchief. My father shook my hand and then embraced me. He had dressed in his best suit to see me off. Clumsily, uncomfortable in the stiff, tight three-piece, he loaded sacks of apples and pears, potatoes, onions and garlic onto the back of the cart for me to take to the city. Adam, one of my father's workmen, sat at the front of the old cart, with a sack rolled as a cushion. Having embraced my father and said a last goodbye to my mother, I jumped up onto the cart and Adam flicked the whip across the smooth flank of the horse.

As the cart bumped down the dirt track towards the forest I looked back at my home with a feeling of both sadness and joy. My parents stood, still watching on the dust road, and behind them, in the doorway of our home, I could see the dark smudge that was my grandmother. By the millpond, a heron, startled, took clumsily to the air. The fields, brown now after the long hot summer months, rolled down towards the village, the roofs of which were just visible. I waved to my parents and then we were in the forest, its cool scented arms enclosing us.

I inhaled deeply the sharp smell of pine. Adam drove the cart in silence, flicking the horse's flank occasionally, uttering a barely comprehensible encouragement to it. He wore an old cap that was pulled down to his ears. Steel grey hair burst out of the cap, bristling against his thick neck. He had the large hands of a peasant, and his fingers were like the oars of a galleon. Adam had worked on my father's farm for more years than I could remember. He had been a brooding, silent presence since I was a baby. On the odd occasions that he spoke I would look at him in terror, as a child, incapable of understanding his thick Polish dialect. Even when I learned to speak Polish myself, it had hardly helped; his pronouncements remained as unintelligible as the growl of a dog.

Adam lived in a hovel on the edge of the woods. The floor was of beaten earth and the walls were bare plaster, dark with the damp and dirt that rose from the floor. The cottage consisted of two rooms and little furniture. It had a small well in the garden where each morning Adam would wander, badly hung over. Summer and winter he would draw up a bucket of water from the depths of his well and balance it on the crumbling wall. He would plunge his large, spade-like hands into it and throw the water at his blunt red face. In the winter months it took him a while to break through the ice to get the water. When he staggered back to the door of his home, his steely hair would be stuck up in a frozen halo about his face.

I was glad of his silence as we drove through the forest. My last weeks in the village had been like the torturous itch of a mosquito bite and it was good now to be on the road, to be gone. I lay on my back, amid the sacks of food and layers of fresh hay my father had strewn for the journey, and watched the delicate wisps of cloud caught and pulled at by gusts of wind far up in the sky.

I had not said goodbye to Rachael, nor to her grandfather, Old Mendle, to whom I owed a debt of kindness. To my shame I was awarded first prize for the best poem at the poetry festival. I collected it red-faced, my ears burning at the applause of the rowdy audience of village drunkards and raucous nationalists. Wojciech Rudnicka handed me the prize awkwardly. He patted me on the shoulder, noticing the look of mortification on my face. My eyes scanned the noisy, red-faced crowd, but tears had welled up in them and all was a blur. I knew that Rachael had gone, though. I could see the dark space at the back where she had been. I could see her absence.

As soon as I decently could, I tried to escape the fetid, smelly village hall. The poet collared me as I made for the door, and for fifteen minutes I had to stand patiently as he stood, fleshy hand holding my shoulder. He bent his soft pink face, with its large moist lips, close to mine. His breath smelt. 'Good poem,' he said. I muttered my thanks and tried to struggle free, but the fingers remained tight.

'You remind me of when I was young. Passionate, full of love.' He looked at me meaningfully. 'Obviously there were faults in the poem, but that is to be expected of a young boy in the sticks. Still, it had promise. The spark was there. I was moved.' He shook my hand damply, holding on to it too long so that droplets of perspiration beaded my own forehead.

The air outside the hall was still warm, though the sun had fallen below the trees. Dark clouds rolled across the dusky sky, swelling thick and morose. A storm was brewing. I pulled my starched collar from my neck. Perspiration had defeated it and it hung limp in my hand. Noticing the glances of the drunken men by the horses I fled quickly from the village hall, up the street past Young Mendle's blacksmith shop which was shuttered up and dark. As I ran the angry taunts from the village hall pummelled my brain. Yid. Pig. I had been the cause of that hatred, that rage. I had roused that feeling through my poem. I recalled how Itzikl had shied away from me when I sat down. I saw, again, the fear in his eyes. A shiver of horror ran through my body.

I kept on running up the hill, beyond the path to our farm. In the distance I saw the lights shining from its windows as the inky clouds rolled heavily over it. I ran on to Old Mendle's place. Standing at the point where his path forked off the road I looked down towards the old house. There were no lights visible. I dared go no further. I knew I would not be welcome. I slumped to the grass and sat beneath the old birch tree, until the last glimmer of sunshine had been snuffed out and the ominous clouds had veiled the sky. I sat on, still, after the first large drop of rain splashed against my cheek. A cold tear.

School was finished and the days dragged. Itzikl had gone to stay with family in Wilno, I heard. He had got an apprenticeship in a tailor's owned by his uncle. I was glad I did not have to speak to him; I would not have known what to say. My father said nothing when he heard what had happened. He laid his large hand upon my shoulder and sighed. Mother, still, was proud that her son had won an award and started to say so, but my father shushed her angrily. I put all my energy into work on the farm, raising a grunt of amazement from Adam, even, at the ferocity of my labours.

We slept the night at a small inn on the road to Wilno. Adam refused to go inside and slept instead with the horse at the edge of the field. I did not sleep well and rose early to find that, though dawn had barely broken, Adam had already harnessed the horse and was ready to go. Before sundown that day the spires of the city came into view. The roads were busy; lorries and cars roared by, scaring the poor country horse. Adam, too, looked apprehensive despite the fact that he visited the city whenever my father had business there.

The sun shone and the crosses glittered. Wilno unfolded its ancient arms like the boughs of an oak to welcome me. I had lodgings on Giedyminowska Street, in the centre of the city. My father's sister lived there. She was married to a Polish businessman and her sons had gone, one to America, doing business in Chicago, and the other to Moscow to study. The busy cobbled street cut straight like a knife through the city from the cathedral to the Orthodox Church on the opposite side of the river. Between west and east were the Jews. Almost a third of the population of the city was Jewish. Irena was on the doorstep when we arrived. While my father was tall and thin, Irena was short and stout, but she resembled him nonetheless.

'Stepanushka!' she yelled with none of my father's reserve. Her fat arms shot from her sides. The brush with which she had been sweeping the dust from the doorway as she gossiped with a neighbour fell to the floor. She bustled forward, grabbing me as I slid from the back of the cart, and squeezed me hard against her firm, ample bosom.

Turning to her neighbour, with tears in her blue eyes, she said, 'My brother's son. What a fine boy, just look at the size of him. As big as our Tomasz.' The neighbour nodded her head and clicked her tongue.

'Come in. *Davai*, let's go. Adamushka, take up the bags and come in. I have been expecting you. You must be hungry.'

I shook my head in protest, barely able to edge a word into her ceaseless flow. Her Lithuanian was fractured by Polish. The two seemed to have been mangled into an unwieldy hybrid that caused spittle to fleck her lips as she chewed the words out. Without releasing me she turned to the opened doorway and pushed me towards it. Adam tied up the horse and picked my bags up from the cart. He sloped in behind us, through the doorway, into the dark stairwell. My aunt lived on the third floor, and she huffed up the stairs, slowing with each flight.

'Oi, oi, oi!' she lamented by her door, trying to catch her breath, her bosom heaving like an earthquake in the mountains. 'A nice house in the country, that is what I need. None of this up and down the stairs all the time. Will he listen to me? Phhh!' Her hands indicated her despair. 'No. How would his friends survive without him to drink with them, heh? Oi, so I have to suffer. To the devil with him.'

He, my uncle, was sitting reading the newspaper when we opened the door. He was a lean cultivated businessman with a large grey moustache that drooped over the sides of his mouth giving him a rather hangdog look. He stood up and stretched out his hand to me, a smile struggling against the confines of the moustache. He was rarely ever to be seen without a suit and wore a smart if fairly old one now.

'Steponas,' he said. 'Good to see you, boy.'

Adam lingered in the doorway, darkening it with his

unkempt mass, the bags in his hands. I went to take them from him.

'Adamovich, come in and sit yourself down,' Irena shouted, stowing the broom behind the door of the kitchen.

'No, I won't,' Adam demurred gruffly. 'It'll soon be dark. I must be gone.'

'*Nu*, Adam, as you wish.'

I shook his hand and he turned stiffly, avoiding my eyes, and was gone down the dark stairs.

'Little better than an animal,' my aunt said, busying herself in the kitchen. 'But he's honest and there's many who think they're better that are not.'

Pawel, my uncle, raised his eyebrows and grinned a canine-like, lopsided grin. Indicating for me to sit he stepped over to a cabinet and pulled out a bottle of Polish vodka.

'*Nu*, Steponas, you are a man now. You will join me for a toast.'

Chapter 40

Shortly before the night of the poetry competition, as I escorted Rachael along the dark road to her home in the moonlight, our hands brushed. We stopped by the old birch, which shone silver, at the point where Old Mendle's path forked off the road. Her breath was ragged with nerves. We stumbled and our faces met, almost lip to lip, in the pale light. I had been in Wilno for almost three months before I saw her again.

I settled into life in the provincial capital. Lectures beginning not many days after my arrival, I soon made friends with a lively group of students who introduced me to the pleasures of the city. Summer drew to a late close; autumn was delicate, golden, and then, on the first of November, out of nowhere, a flurry of snow. Winter. At a café just off German Street I met a group of poets and soon became a member of their fraternity. The leader of the group was a wild-haired Pole, Jerzy Szymonowicz. Jerzy was an aggressive, loud atheist obsessed with the Virgin Mother. Whilst one of his poems would be crude and mocking, the next was full of tender love.

Most evenings some members of the group would be in the café, discussing the latest poetry and drinking beer.

'Mary, the mother of whores,' Jerzy exclaimed, one evening, reading a poem he had been working on. His booming voice carried across the din of the early evening café. Heads turned in our direction. A chair scuffed as a tall well-dressed man rose, his face an angry shade of red.

'Jerzy,' a timid member of the group protested.

The waiter, midway to serving the couple of young women sat at the tall man's table, hesitated. His eyes swivelled between his well-dressed customers and the group of us in the corner.

'Immaculate madam of small town faiths,' Jerzy proclaimed, turning his attention to the red-faced diner. The man strode forward. Dextrously the waiter, switching his loaded tray from right hand to left, intercepted him. He bowed. He urged the man back into his seat, whispered to him and with great display presented the young ladies with their drinks.

'Whose pudenda . . .'

A howl of rage and small, offended feminine shrieks drowned the end of the stanza. The tall man rose, his chair falling with a clatter. A delighted grin crept up Jerzy's face as the offended Catholic beat a path to the corner where we were drinking.

Later I walked Jerzy home through the old, winding city streets. His eye was swollen and the skin around it had begun to turn a deep shade of yellow. He was still giggling at the scuffle that taken place as a result of his poetry reading.

'You're drunk,' I said, a little shocked myself.

'How else should one be at a time like this?'

'A time like this?'

'We're going to be fucked. One way or the other it's coming to us.'

'You think there will be war?'

He looked at me a little incredulously, then patted my shoulder, relegating me to the position on which he had accepted me to the group – country hick in need of a cosmopolitan education (which to him consisted of alcohol, women and poetry).

'It's not a case of if there will be war, but who will get to invade us first, the Commies or the Nazis. One way or the other we're fucked.'

Alcohol I hardly needed educating in; there was little else to do but drink in a Polish village. As to women, Jerzy was insistent I lose my virginity at the soonest possible occasion.

'Come on,' he said, taking my arm. 'Let's go and get a whore.'

I shook my head.

'How can you be a poet if you're a virgin?' he demanded. But I refused, the image of Rachael haunting me.

'I have a poem that reminds me of you,' he said, his arm drunkenly winding around my neck as we lurched through the darkness towards his apartment. Jerzy lived in a run-down apartment not far from the station. The sound of the trains rattled the loose windows in the room he rented. It was cold and damp and, for me, romantic. The boards were loose on the stairs and rattled as we climbed them. The fetid stairwell was filled with the overpowering odour of boiled cabbage and pig's trotters and as we passed a doorway at the top of the second storey a woman's cry pierced the air. I stood stock still, the hairs on the back of my neck standing on end. Jerzy waved his hand dismissively. 'Gypsies,' he explained.

It took Jerzy some time to locate the poem he was looking for. I sat on the unmade bunk in the corner of the room, while he searched through the detritus of his life. 'Ah!' he said at last, pulling a bundle of crumpled sheets from beneath his bed, close to my feet. 'Here we go.' He shuffled through the poems, humming a lewd song that he had been teaching me the words to earlier in the evening.

'David Vogel. He lived not so far from here, in Wilno, at some point. A friend of mine met him in Paris a couple of years ago. These are translations that he made. Vogel writes in Hebrew, can you believe? Can you believe that, heh?' He nudged me in the ribs and winked. 'Almost as bad as you writing your poems in Lithuanian.'

'Hey, what is so wrong with me writing poems in Lithuanian?'

'You mean why write in an anachronistic peasant's language rather than our beautiful Polish tongue?'

'It's not my tongue.'

After the poetry competition I had started using Lithuanian more. When I wrote in Polish I felt a shiver of shame run through my body. Since falling in with Jerzy's band I had translated a few into our common language. I did not tell Jerzy the real reason for writing my poems in Lithuanian; I let him believe I was a revolutionary, a romantic nationalist in the tradition of Mickevicius.

Flicking through the poems, he finally pulled out a dog-eared sheet. '*Nu, va!*' he said, pleased with himself. He scattered the other pages across the bare, rotten floorboards. Taking the poem he went to stand by the window. His smoked voice rolled the words across the dim room.

> *'When night draws near your window,*
> *come to him naked.*
> *Softly will he ripple and darken round*
> *your still beauty, touching the tips of*
> *your breasts.*
> *I shall stand with him there, a stray*
> *wanderer, and silently we shall yearn:*
> *come into our dark.*
> *And let your two eyes travel before us*
> *to light the way for me and my friend.'*

Silence descended upon the room like soft snowflakes, punctuated only by the stray shout of a lunatic woman in the cold street. Jerzy's long dark hair hung across his face and his shoulders slumped as though under a weight.

'Why should that remind you of me?' I asked.

He turned from the window and sloped over to me like an old tired wolf. Slouching on the bed he rested his feminine poet's fingers on my knee. 'Because,' he said, 'you are a lonely soul. You stand outside the window and look in.' He pressed my knee. 'Why don't you come in, Stepanovich?'

He pulled a bottle to his chest. 'Look at this,' he said, displaying the thick red liquid. 'Baba made it for me. She picked the cranberries herself in the forests. Granddad distilled the spirits in his little wooden hut down by the lake. That's the life. Here we are in the city, rotting in hell, surrounded by ignorant bastards!' He paused. '*Nu*, what do you say? Let's rent a cottage down by the river. We'll fish and gather mushrooms and berries in their season. We'll lie on our backs and watch the wind in the birch trees, watch the heron swoop down over the lake glittering in the sunshine. No Nazis or communists or anarchists.'

'You think that there aren't enough ignorant people in the villages?'

'You're right, you're right, but sometimes I look at Baba and her simple life and I just can't help but wonder.'

'You're drunk and Polish, which is saying the same thing.'

'Ha! Listen to the Lithuanian speak!' He laughed. He raised the bottle. 'To Mother Poland, and her sons who are heroes and poets!' He took a long slug of the spirits, wiped his mouth with the back of his elegant hand and passed the bottle to me.

I raised it. 'To poetry, our one true mother.' And took a swig. I coughed and water sprang to my eyes. 'That's ninety per cent spirits,' I told him. He grinned and took the bottle back.

'To the virgin queen. May his maidenhead soon be plucked!'

'To the husband of whores.'

He perked up at that. 'To whores and their daughters.'

The bottle shook as I took it back from him. Its neck was warm and sticky. I raised it.

'To peaceful times to enjoy them.'

'Peace? To the hours we have left to us. To these last moments. To the vodka that makes us forget and the whores and songs and friends we shall always remember.'

My head had begun to spin. My vision leapt between a seemingly preternatural clarity and a foggy blur. Jerzy was grinning stupidly. A fierce heat billowed out from my stomach and coursed up my body, exploding through the top of my skull. I wrapped my fingers with delicate precision around the neck of the bottle. Solemnly I raised it, gazing intently into its depleted, bloody contents.

'Never forget,' I said, my lips thick and rubbery, a little numb.

Jerzy tapped my knee. Two careful little slaps that none-theless almost missed their mark. 'Now,' he said. 'My stray wanderer, standing forever outside the window. Now you tell me. Tell me all. Tell your uncle Jerzy.' One more slap, for effect, executed a little too quickly; his hand slipped off and onto the wooden floorboards.

'Wha' you talkin' abou'?' I asked.

'Who is she, Steponushka? Tell Jerzy, tell Baba.' He patted my head delicately, flattening the hair slightly. 'I'll be Baba,' he said, his eyes focusing on a space somewhere inside my skull, or perhaps a couple of feet behind it. '*Mociute. Motule. Motute . . .*' Granny, nana, nanny.

Rachael. Rachael with your dark eyes, dark, mysterious eyes. Rachael with your hair that falls in waves upon your shoulders. Your voice is like the singing of a brook in the summertime. Your fingers, as they stroked my forehead that one time, like the whisper of grass in the spring breeze. Rachael. I recall how we walked in the forest, how we sat in the fields watching the beavers down by the lake building their home. Rachael. Your hair shone in the moonlight. The birch tree was silver beside us. Its leaves rustled. The insects sang. Your breath was warm and your skin scented. Your lips . . . Rachael.

Snowflakes settled on the window pane. The first few dissolved in the weak light, but one by one they grew braver, stronger. A thin layer of crystals formed. The apartment settled into a night silence. A silence almost as profound as that in the woods when the snow is two feet thick and you are alone. Then Jerzy, sleeping, caught a breath. He snorted and turned uncomfortably on the floor. I struggled to pull him onto his small bunk. He murmured in his sleep and the empty bottle fell from his grasp and rolled across the floorboards. I piled what clothes I could find on top of the thin blanket I had covered him with. He opened his eyes, as I was about to leave.

'Forever outside the window,' he said and grinned.

Chapter 41

Not many days later I saw her. I was staring out of the steamy window of a café having just finished a cigarette. For a moment I thought my eyes had tricked me. I almost rubbed them to be sure. She was walking down the narrow street, shadowed from the fine winter sun by the walls of the buildings. On the pavement a thin hard crust of snow glistered brilliantly. The air was sharp and fresh.

I had been sitting in lectures since the early hours and the last thing I felt like doing when they finished was returning to the stuffy flat on Giedyminowska Street. Instead I wandered around the old streets of the city, enjoying the bright winter weather. After an hour I was chilled to the bone and found a small café on Pilies Street. It was mid-afternoon, and the café was quiet as I sat by the window drinking sludgy coffee and smoking cheap Russian cigarettes. I was about to order another coffee from the emaciated girl behind the counter when Rachael came into view.

I sat transfixed. She was lost in thought, kicking the toes of her boots absently at the crust of snow as she walked, billowing it into sparkling showers. A fashionable scarf covered her dark hair. I rose immediately, dropping a pile of kopecks onto the wooden table.

'God in heaven!' she exclaimed when I caught her elbow.

'Rachael.'

'Steponas!' She looked dismayed.

I held her elbow and pulled her to a halt. Her dark eyes looked into my own questioningly.

'It's good to see you, Rachael,' I stammered.

'Listen, Steponas, I am going somewhere.' She glanced around as if worried somebody might see her. She tried to pull her arm away.

'Rachael, please don't just run away.'

'I really am in a hurry.'

'Have a drink. A quick one.'

She shook her head. A strand of chocolate dark hair broke loose from the colourful silk scarf and curled across her forehead.

'Rachael, you must. I won't keep you long. Please.'

She melted a little. She shook her head again, but not so confidently. Again her eyes flicked around the street and she seemed nervous. 'I don't know,' she said.

'Come,' I said, directing her to the little café from which I had just emerged.

'No,' she said. 'Not there.'

We ducked into a narrow alley-way and she led me to a small Armenian café with room for little more than one wooden table.

'I know you're angry with me,' I said. 'Rachael, you do not know how sorry I am for what happened at the competition. I had no idea.'

She shook her head again and I feared that she would not allow me to apologise; that she would not find it in her to forgive me.

'You know I am not like that,' I told her. 'It was a mistake that they reacted that way. I would never have read the poem if I knew that they would respond like that.'

She shook her head again and laid one of her hands on my sleeve. She wore elegant black gloves. 'You don't understand,' she said. 'I know you did not mean to cause the problems with your poems. I know you are not one of those Polish shits.' She smiled weakly. 'But still, you know, your poem did that. And after all you are not a Jew, such poems will not be visited upon your head. Such mistakes will not bring bottles through your window, or cause drunken men to jeer at you in the street.'

It was my turn to shake my head.

'Steponas, you do not understand, and how could you unless you had been born a Jew? All that night I held my little cousin in my arms because a crowd of yobs gathered outside Rivka's house, singing and cursing and threatening to burn it to the ground. Thank God nothing happened.'

'I'm sorry.'

'I know you are sorry, Steponas. I know that, you fool.' She squeezed my arm. My eyes lit up once more and a little of the painful guilt lifted from my heart.

'Could you forgive me?'

'What is there to forgive? You didn't mean any harm. It's not your fault the world is so full of fools.'

The old Armenian clattered in the kitchen of his tiny café. The room was filled with moist clouds of steam, fragrant with spices. Rachael was well dressed, she looked more beautiful than ever. I took her slim gloved hand. She quickly pulled it from me.

'No, Steponas.'

'But, Rachael . . .'

'You don't understand.'

'You said . . .'

'I said you don't understand.' Her voice rose and she flushed red. A pained look passed over her face. The Armenian bustled up to the table, cauterising her words. He took the two small cups in his large paws. She looked down. The Armenian grinned. His large face was accentuated by a moustache, which bristled out like an unruly thorn bush.

'More?' he demanded in heavily accented Russian.

I looked at Rachael but her face was down. 'Yes,' I said. 'Yes, two more.'

When he had retreated I put my hand beneath her chin and lifted it. She resisted.

'What is it, Rachael?'

'I am to be married.'

'Married?' The word stumbled from my lips.

Her eyes flashed. 'Yes, married,' she said. 'Is there anything wrong with that?'

I was wounded. My hand fell from her delicate chin. I was glad when the large Armenian intruded once more. He set the small cups of wickedly strong coffee before us and then lingered. 'A couple of small pastries to go with these perhaps?' Rachael shook her head. He withdrew to his steaming kitchen.

'What did you expect, Steponas?'

'Not this.'

'Then what? Did you think that there could have been any other way? I am a Jew, Steponas, and you are not.'

'We would not have been the first.'

'You know others?'

'Love does not care for these things.'

'Love may not, Steponas, but Hitler does. The Poles do. My father does.'

'I thought your father was a socialist.'

'He's a socialist and a Jew. And if I mentioned your name after that poetry competition he would have thrown me out of the house.'

A gloomy silence descended upon us. What had I thought? What had I expected? I had, I realised, thought nothing. The future had been shrouded in a rosy haze. It could not have been any other way than this.

'Who are you marrying?' I asked.

'Rivka's cousin. He is a good person and his family own a haberdasher's.'

'Where?'

She shook her head and would not answer.

'And you are happy?'

The ironic edge to my voice did not escape her. She laid one of her elegantly gloved hands on my arm.

'Yes, Steponas. I am happy. What else could I have asked for?'

When she left I stayed on at the table. I ordered another coffee from the hirsute Armenian and stared gloomily from the steamy windows into the dark, narrow alley-way. The words from Vogel's poem came back to me. 'I shall stand with him there, a stray wanderer, and silently we shall yearn.' Maybe Jerzy had been right; it had been allotted to me to be ever standing outside the window looking in. A wave of bitter feeling for Rachael washed over me. I had loved her. I did love her. Why had it been so easy for her to forget me? I moodily pictured her bourgeois fiancé.

'Women trouble, eh?' the Armenian said, rubbing his large hairy hands on a grubby rag.

I nodded.

'Oi, the women, always they are a problem,' he said. 'You need some medicine.'

'Medicine?'

'The fix for all the broken hearts.' He disappeared into his steaming inferno, reappearing seconds later with some Armenian brandy. He set it down on the table with a thump and clinked two small glasses down beside it. Deftly he flicked the lid from the bottle and sloshed a sticky amber substance up to the rim of the glasses.

'Well, *gaspadin*! Let us drink to women.' He licked his lips, whether at the idea of women or in anticipation of the brandy I could not tell. '*Na zdarovje*.'

'*Na zdarovje*,' I said, raising the sticky glass to my lips. I winced at its sweetness. The liquid burned a sticky rivulet down my throat.

'Jewish?' the Armenian asked, nodding his head sideways at the door through which Rachael had left. 'Not a bad looker. A special toast to this girl of yours, eh?' We tossed back two more of his undrinkable brandies. The Armenian smacked his lips. The brandy hung in golden droplets from the bottom of his bushy moustache.

'You don't move,' he told me. He disappeared, a few moments later reappearing once more, bearing chipped plates on his large arms.

'Not a good idea to drink on an empty stomach,' he said, poking at his head as he spoke. He spread the plates between us. Pickled green peppers stuffed with chopped vegetables. Thin Armenian cracker bread. Cheese. A dip of crushed chickpeas and crushed sesame seed. He pointed at the bread. '*Patz hatz*. Armenian bread. Great with the dip. Eat.'

But when I left, the feeling of bitterness had not dissipated. I kicked down Pilies Street keeping to the icy shadows. Not having anything better to do I pushed in through the large doors of the cathedral below Gediminas Hill. It was quiet and I sat for some while contemplating the painting of the Virgin Mother. Her benign face regarded the child in her arms, a fat healthy baby boy, the blue cloth falling away from his ruddy body. My grandmother kept a small icon of the Virgin by her bed and prayed to it night and morning, touching it till the face shone in the candlelight with the grease from her fingers. The image did not move me. I tried to pray to Her as I knew that my grandmother would be praying on my behalf. But no words came.

I left the mother and her child, the bitterness still burning my insides, like cheap brandy. I pushed open the doors to see the sun setting, violet, above the spires and tumble of city roofs. I turned in the direction I knew I would find Jerzy.

Chapter 42

Snow settled deep upon the city. The clouds that clipped the tiled roofs were heavy, pregnant. Men and women huddled around their radios listening for news. Jerzy and I took to the streets, trekking from one drinking den to another. The city opened up to me. It opened like a flea-bitten mongrel wanting to be scratched. And I delighted in scratching it. Poems flowed from me as they had never before. Late into the night we sat around a bottle and the stub of a cheap candle that burnt an acrid smoke, to argue over the merits of things we had discovered in our reading.

Our poetry group moved out of the café off German Street following the scuffle Jerzy's Virgin Mother poems had provoked. We were no longer welcome. We set up in Chaim's, closer to the station. There the clientele of drunken Jews did not mind our poems, oblivious in the fug of cigarette fumes. On Saturday evenings an old man, his beard tickling the whistling lungs of his accordion, sat up at the back of the spartan bar. We forgot our poems then, losing ourselves in the wheezing chords, the stamping feet and the cheap vodka.

I moved out of my aunt's flat on Giedyminowska Street and set up with Jerzy in an apartment on Rudnicka Street. There was a church nearby, outside which stood an old and beautiful maple tree, denuded by winter. The block had once been grand. Time had not been generous to it, however, and the plaster in the stairwell fell in chunks onto the decorated stair tiles. It was, still, grander than we could have afforded as students. What we could not afford in money, I came to realise, Jerzy paid the landlady, a widow in her forties, in kind. 'Who am I to complain?' he protested when I found out.

And indeed, in the end, it was to her, old enough to be my mother, that I surrendered my virginity. Her name was Tzalka. She was a dark-haired, faded beauty, half Karaite, half Pole. She arrived late one night on our doorstep looking for Jerzy. Jerzy had gone out to scavenge some food for us and I was expecting him back. I invited her in. She wore a thick, bright wrap pulled tight around her shoulders, a present from the elderly husband who had widowed her young, she explained. The same wrap she would be wearing when the Soviets pushed her onto the cattle car that took her to the freezing steppes to die. She sat on the old chair we had been given by another of Jerzy's friends, with a wry grin on her pretty face. I suspected she had been drinking.

'So, you are Mr Szymonowicz's young friend,' she said, regarding me squarely. She spoke a correct but slightly accented Russian. When I replied in Polish she frowned. 'You are a poet, are you not?' she told me. 'You should speak in the language of poets. Polish is just so . . . parochial.'

'Poland has its poets, too,' I ventured.

She ignored me. 'My husband was Russian. He was acquainted with members of the royal household. He was a great but very modest man. He once dined with Mayakovski, you know, the year before he died. My husband, that is. They were in Nice. "You are wrong, wrong, wrong," my husband told him. He could not agree with the Bolsheviks. But what a handsome man he was, Mayakovski.

> *The skin proliferates in wrinkles.*
> *Love flowers,*
> *and flowers*

and then withers and shrinks.

Jerzy quoted me that one.' She looked suddenly miserable. 'The young fucker.'

She jumped up from the seat restlessly. I stood by the door to the small kitchen watching her nervously. Her wrap had fallen from her shoulders to reveal a rather flimsy dress of the type you would wear for an evening at a club. It seemed a little insubstantial, considering the snow outside. She strode over to an old gramophone that stood in the corner on a low table. It had been in the apartment when we moved in with a small collection of wax discs. She chose one and wound up the machine. Music blared from the dinted horn. She twirled round, flaring the bottom of her dress, displaying shapely calves.

'Come and dance,' she told me in her accented Russian. 'Do you have a girl?' she asked.

I almost told her about Rachael but did not.

'Do you think I look old?' she demanded, pressing close to me. She glared into my eyes. Thin lines explored the edges of her fiery eyes and her skin was olive-yellow. Her body was supple and her closeness aroused me. Her heavy perfume filled my nostrils and her firm, strong hands caressed my back, pressing me tight against her breasts.

Jerzy discovered us in bed. He stood in the doorway laughing into the darkness, waking me. I sat up quickly.

'I'm sorry,' I began.

He tiptoed theatrically towards me and caught my head in his hands. 'I love you, baby,' he said in English and kissed me drunkenly on the forehead. 'The whore has made a man of you.'

She snorted in her sleep. Jerzy and I collapsed in silent laughter.

* * *

Jerzy had a steady stream of young women to distract us from the news of the coming war. We laughed in the face of darkness. 'We're going to be fucked any which way, so let's fuck,' Jerzy reasoned. I did not argue. Jerzy had started to drink harder than ever.

I stood in the snow outside a haberdasher's in an old winding street in the Jewish quarter. Muffled figures passed quickly in the street muttering in Yiddish, old men going to study at the Beth Midrash. Ravens against the deep pure snow that had fallen overnight. A light burned in the shop. The windows were steamed up so I could not see in. But I knew she was in there.

I had been on my way home as the sky was beginning to lighten. Lidya, the Polish whore, lived in the courtyard of an apartment across the river and it was a long trek back to Rudnicka. I saw Rachael hurrying through the uncleared drifts past the Church of Mary the Solacer. I fell into step behind her, keeping a safe distance between us. She walked fast and did not look back. She ducked, finally, into the haberdasher's shop in a narrow alley.

'Where have you been?' Jerzy muttered when I pushed open the door of our apartment. He was sat at the table, fully dressed. An empty bottle had fallen over onto the floor. His eyes were like hollow pits in his lean face. I was cold and went to pull the thin blanket from our bed. I wrapped it around me and joined Jerzy at the table.

'Lidya's,' I told him. He gazed blankly at the table, his unshaven chin resting on his arm. 'Have you slept?'

He grunted derisively. 'Sleep?'

'Jerzy, you need to take it easy,' I said, getting up and moving closer to him. He pushed my hand away from him, irritably.

'There'll be plenty of time for sleeping,' he said ironically. 'An eternity of sleep. It can wait.'

'Come,' I said and took him under the arm. 'Let's go and catch some sleep. I didn't get so much myself.' I forced a grin.

Jerzy grinned too. 'Good old Lidya,' he said.

We lay on the sagging mattress, sharing the blanket, huddling up for some heat. Jerzy's body was thin, not much more than a covering of skin across his bones. He kicked around in the bed and sloped off some time after I had dropped into a fitful sleep. As the days wound around past New Year, he wrote fewer poems and those that he showed me now were more vicious. 'What is the point of poems?' he asked one night as we drank our way down a bottle of spirits.

I returned to the haberdasher's on a fairly regular basis, drawn by a compulsion I felt unable to control. Usually I would find my way there after a night with some whore Jerzy had found for me. I stood in the ice and snow, watching the comfortable light burning in the window, resenting Rachael her happiness. Often I was overwhelmed with self-loathing, and would stalk away determined to leave her alone, but I could not stay away from the shop for long. I did not go in. I was nervous of talking to her and I had no money to buy anything. Her clients were fashionable Jews. Elegant, well-groomed men, hats pulled low against the weather, hurrying from their cars left in the small square, to her door. They re-emerged with packages neatly wrapped under their arms and scurried back up the alley. Water was dripping from the long icicles that hung from the eaves by the time I saw her next.

The door of the shop opened and I heard the bright tinkle of her laughter drift out across the dark slush. I stood suddenly alert. My legs were stiff and I was very cold. I had not even been thinking of her. I had been standing for perhaps half an hour in the opposite doorway deliberating on whether to change my discipline at the university. Jerzy had been urging me to move to the literature department where he was finishing his studies. My legal studies were dreary going and I was only continuing with them to keep my father happy.

For a moment the door stood open. From the shadows I watched intently. No customers had gone into the shop. They had hired a young girl some weeks earlier and it was usually she who popped out mid-morning. I had half formed the intention of getting acquainted with the girl and had on one occasion followed her. She had walked several blocks and perhaps suspected I was following her. She had glanced over her shoulder a couple of times, then she turned suddenly into an old courtyard and when I slipped in through the crumbling archway she had disappeared. I felt so ashamed after this incident that I didn't go back to the shop for another week.

It was not the girl though. A short man appeared in the doorway. He stopped on the threshold, his fingers reaching out to the small box on the door-jamb. He was dressed in a smart suit. He pulled on an expensive overcoat and fastened it up against the cold. He was smiling. He called back into the shop, jovially, in Yiddish. And a moment later she appeared at his side. She, too, was dressed stylishly. A beautiful scarf wrapped around her throat and hair, revealing only the soft olive oval of her face. She stopped in front of her husband and carefully buttoned his coat. He laughed. She was smiling. She slipped her arm through his then and they stepped out into the dirty melting snow, the door swinging firmly shut on their bright and inviting shop.

I pressed myself back into the shadows. I felt then the stubble on my chin. The lankness of my hair and the damp unwholesomeness of my clothes, which needed both washing and pressing. I felt the loose unhealthy quality of the skin on my hands, the dirtiness of my broken nails, the corns pressing on my too tight shoes. I felt the hunger in my stomach and the longing in my heart. I watched her step quickly down the alley-way by the side of her short, smart husband. His hair was thinning, but he pulled a dashing hat over it, tilting it rakishly over his forehead.

I pressed my own forehead against the cold damp plaster in the dark doorway. In the moonlight, our hands had brushed. We stopped by the old birch tree, which shone silver, at the point where Old Mendle's path forked off the road. Her breath was ragged with nerves. We stumbled and our faces met, almost lip to lip, in the pale light. Had it been allotted to me to be ever standing outside the window looking in? Rachael?

Chapter 43

It was late summer and we were sitting in a café when Nathan Fisk, a young, red-haired communist, burst in with the news. 'They're coming,' he called. His face was alive with excitement and he could not keep still when he reached our table. Hopping from one foot to the other, he pounded a fist into the palm of his ink-stained writing hand. Jerzy pushed back his chair and ran a hand through his hair. A sardonic smile flickered over his face.

'Who is coming?' asked Jankowski, an expressionist painter, his head lowered almost to the rim of the bowl from which he was supping beetroot soup. He lifted a potato from the creamy, red liquid and sucked at it noisily.

'The Red Army,' Fisk said breathlessly.

Jerzy snorted derisively.

Fisk's excitement was dampened by Jerzy's withering gaze. He squirmed a little and then dropped into a free seat at the table. 'It was on the radio. They should be in Wilno before darkness falls.'

'Hurrah for the Red Army,' Jerzy jeered.

'Daumantas should be happy,' Jankowski said, his mouth full of potato.

'And why should I be happy?' I asked.

'They've made a deal, haven't they? With your government in Kovno. Wilno will be handed back to Lithuania.'

Fisk looked anxiously from Jankowski's face to mine, trying to weigh our feelings. I shrugged. I had heard the news from a soldier I had met at the railway station earlier in the day. Jankowski went back to his soup. It was early afternoon and Jerzy was in a foul mood, recovering from a night with our landlady, Tzalka. He kicked Fisk's chair hard. Fisk started back, a look of panic on his creamy-pink face.

'Fuck off, Fisk. Go and share the good news with some of your commie friends,' Jerzy growled.

Fisk's face reddened. Kicking back his chair, he attempted something like aggression. When he turned, however, he was forced to right the chair in order to pass it. Huffily he left the café. Jerzy stared after him, blackly.

'Got to be going,' I said. 'I'll see you later.'

I caught up with Fisk outside All Saints' Church, near our apartment. He looked reproachful when I caught his arm.

'If you've come to jeer, forget it, I've got to get to a meeting.'

'I'm not jeering, Nathan.'

'What's wrong with Jerzy?' he whined. 'Is he a fascist? Would he prefer that it was the Wehrmacht marching into Wilno?'

'Jerzy's just in a bad mood,' I reassured him. 'You know that he isn't a fascist.'

'Yes, well, it's all right him thinking he is above it all. He takes this grand detached view, as if he is such a great poet that it is all irrelevant. But you tell me, what is the use of poetry unless there is something in it that can make our world a better place? It's up to us poets to set the moral agenda. It's up to us to voice the feelings of the masses, those not able to make their voices heard.'

Fisk's pink face had gone red. He was punching his fist into the palm of his hand again, too, as we walked down the narrow lane.

'Yes, yes,' I reassured him, though my own poetry was defiantly resistant to the ideological programme he held so dear.

'It's not just that I am a communist,' Fisk continued. 'Who knows what the Germans will do if they invade? Listen, Steponas, my uncle went to Germany, to Augsburg to attend my cousin's wedding. He was arrested. You don't know what it is like for the Jews there. Every day their lives get harder. They are being forced out of their jobs, intimidated. The police pick them up without any justification. My uncle is kept in Augsburg still.'

I nodded. 'I know, Fisk, I have heard these things.'

'I hear that your government has been in negotiations with Berlin as well as Moscow, to get Wilno back?'

I stared back at him blankly.

'I heard it at a Party meeting.'

We walked on in silence. Despite the nationalist reputation I had gained, as a result of writing my poems in Lithuanian, that country's attempts to claw back the old capital held very little interest for me.

'Fisk, I wanted to ask you something.'

'Yes?'

'Do you know a certain Troiman? Owner of the haber-dasher's.'

'Ira Troiman? Oi! What do you want with him?'

'You don't like him?'

'What's to like? He's a bastard. The whole family is. How do you know him?'

'A bastard, eh?'

'Listen, they're big in the textiles and treat their workers like shit.'

'Capitalist bastards?'

'They have a factory. A couple of months ago a worker there got his arm ripped off, working on one of their old machines. His fault, Troiman said. They refused to give a kopeck in compensation to his family. They said he wasn't married, despite the fact this woman had been with him near enough fifteen years and they had five kids. The Party tried to intervene on his behalf; the foreman at the factory was a Party member. So they sacked him. Spread his name around as an agitator, trouble causer. Tried to stop him getting another job.'

'This Troiman owns the factory? Ira Troiman?'

'His father. Ira stands to inherit when the old man goes. When the Soviets come we'll kick the filthy bastards out. That'll teach them.'

'Ira Troiman is married?'

Fisk shrugged. 'What do I know? Do I look like the local gossip? Why are you so interested?'

I shrugged. 'Come for a drink?' I asked.

'Meeting,' he said. 'Why don't you come along?' I shook my head and left him on the corner of Stefanska.

The Soviet troops began entering the city after darkness. The sound of tanks and rattling engines disturbed the city's sleep. We lay in our beds trying to interpret the sporadic outbursts of gunfire. By daybreak Wilno was theirs.

The streets were noisy. A group of young Jewish communists hailed the armoured cars rattling through the city. '*Da zdravstvuyet krasnaya armija!* – Long live the Red Army!' I slipped through the thin knots of pedestrians idling on street corners watching the liberators.

I had discovered from another contact that in the summer Ira Troiman spent much of his free time down by the Wilja at the Maccabee athletic club. He was a keen rower. For a couple of Sundays I kept a watch on him. He drove down to the club dressed in smart sports clothes in his imported scarlet Tatra 57. The banks of the river were lined with young women in their bathing costumes, swimming, sunbathing, gossiping, watching the young athletes pulling hard at the oars on the sparkling surface of the water.

I borrowed a bathing costume from Tzalka. It had belonged to her husband and was hopelessly old-fashioned. I invited her to join me by the river, but Jerzy had been cruel to her and she would not come out of the darkened room I found her in. In the end I went alone. I had half hoped that Fisk would accompany me, but he was busy meeting with Party members. Later in the afternoon I saw a group of them waving flags and placards, cheering a group of Kazak soldiers in battered green lorries.

Rolling the bathing costume into an old towel I made my way down to the river. The day was hot. The church spires reached up into the magnificent September sky. The war seemed a long way away, despite the Soviet tanks and battalions streaming into the city. It was hard to imagine that on this pleasant day the German forces were pounding their way across France. On the banks of the river there were a fair number of bathers and sun-worshippers catching their last rays before the winter set in.

Changing in one of the booths, I sat on the grass watching the rowers work their way up and down the Wilja, which glittered in the sunlight. I could not see Rachael or her husband, Ira. To escape the sun, I took a walk in the pine forest. The air was fine and fresh. As I made my way back to the road I noticed the scarlet Tatra parked in the shade.

It was a lovely car. The hood was folded back and I could smell the leather of the seats. A silk scarf lay on the passenger seat. Hers. Furtively I glanced around and picked it up. The silk was cool and fine when I held it to my lips, like the smell of the pine forest. Faintly there was the scent of the soap she used. I closed my eyes and drew in a deep breath.

'Hello?' a man's voice called in Polish.

I whirled around to find him close behind me, tense in his pale flannels. He was shorter than I, but stronger, evidently fitter.

'Steponas.'

She was a step behind him. She was pale. Her husband turned to her, an enquiring look on his face. 'You know him?'

She did not answer immediately. Her eyes were on the silk scarf I held in my hand still, suspended close to my lips. Slowly the dark eyes travelled up to my face and I felt them searching it. I felt weak with shame. Her deep, immeasurably deep, eyes came to rest upon my own. Silently she held my gaze.

'Yes,' she said. 'Yes, I know him.'

I flushed scarlet, to match the smart sports car. I turned and dropped the scarf back onto the pale leather seat of the car.

'Steponas Daumantas,' Rachael said to her husband. She seemed to have recovered. 'We're from the same village. We went to school together.'

Ira's face relaxed. A friendly smile spread across it. 'No kidding? Really? Hey, that's great.' He was about thirty-five years of age, a compact man. His hair was cut short and his skin glowed healthily. He proffered a hand. He wore a large golden ring. His handshake was firm, manly and warm.

'Ira Troiman,' he said. 'Proud husband of your school friend.' He spoke with a slight American accent, an affectation popular then among the fashionable businessmen who regularly travelled abroad. He gathered Rachael into his large brown arm. She smiled faintly, her eyes not leaving my own. I nodded in acknowledgement.

'Well, what a coincidence to find you here by my car,' Ira continued gaily. 'She's a beauty, isn't she?' He slapped the side of the car affectionately.

'Yes,' I said. 'Yes, she is.'

Chapter 44

'Why don't you join us,' Ira said. 'We were just going for drinks. It'll give you two old buddies a chance to catch up.'

I shook my head quickly. Though it had been my very intention to somehow insinuate myself into their company, now the opportunity had arisen I felt ashamed; the thought of going for drinks horrified me. Ira opened the door of the Tatra for Rachael. He held it while she lingered.

'Come on,' she said quietly.

Mutely, I got into the car, feeling my legs sticky against the soft cream leather of the seats.

We drove to a quiet restaurant on Giedyminowska, not far from my aunt's. It was early evening, the city was quiet but for the small groups of young communists exultantly wandering the streets. Ira laughed at them good-humouredly. I considered telling him Fisk's views on his capitalist activities, but did not. At the restaurant Ira drank German schnapps and ordered champagne for his wife.

'What are you drinking, Steponas?'

Since arriving in Wilno I had drunk little other than cheap vodka, but I indicated that I would join him with the schnapps. He raised his glass and we drank a toast to old friends. I struggled to keep the irony from my voice. Rachael sat in silence as Ira chatted, regaling me with his opinions on the Soviet occupation. We had not been sitting long before Ira glanced at the smart watch on his thick wrist. He raised his eyebrows.

'Got to be going,' he said. 'I'm running late.' He stood

up and leant over to Rachael. 'Why don't you stay and chat?' he said, kissing her briefly on the cheek. He shook my hand warmly, looking me in the eye. 'Nice meeting you, Steponas.'

As he passed I smelt the subtle scent of his aftershave. Rachael studiously inspected the champagne she had scarcely tasted.

'I should go too,' I said. The schnapps was sweet and I found it quite undrinkable after the samogonas.

I had risen from my chair before she spoke.

'I'm sorry,' she said, not looking up from the champagne.

'What do you have to be sorry for?' I replied, belligerently.

'Just sorry,' she said. She looked up. 'Sorry for this whole mess.'

'It doesn't look such a mess for you.'

'You think you are the only one to feel anything?' she said. 'Do you think that I never felt anything? What was I supposed to do, would you like to tell me that? Would you like to tell me why what I did was so wrong?'

'I loved you,' I said petulantly.

'And I loved you, Steponas. But we were children. We were playing. This is not a world for children. I don't know whether you noticed but there are soldiers in the streets. They are Russians and God knows what that will mean for us, but, thank God, at least they are not the Germans. And still, if it were not for the war, this is Poland. I am a Jew and you are not. What are you asking for? I don't understand.'

'How can you be so cold?' I dropped back into my chair, opposite her. 'You reason about love and then just cut it from your heart?'

'Ach, you are a poet! What is reason to you? But do you remember where your poetry led, Steponas? Reason is important. Maybe for you there is more room for risk, but I do not want to sit up at nights cradling my children, fearing for what might happen to them. I fear life without reason. I fear your poetry and all you poets. You are dangerous.'

She looked at me furiously, filled, perhaps, with the resentment she had felt the night of the poetry competition when she had sat holding her young cousin, listening to the jeers of drunken village men outside her window. I regarded her, stony faced. Shamed but bitter. She reached out her hand and rested it on my own.

'You're right,' I relented.

'Sometimes I wonder,' she said, half burying her face in her hands. 'I mean, I wonder if there is right and wrong. I have such dreams at night. I have such fears for the future.'

'Things will turn out fine.'

'I pray to God.'

'Ira seems confident. He doesn't seem to be worried about the communists.'

Rachael smiled. 'Ira is incurably confident.'

'He seems like a nice man, anyway,' I said morosely.

'He is a good man, Steponas. He is kind and hardworking.'

'And rich.'

The corner of her mouth screwed up. 'How did you get so cynical? Is that how the poets must be here?' She regarded me disparagingly.

'I'm sorry,' I said and paused. 'Rachael, the things I would like to say just don't come out. I'm afraid. My friend read me a poem, he said it reminded him of me: "I shall stand with him there, a stray wanderer, and silently we shall yearn". I am afraid of being that – a stray wanderer, forever outside the window.'

She placed her hand on mine again and smiled faintly.

'I used to enjoy the talks we had,' she said. 'I miss them.'

'Me too.'

'Maybe you will come for dinner with us one day? Ira would be pleased, I am sure.'

'Yes. Maybe.'

Rachael pulled a jacket across her shoulders. 'I have to go,' she said. I nodded. She turned and waved, briefly, as she left the restaurant. I downed the schnapps with a grimace and ordered vodka. Rachael's champagne stood barely touched, a semi-circle of her red lipstick printed at its rim from where she had sipped at it. I rubbed it, smudging the lipstick onto my finger. I brought it up to my own lips and tasted it. Sweet.

Chapter 45

The Soviets, after gaining control of the city, turned it over to the Lithuanian government in Kaunas, and then withdrew. Almost immediately rioting broke out. Bands of Lithuanian thugs roamed the night-time streets, drunk and enraged. Searching out Jews and whatever other trouble they could find.

It was October and the air was cold and damp. Jerzy and I tumbled through the half-lit streets on our way home from the Staromiejska. A thick fog had drifted across the city, blanketing it. Rounding a corner by the university we were set upon suddenly by a gang of youths. A short, stocky young man dressed in a worn dark suit and no overcoat grabbed the lapels of my coat and thrust me against the wall of the old university. Without my support Jerzy dropped to his knees and before any words were spoken a boot landed in his stomach. He doubled up with a faint groan and rolled onto the glimmering, wet cobblestones.

'Where you been?' the stocky youth growled in Lithuanian. There was no sense to his question beyond ascertaining what language I spoke.

I was taken aback and concerned for Jerzy, who was not moving. For a couple of seconds I did not answer, as my fugged brain tried to clear itself. I was too slow. The wind was suddenly knocked from me and my body crumpled in a painful spasm.

'*Palauk*!' I gasped. 'Wait! I'm Lithuanian.'

My short attacker paused. He grunted. Without another word they turned and disappeared into the fog.

Jerzy had not moved. I knelt over him. The cobblestones cut into my knees painfully. A gash on his forehead was bleeding darkly. I lowered my cheek to his lips to see if he was breathing. He grimaced as I put my face close to his.

'Don't kiss me.'

'You piss-head,' I said. 'I was hoping they had killed you. I was just going for your wallet.'

I pulled him up and looped his arm around my shoulder. Slowly we trudged up the hill winding into the ancient lanes of the Jewish quarter of the city.

'Can't you sing a Lithuanian song or something?' Jerzy joked. 'Just to let them know.'

The fog thickened, drifting down the narrow, cobbled streets. The city was full of noises it was hard to determine. We listened uneasily as we walked. The fog was illuminated suddenly as we turned into Stiklu. It glared red and the muffled sound of shouting seeped out from the glow. Oaths and a woman's scream. Glass cascaded onto stone and there was the sound of a sudden huge intake of a monster's breath. Flames tore through the fog. A man was shouting somewhere, discordant accompaniment to the woman's cries. Pleading. We stopped on the corner, staring into the dim glow. The male voice was broken Russian, Polish; the woman, without control, screamed Yiddish pleas to the invisible sky. The cries were strangely muffled by the fog, so that the scene was like a drama played in a too small theatre.

Jerzy turned. 'Let's get out of here.'

I stood transfixed, holding him. The fog shifted, giving a surprise glimpse of the narrow lane, like a tableau, figures arrested in violent postures. And then it closed in once more, enveloping them. Jerzy pulled at my arm but I resisted.

'The Jews,' I muttered. 'They're after the Jews.'

'The Jews, the fucking Poles, who cares.'

A figure sprang from the fog, almost colliding with us. The

man started, his face a plastic mask of fear. His forehead and cheeks were blackened and his hair oddly cut. It was only when he passed I realised it had been burnt away at the front. Jerzy broke into a shuffling run after him. The fleeing figure, looking back over his shoulder, must have thought he was being chased. He let out a piteous shriek and doubled his speed, disappearing within seconds into the hulk of the fog.

'Jerzy,' I called. He stopped and turned on the edge of visibility. When I did not move he sloped off.

I stood rooted to the street corner. This was the rage I had provoked in the village with my poem. That night they had gathered outside the homes of the Jews in the village. Perhaps they were outside her window tonight, too. Perhaps she was huddled behind shuttered windows, whilst they threw stones. I broke into a run. I ran through the ghostly city streets. Surreal pockets of animated hatred punctuated the dead silence. The fog isolated the attacks. It muffled the shouts, the explosions of glass, the shattering wood, preventing them from carrying beyond a few metres. In my haste I stumbled upon attackers prising cobbles from the street to lob at the windows of shops. Gelbhauer the Shoemaker. Fiszlinski the Baker. Haberkorn the Photographer.

When I reached Zawalna, it was quiet. Not even the fog stirred. I walked slowly to her house, treading the damp leaves underfoot. No lights showed in the windows. The whole street was in darkness. I lingered in the gloom, unsure what to do. For some time I paced backwards and forwards until my mind had cleared totally of the effects of the vodka we had drunk at Staromiejska. The fog made my clothes damp and the cold wet air crept in through the thin cloth and chilled my body. I stamped my feet to warm them, but the sound echoed hollowly and dark faces appeared behind windows, staring out into the street wide-eyed with fear, watching, afraid I was a rioter.

I stumbled back to our apartment. Jerzy lay sleeping and I huddled down in the bed with him, fully dressed, letting his fragile warmth soak through the damp clothes.

In the morning the city was quiet. The fog had dispersed and we walked with our heads down. But with darkness the rioting began again. The streets of the city were littered with glass and the air was acrid with the smouldering fires ignited by primitive hatreds.

Chapter 46

On 15 June 1940, as Hitler's tanks rolled into Paris, Stalin's returned once more to the streets of Vilnius. Smetona, the right-wing Lithuanian president, slipped out of the country in the night, along with other influential politicians and intellectuals. We had been liberated. 'Long live Soviet Lithuania – the Thirteenth Soviet Socialist Republic' read a leaflet the ebullient Fisk pressed into my hand.

'It's a blow to the head of the fascist thugs that ran this country,' Fisk expostulated loudly as we walked along Giedyminowska, now Gedimino. I cringed at his high-pitched confidence, wondering how many of those in the crowds pushing along the pavement, glancing at us, were those self-same thugs who had been burning Jewish homes and murdering unfortunates in dark streets.

Fisk laughed when I shushed him. Excitedly he waved his hands at the street. 'Look,' he said, pointing to the Soviet tanks and the soldiers leaning up against them, guns slung over their shoulders. 'Why should I be quiet? The revolution is here.' I managed to escape him at Cathedral Square. I joined one of the long snaking queues that had formed outside a food store. Jerzy had gone to the market by the station to see if he could get bread and other basics. Rumours had been spreading that shops were running short of supplies and every shop in the city was besieged by panicked citizens trying to build up a supply to last the crisis.

'The shops are empty, but you know why?' a wizened babushka observed in front of me. 'They've got the stuff in the back. They're holding on to it, pretending it's all gone, then they'll bring out a few loaves at a time and a bit of flour and charge the earth for it.'

The old man with whom she was standing nodded knowingly. '*Tag, tag*. That's right, the bastards. That's if the Russians haven't confiscated it all for their soldiers.'

'No, you listen to me, somebody's making a tidy packet here. Believe me. Oi! The bastards. Let us poor old people starve, they'll be sitting pretty.'

'They caught some Jew hoarding a warehouse full of flour and legs of pork,' another crone chipped into the conversation. 'He was holding on to it, waiting till prices rose.'

The shop was bare when finally I managed to fight my way in through the doorway, battling with a seventy-year-old baba. A large, red-faced man was shouting at the staff behind the counter. An evil looking scar split his face in two, intimidating the usually indomitable women. One stood in tears while another railed at him.

'One only. No more.'

'What's the use of one loaf? I've got to feed a family of ten.'

'The rules are the rules. You can get only one. I don't give a fuck how many you have to feed. What will everybody else eat when your belly is full? Eh? Tell me that? Look.' She swooped her hand angrily, indicating the rest of us. 'What are they going to eat, tell me?'

'It's a shame,' the man argued, his face growing redder. 'It's a shame, I say.'

The manager of the store, a nervous dark Pole, sidled through the doorway in his neat white apron. He glanced at the crowd and the angry man, trying to assess the general mood. Various shoppers offered their opinions in rough tones.

'Just take your loaf and let us get ours.'

'What do they care about us? They're making a profit, aren't they? I bet they've got the back of the shop packed with goods.'

'*Tag!* Bring out the stuff and let us have it, you mean bastard! You think you'll enjoy your riches knowing how you got them?'

'May God in heaven look down on you and see what you are doing!' an old woman shouted, her small white face quivering beneath a heavy black scarf.

'Please, please,' the dark nervous shopkeeper pleaded. 'It is not our fault. We have not got enough. The government has said one each. We have to make it fair. No speculation.'

This Soviet phrase incensed the crowd. The shop burst into an uproar of vitriol at the communist invaders and their slogans.

'What have you got?' Jerzy asked chirpily when I arrived home tired. He laid his goods out on the table. He had managed to get a loaf of bread, milk, potatoes, sugar and a small bag of fresh curd. I laid down all I had been able to get, the smoked sausage and the small loaf.

'You leave it to me, my boy,' he said heartily, clapping me on the shoulder. 'You leave this to Uncle Jerzy.'

'What's the swindle?' I asked.

His face took on an expression of child-like innocence. 'Swindle?' Then he grinned like a satisfied cat. I did not ask any more. I assumed he had found another generous lady benefactor. And I was right. I found out a few days later he had set about seducing a string of shop girls all of whom he milked for goods in return for his attentions.

Jerzy looked little healthier than he had during the previous winter. His pale skin was almost translucent and his hair wildly long. Despite the warm weather he had a hacking cough that he could not shake off. His energy, though, seemed to be undiminished. He had given up his studies and spent his time working on intense little poems, which he refused to let me see. Late into the night he paced back and forth mumbling to himself. 'The words,' he said. 'Each word must be the exact word. Nothing superfluous. Not one letter should detract from the lyricism of the poem.'

We published a small book of our poems in late October called *The Cataclysm*. Jerzy managed to get it stocked prominently in the large bookstore on Gedimino and it sold well. He also befriended some Russian officers. From these he got hold of good vodka that had been impounded by the military police. The Russian soldiers, from poor villages, revelled in their wealthy position. The new Soviet puppet government pegged the Lithuanian currency at 0.9 roubles rather than the four or five it was really worth, making the poor Russians artificially rich. Jerzy introduced them to Polish girls with whom the young peasant soldiers swaggered around the town like fashionable aristocrats.

'You should be careful,' I warned him one day when he returned merry, giggling over a gambling swindle that had just helped him relieve some drunken communists of a small fortune.

'Ach, they had stolen it themselves,' he said. 'Anyway, have you seen what your friend Fisk is up to?'

'Fisk? No, I haven't seen him for days.'

'He's working with the NKVD. He was talking about that Troiman you know.'

'What about Troiman?'

'Fisk informed on him and his father for exploitative behaviour and suspected collaboration with Western security forces.'

'He accused Troiman of being a spy?' The blood drained from my face.

'He was off to arrest him.'

'Fisk?'

'The NKVD. I assume Fisk was just tagging along for the thrill of it.'

I pulled on my jacket and dashed from the room. By the time I had run across the old town to Zawalna a large crowd had gathered outside Troiman's house. A cordon of rifle-bearing Russian soldiers kept the curious crowd at bay. Fisk stood sharing a cigarette with one of the soldiers. He wore a pompous, self-important expression that looked ridiculous when you regarded the dirty, frayed collar and cuffs of his old shirt and the suit shiny with wear. I pushed through the crowd to get close to him. He grinned gleefully when he saw me.

'Steponas, comrade,' he said, passing the cigarette to the large-boned peasant lad in the soldier's uniform.

'What's going on, Fisk?'

Fisk waved his hand dismissively, as if it was of no importance. 'Just doing what is necessary.'

'Jerzy told me they're arresting Ira.'

Fisk grinned. 'I told you the bastard would be dealt with, didn't I?'

At that moment the door of the house opened. Two officers emerged. Ira was between them. His healthy face was pasty and he looked unusually dishevelled. Seeing the large crowd gathered outside his door seemed to make him nervous. His startled eyes flicked around the pack of faces. It was strangely unnerving to see this self-possessed, confident man looking so frightened. The heavy wooden door closed behind them. There was no sign of Rachael.

As Ira passed by, he noticed me. His step faltered a second and a half smile rose to his lips. Then he saw Fisk by my side. His expression changed. He did not look angry, rather his fear seemed to increase. He stumbled on quickly after the soldiers, who forced a passage through the quiet crowd.

They bundled him into the back of a van and drove away. The crowd dispersed.

'Coming?' Fisk asked. I shook my head.

When he had gone, I lingered on the pavement. Not by the house, where a soldier hung around outside the door for a while, smoking, his gun propped up against the door-jamb, beneath the mezuzah. After a while the door opened. A small group of men in civilian clothes and one uniformed officer appeared. The soldier stood to attention. They walked by him as if he was not there. The officer called for him to follow. The NKVD jumped into a black car and the two soldiers wandered away back into the city.

When I knocked at the door there was no answer. A frightened face appeared behind the net curtains in the house next door, but the Troimans' did not stir. I looked through the brass letterbox. The long hallway was dark and quiet. At the far end, in the light cast through an open doorway, there was a broken picture frame propped up against the wall. Slivers of glass shone in the faint sunlight on the floor. In the gloom I caught a sudden movement.

'Rachael,' I whispered through the brass slot. The figure froze at the bottom of the staircase and for a moment did not move.

'Rachael?'

'Who's there?' a hoarse voice I could barely recognise called from the shadows.

'Rachael? It's Steponas.'

My words were met with silence. The figure did not stir. I could barely make out if she was standing or sitting at the bottom of the stairs. A car grunted slowly past in the road and nervously I straightened up, glancing over my shoulder. It shuddered its way down the street and disappeared. A panicky sweat had broken out on my forehead. I bent down to the letterbox again and pushed it open.

'Rachael, it's me. Open the door.'

She stirred then, seemingly reluctantly. Her body emerged from the darkness and shuffled across the polished wooden floorboards, kicking splinters of glass. She was hunched over. I allowed the brass flap to drop and stood up. The door opened slowly, just a fraction, not revealing her. I pushed into the darkness, checking the road to see that I had not been watched. She stepped back against the wall behind the door. With the door closed it was still hard to see much more than her vague shape in the darkness. She did not look up at me.

'I saw you with Fisk,' she said finally. Her voice was husky as if she had been screaming. 'Through the window. I saw the two of you standing there laughing.'

'No. Rachael, no. You misunderstood,' I protested. I moved towards her but she started back, whether with disgust or fear I could not tell.

Chapter 47

I followed as she padded softly down the hallway. There was a patch of startlingly red blood, I noticed, on a large glass shard that had fallen from the picture. It puzzled me because, despite his pasty look, I had not noticed that Ira had been cut. When we entered the drawing room the sunlight streaming through the high windows exposed Rachael. A large gash marred her cheek, beneath the left eye. I gasped and, seeing me look at it, she fingered the wound delicately.

'You're hurt.'

Her eyes turned on me reproachfully. 'Not here,' she said, her finger on the gash. 'This does not hurt.'

'I had nothing to do with this, Rachael. I just met Fisk at the door. It was he that informed on Ira.'

She did not seem to believe me. Or perhaps she did not care. She turned away from me and wandered to the large windows. She pushed back the net curtain and looked out. I stood behind her not knowing what to say. I could not bear the fact that she seemed to suspect me of collaborating with the communists but could think of nothing to say that might convince her of my innocence. Her shoulders twitched. It was a small movement, as if she was shrugging. At first I thought it was simply that. But they shrugged again and a moan escaped her lips involuntarily. She buried her face in her hands and the emotion seemed to wash violently over her like a powerful breaker. She collapsed to her knees.

I rushed over, taking her in my arms. She was stiff. Each breath seemed to rip her body open painfully. I held her tight,

249

stroking her hair. Her scent cut delicately into my nostrils. It was, I realised, the first time I had held her. I caressed her. I whispered in her ear, my lips close to her olive flesh. Her body relaxed a little. Her breaths, though ragged, came a little easier. Tears rolled from her eyes. She clenched her eyelids tightly shut as if to stop the flow. I kissed her hair.

'Ira,' she groaned. 'Ira, my Ira.' She repeated his name time after time; her eyes clenched tight, her hand gripping mine.

The light in the window turned violet and slowly died. We did not move. Rachael's tears receded. For many minutes we sat in silence watching the day steal away. She leaned against me and I felt her sweet weight press me to the wall. How many nights had I fallen asleep in my dark village room dreaming of such a moment as this? I closed my eyes and felt her. Smelt her. Sensed her.

'Tell me what happened,' I said later, in the darkness. I traced my finger delicately down the cut on her cheek.

'There was a knock on the door. Ira knew there would be trouble. His father had warned him that the communists had their names. We were going to go away for a while, until things had quietened down. I told him not to answer the door. He wouldn't listen. He said they would break it down anyway. It was better to talk to them now, rather than making them angry. Talk!' She laughed bitterly. 'They burst through the door. Maybe five of them. The soldiers shoved him down the corridor, pushing their rifles into his face, shouting at him.' She paused and closed her eyes again as if to shut out the memory. I took her hand in my own.

'They pushed him to the floor. One of them grabbed his hair and pulled up his head.' She mimed, her eyes shut firm. 'Another took out a pistol and placed it at his temple. "Capitalist pig," they shouted at him, over and again. "Fucking Jewish exploiter".' The words sounded strange on her lips. 'I could not bear it. I ran forwards to beg them. One turned and struck me. He knocked me back against the wall and my head smashed the picture.'

She paused. Her eyes opened and she looked off into the pitch-black recesses of the room. From somewhere, far down the road, came the sound of a drunk singing. The comic song sounded frail and sad in the darkness of the evening.

'After a while they took the gun away from his head. They brought us through into here. The NKVD took over. Who did we know? Which government was paying us? Why had Ira been seen talking to that official from the British embassy? What had he been doing on his last trip to Paris? And on and on. Endless questions. What was the point in Ira answering? They were not interested in his replies. Then they said he must go for further questioning. Ira said I should go to his cousins, but I haven't the energy to move.'

She brushed a hand through her hair. 'They took him,' she said; her voice sounded strangely hollow, as though she had been emptied out. 'A couple of them stayed on. "It would be better for your husband if you told us what you know," they said. "It will be worse for him if you don't tell us."'

'What did you tell them?' I said.

She looked at me. 'What would I tell them? What is there to tell?'

A little later she made tea and we drank it with honey. She did not switch on the light. 'It's like in the forest,' she said. I nodded in the darkness, remembering walking up through the pitch-black forest taking her home. I moved closer to her. 'I still dream about the forest,' she said. 'I don't know whether I miss it or not. A part of me misses it, but whenever I dream of it I am afraid.' Again I nodded rather than answering. I took her hand in mine. She leaned closer to me. My lips softly brushed the jagged cut on her cheek. Her skin was cool. I searched in the darkness for her lips.

Rachael jerked back. She wrenched her hand from mine.

'What are you doing?' she demanded. Her voice was sour with surprise.

'I'm sorry,' I muttered.

'What are you thinking of?'

'I didn't mean anything.'

'My husband has just been arrested by the secret police. What did you think that I would . . . ?' Her words faltered in outrage. I heard scuffling as she got up. There were footsteps on the wooden floorboards and I saw her silhouette against the window. A match struck. The flickering light of a small lamp illuminated us. Her eyes sparkled with anger.

'I think you had better go,' she said.

I stumbled to my feet, red-faced in the weak lamplight. I approached her but she backed away, as if she was repulsed. The words of apology caught in my throat. When they came out they seemed insincere, even to me. I stood behind her, speechless, my heart aching with misery. 'Rachael,' I said, 'I did not mean it like that, I had no desire to hurt you.' I flushed with shame, knowing that, truthfully, she was right to despise me. I had held her in my arms, had felt the soft weight of her body against mine, I had buried my head in her hair and held her hand, I had been overwhelmed by her closeness. I had longed for her for so long. And though now she was close enough for me to reach out and touch, I realised at last how far she was from me.

'Go,' she said.

I turned and left, stumbling in the darkness, tears stinging my eyes. As I was about to put my hand to the door there was a soft knocking. I stopped short, my hand hovering above the door handle. Rachael, in the drawing room doorway, froze. As we stood silently, the knocking was repeated inches from me. Soft and hesitant. Rachael approached reticently. 'Who is it?' she called quietly through the door. The brass letter flap rattled and a pair of eyes appeared, indistinctly.

'It's me,' an old man's voice whispered.

'Reb Azriel,' Rachael breathed.

She unlocked the door. Outside stood an old man whose long white beard straggled limply over his dark clothes. The skin on his face fell in folds, as if once he had been fat. Behind him stood a small woman, smaller even than he. Her scarf was pulled tight around her walnut face. Her eyes betrayed both fear and concern. I slipped out of the door around them. I hurried out into the street without looking back. Rachael did not call after me and before I had taken many paces I heard the door click softly shut.

Chapter 48

I felt so ashamed of the way I had behaved that evening that I took care to avoid Rachael. I could not avoid hearing about her though. I was sat in a small café near the station when Fisk walked by. He noticed me and grinned. Before he entered the café he checked carefully that Jerzy was not around. He was in a cheerful mood and offered to buy me another drink. I agreed despite the fact that I did not want to speak to him. He insisted that we spoke in Russian even though we both spoke better Polish.

'No Jerzy?' he asked jovially but rather apprehensively.

'No. He's working on a play with Marcin Lunski.'

'You should be careful with him.'

'Lunski?'

'Jerzy Szymonowicz.' The name rolled from his tongue like a bitter cherry.

'Jerzy? Why should I be careful with him?' I asked coldly, over the top of the volume of poetry I was reading. Fisk winked at me, knowingly. The action infuriated me. I closed the book of poems and slipped it into the pocket of my coat.

'Going?' said Fisk unhappily. 'You haven't drunk your coffee.'

'It doesn't taste so good,' I said.

'Hey, I have some news for you,' he said, grabbing my sleeve as I stepped by him.

'I'm not interested, Fisk.'

'The government has nationalised the Troimans' factory and the shops too.'

'Ira's haberdasher's?'

Nathan Fisk nodded happily. A smug smile spread across his pasty face. His cheeks were rosy red and his blue eyes twinkled brightly. I should punch you, I thought. I imagined doing it; the feeling of my fist contacting with his soft fleshy cheek, the shock registering in his eyes, the impact catapulting him backwards, his chair overturning, his head bouncing from the dirty concrete floor.

'What about Ira?' I asked.

'Still in prison. Lucky he hasn't been deported to Siberia. Not much left for him here now, though.'

'He has a wife.'

'I heard that she had been taken in by his cousin.'

If Ira was lucky to have avoided deportation, all did not share his luck. I met Jerzy on my way back to Rudnicka. He was running full tilt up Stefanska, his long coat billowing out behind him, giving him the appearance of a vampire. Seeing me he shouted. He could not speak when he reached me; he leaned forward, his hands clutching my shoulders, gasping for breath. His face became quite grey and he began to retch. When after a couple of minutes his breathing had calmed, he tried to speak. He was so agitated that he made little sense.

'Steponas, thank God.'

'Jerzy?'

'She's gone.'

'Who?'

'They've . . . taken her.'

'Taken who, Jerzy? Who have they taken? Who has taken her?'

'The communists . . . the bastards.'

'But who, Jerzy? Are you talking about Rachael?'

'Rachael?' He stared at me puzzled. 'Who is Rachael?'

'You know who Rachael is,' I snapped angrily. 'You're

making no sense, Jerzy. Start from the beginning and tell me slowly. And clearly.'

'They came early this morning. I was with her. They burst in through the door, swinging their guns at everything in sight.'

'Who, Jerzy? For God's sake, who?'

He looked at me blankly for a second and then said, as if to an idiot, 'Tzalka, stupid! Who else?'

'*Blyad!*'

'I couldn't do anything, I really couldn't.' He collapsed against me. A sob caught in his throat and racked his body. I held him. He began to cry; raw, ugly tears scarring his face.

'Jerzy, Jerzy,' I said, patting him uncomfortably, 'what did you think you could do?'

'They took her away. They grabbed her by the arm and dragged her naked from the bed. "Get dressed," they said. She pulled on some clothes and they pushed her out of the door. When I tried to follow they pointed a rifle at me and told me to get back into bed unless I wanted to lose my balls.'

We rushed together through the streets to the NKVD dungeons on Gedimino, overlooking the large square where later Lenin would stand and fall. From a distance we saw the commotion. We hurried towards it. Rows of Soviet soldiers were pushing civilians up onto the backs of trucks. A crowd had gathered. While some stood silent, wide eyed, others were calling, wailing to the unwilling passengers. The lorry at the front of the queue started its engine, farting acrid fumes over the distraught crowd. Tzalka was there on the back of the truck. We did not see her at first. She was crouched quietly. She wore around her shoulders the thick bright wrap given to her by her Russian husband years before. It was that which caught our eye.

The lorry rolled past us, its tyres hissing on the cobbles.

Her eyes met ours as she passed. They were red from crying. She looked old. She blew a kiss and the young Soviet soldier stood by her blew one too, a big grin on his pleasant peasant's face.

Chapter 49

They kept Ira in prison over Christmas. Visiting was not allowed and, ironically, in the end it was through Fisk that I was able to get information about him. Fisk had become a full time informant hoping to curry favour with the new puppet government. I asked for news on Troiman whenever I saw him and he was only too happy to revel in the haberdasher's misfortune. Whenever I had news from Fisk I wrote a short note to Rachael, telling her what I knew. She had moved into the home of her cousin. The notes I left unsigned. She would, I knew, recognise my handwriting but the pretence of anonymity would free her from feeling that I felt any debt was being incurred, or that I was doing what I did from feelings of guilt.

Christmas 1940 I returned to my village. I sat by the kitchen window looking out across the glittering blue-white fields. Crows, black as coal, dark as death, lingered in the naked treetops. Jan had been killed in the autumn, fighting in the Polish army. His mother visited wrapped in thick black clothes. She sat in the corner of the kitchen weeping. Pressing my head to her she thanked God for my mother's fortune, her voice trembling with bitterness. She nibbled at the bread my mother had baked, choking on the crumbs. Crumbs her young son could not taste, buried beneath the ice-iron earth.

Christmas Eve was more sombre than sober, as ritual demanded. The house was cleaned. We fasted, as was the custom, and my mother and grandmother prepared the Kucios table. A new white tablecloth was laid and beneath it spread stalks of hay to remind us of the birth of Christ. The best cutlery was brought out and places were laid for us all and a place set too for my dead grandfather. His chair was pulled up and a candle lit and placed on his plate. The twelve traditional dishes were set on the table. Herring, slizikai with poppy seed milk, pickled mushrooms, steaming boiled potatoes. Only meat was missing, according to tradition. My father took a wafer and said, 'God grant that we are all together again next year.' Mother said 'Amen' fervently and crossed herself. I crossed myself too.

Later, the sound of the village church bells drifted up over the fields. I stood in the snow smoking a cigarette. My father came out of the house and stood beside me. The night was dark and the stars seemed very small and far away. For a while we stood silent just outside the soft glow of the lamp in the kitchen.

'Old Mendle died,' my father said.

'Really?'

My father nodded in the darkness. 'They buried him a month back. The earth was like rock, it was a wonder they got him in.' The night's silence drifted between my father's sentences.

'He had lost the farm. They took it from him. It cut the heart out of him. He withered away to nothing.'

'Who took the farm?'

'Who?' said my father, his breath small frail clouds in the freezing night. He clicked his tongue and turned and trudged back through the thick snow to the kitchen door. 'Don't stay out too long, you'll catch your death . . .'

I left the day after Christmas.

On New Year's Eve Alexei Jankowski, the expressionist painter, invited us to a party. It was there I met Rita, a Lithuanian girl with flaxen hair and a face as white as the village snow. She was a painter. She was very pretty and I was gratified that she knew my name and had read some of my poetry.

'Did you like it?'

'It is very sad.'

'I have a lot to be sad about.'

'Do you?' she asked, smilingly sceptically.

'What do you paint?'

'Perhaps you would like to see?'

Jankowski had introduced me to her. She was sitting on an uncomfortable wooden chair near the back door of his house. Through the open door it was possible to catch glimpses of streetlamps reflected on the iced surface of the river. From the way he introduced her I gathered that Jankowski was having a relationship with her.

'I would love to see your paintings,' I said. 'Is your studio far?'

Jankowski was drinking with Jerzy. I pushed her out through the door into the snow. She looked a little startled but did not protest. We walked slowly through the silent streets. Thick frost sheathed the trees, giving the impression of a thousand stumpy fingers stabbing at the brittle air. She held my arm to avoid slipping. Her frozen breath seemed delicate beside my own.

Her studio was cold and I made love to her angrily. Almost violent. She lit a thin feminine cigarette and slouched against the wall in the darkness. 'It's midnight,' she said after a while. I grunted. I had found out from Fisk earlier in the evening that Ira had been released just after Christmas. I lit the stub of a candle and examined the canvases leaning up against the wall. What were they doing?

'Are you angry at me?' she asked from the shadows.

'Angry? Why should I be angry?'

Her easel stood by the small window. I picked up the candle

and wandered over to it. Were they celebrating together? The canvas was covered with a thin cotton cloth. Rita shuffled to her feet. Her flaxen hair fell loose across her shoulders. When she walked close to me her blue eyes shone in the candlelight. Clear and as blue as the spring sky. She lifted her hand and caressed my cheek softly. Were they embracing? Kissing? Rita leaned forward and pulled my head gently towards her. 'It's customary to kiss at the turning of the year,' she whispered. Her breath was sweet, tainted only vaguely by the tobacco.

Kissing? Loving? His hand slipping up under her blouse as my hand now slipped beneath the loose shirt that Rita was wearing? Rita's flesh was cool, rough with goose bumps. And hers? And hers?

I grabbed Rita's young breakable body and made love to her again. Thrashing, desperate, sad lovemaking. Love-making to forget. To bring on oblivion. Fucking to annihilate thought.

'Hey!' she protested. But I paid no heed. And when I had finished we lay together on the floorboards and cried.

Later she showed me the painting that she was work-ing on. It was of a young woman seated on a vivid, red, plump chair. Her eyes were large almonds and her hair was caught up in buns on either side of her head. Yel-low ribbons held the buns. In her arms was a baby. It was planted there almost like a doll. A Russian doll from which might be pulled another. The painting radiated warmth and love.

'This is beautiful,' I said.

'Madonna and child. The priest in my village asked me to paint it for him. Do you think that is shameful? I haven't shown Alexei. He would be furious. It's part of a triptych. Would you like to see the central section? You won't tell Alexei?'

I shook my head. She rummaged in the dark corner of the

room and pulled out a larger canvas. She turned it around and I illuminated it with the stub of candle.

'But you have crucified the Madonna,' I said.

'Yes.'

Christ was cradled still, a Russian doll. The young girl was no different. The plump red chair had gone and in its place hovered a yellow cross that matched her ribbons and a cobalt sky.

'The Madonna has always been crucified,' she said, her eyes as blue and untroubled as before.

'I would have thought that Jankowski would have liked this kind of thing.'

'Oh no, you're wrong,' she said earnestly. 'You're reading it wrong. Does it seem blasphemous? No, no.'

When I returned home on New Year's Day, Jerzy was crouched on the floor by the bed. His body shook. When I lifted him he was frail and edgy. I laid him on the bed and made some soup. He shook his head when I brought it for him. His face was grey. His eyes were hollow pits. His lips thread-like. His hair hung in oily, spidery curls down the sides of his face.

'You must,' I whispered, trembling with fear at the state of him. He allowed me to spoon him some of the warm liquid. Just minutes later he turned his head, attempting some decency, and vomited it back up again.

I hovered over him, a nervous nurse. He lay for many hours motionless on the hard dirty bed. When night fell he opened his eyes again and I once more tried to feed him the soup. I lay through the night beside him, listening to the catch of his breath, holding my own when I did not hear his.

As the year grew older Jerzy grew a little stronger. For much of the day he sat at home brooding. He remained weak and did not put much weight back on to his body. I took a job at a hospital and it was only the groschen I earned that kept us from starving. The winter months were bleak. The heating had disappeared from our flat and in the mornings our breath rose in little fragile clouds. The Soviet government continued its programme of compulsory nationalisation and the icy rain lashed the faces of the dispossessed. In the forests the partisans froze.

Often, after finishing work, I walked to Rita's studio. Invariably I found her painting. Many times I simply lay on the sofa watching her work. At other times we pulled on our coats and scarves and boots and gloves and went to trudge our way along the frozen Wilja. It was whilst walking there one Saturday evening that we bumped into Rachael and Ira. I had been skimming pebbles across the dirty yellow surface of the ice. Rita called from higher up the bank. She was shivering in her old coat. For many minutes I ignored her, listening to the electric click of the pebbles on the ice. When I turned there were two other figures on the bank behind her.

'Steponas,' a familiar voice called out.

For a few moments I did not recognise the voice, for while it was familiar there was something strange about it too. The figure silhouetted against the weak sun was also strangely familiar. As I drew closer I realised that the small stooped figure was Ira. It was impossible to hide my surprise. He looked at least ten years older than when I had last seen him. Perhaps more. He was completely bald on top and the hair at the side of his head grew in untidy grey tufts. His face was sallow and his previously upright, stocky figure was thinner and bent. He held out his hand. I took it firmly, almost crushing it in my own.

She did not look so different. In fact she looked more than ever like the young girl I had known from the village. She was not dressed elegantly, but her hair was luxuriant. Its fresh curls burst from the plain kerchief that she had tied over it. Her eyes were luminous. She was radiant. My heart contracted. A spasm of pain almost brought tears to my eyes. When Ira said something, I missed it. My heart rooted itself painfully in her and I could not draw my eyes away.

'I'm sorry?' I said.

'You're looking well,' Ira repeated, jovially, his voice reedy, older.

She laid her hand softly on my sleeve. 'Thank you.'

'For what?' I said, my heart labouring to squeeze each painful beat. She did not answer and I shrugged. Only then did I notice that her figure had changed too. Ira noted the track of my eyes. He grinned. Reaching over he patted his wife's slightly swollen stomach.

'What do you think?' he said joyfully. 'Doesn't she look beautiful?'

'Oh, you must come and sit for me,' Rita begged.

'You're a painter?' Rachael asked.

For some while we walked slowly together along the frozen riverbank. Rachael took Rita's arm and they swung along chatting before us. When we parted we went back to the studio. I made love to Rita so angrily, so violently, that she cried and would not speak to me. I left her in the darkness and walked the silent city. I walked for so long in the snow that I developed a fever and lay for the next couple of days in bed, sweating and hallucinating.

Chapter 50

By March there was a rumour of green in the trees and bushes. The city uncoiled tentatively from the numbness of winter. It snowed again, briefly, in the middle of March, the small crystal flakes glittering in the nascent spring sun. Children appeared and their shouts sounded oddly loud in the streets after their long absence. By April the last of the grimy snow drifts, packed in dark corners, had melted away.

Jerzy managed to get his hands on a car and we drove out to Trakai, with Rita and Lunski. The lake shimmered in the sunlight and the trees were fresh with colour. We hired a small boat and rowed out onto the lake. We did not speak of the war. We had all heard the rumours, the stories, speculation, but we spoke of art, of plays, of poetry and beauty and all the things that normal young people may speak of in times of peace.

In the afternoon a sudden shower surprised us and we were forced to row to a low, wooded island for shelter. We sat beneath the trees and listened to the rain approach us across the surface of the water. I lay on my back, cushioned by thick layers of pine needles, and Rita lay by my side. Listening to the softness of her breathing and the patter of rain on the water it struck me that I should be content. While half the world was fighting, I was there beneath the trees savouring the loveliness of being. However, rather than feeling joy, a heavy weight oppressed me. I closed my eyes and thought of her – the soft swell of her belly, the quiet pride that flushed her cheeks.

'You're crying,' Rita whispered in my ear.

'No,' I said. 'It's just my eyes watering.'

When the shower had moved on we rowed back to land and drove into the small town of Trakai. Whilst Jerzy and Lunski settled down to a beer in a café overlooking the lake, Rita and I wandered across to the section of the town inhabited by Karaites. Their houses shone brilliantly in the sunshine, yellow and blue, each with three windows looking out onto the road. Legally the Karaites were not Jews though they were great Hebrew scholars. They differed from the Jews in that they rejected the Talmud. Legend had it that the Grand Duke Vytautas had brought them back from Asia, and they retained their Turkic culture. I sat on a grass bank and watched as Rita sketched their prayer house.

Vilnius was enjoying a wary spring. We drove back to the city, the car loaded with flowers. So overpowering was their perfume to our deprived senses that we had to open the windows. Rita arranged bunches around her studio, and their petals were liked polished gold in the sunlight. Jerzy wanted to take an armful to sell, but Rita refused to give them up.

'Go fuck one of your shop girls, if you want bread,' she said to him.

'You don't need to eat?' he answered morosely, eyeing her.

Rita had lost weight over the winter. She had lost the soft fullness of her body; her shoulders were sharp and her cheeks slightly sunken. The paleness of her skin had begun to look unhealthy as opposed to richly virginal.

'I need to see something beautiful,' she said, her hands ranging delicately over the fresh petals, caressing the swelling buds with a hunger she did not display for food.

'Artists!' Jerzy spat, angrily.

Late one afternoon I returned from drinking with Jerzy to find her painting a young woman. The woman was bent with her back to the door and I did not recognise her. Rita, seeing me, looked around uncomfortably. With a swift, deft flick of her arm, she turned the canvas that she had been working on and covered it with a loose cloth so that I could not see.

The young woman straightened up, her arms resting at the base of her back, as though she found it difficult or painful to rise. I noticed then the large swell of her stomach, the way that her hair fell back across her shoulders, and before she turned, recognised her.

'Rachael,' I said.

She glanced over at me, surprised.

'Steponas,' she exclaimed and sneezed. She grinned and sneezed again.

I noticed then that she had been bending to smell the flowers. She must have pushed her face deep into the bunch as it was dusted all over with golden pollen. Rita noticed and stepped over to her. She drew out a handkerchief and caught Rachael's face in her hand to wipe away the pollen. My chest tightened.

'Rachael has been sitting for me,' Rita explained.

She was heavily pregnant. Whilst Rita looked drawn and pale, Rachael was radiant with health. She sneezed again, and laughed.

'The pollen has got up my nose,' she explained.

Rita smiled and handed her the handkerchief, which was prettily embroidered, with Rita's initials in the corner.

'Keep it,' she said.

'Thank you,' said Rachael. She admired the needlework then slipped it into her pocket.

Rita took her arm and moved her past me before I could say anything. She turned at the door and smiled. I slumped into a chair. The mixture of feelings that assailed me was bewildering. At the same time I both loved and hated her.

I longed to go after her, yet felt a mounting, irrational fury that Rita had invited her here.

Hearing their voices, soft outside the door, I jumped up quickly and strode over to the canvas stood on its easel in the light, by the window. Stealthily I pulled back the cloth to look at the painting. Rachael sat looking out from the picture, her hands resting gently on her swollen stomach.

I heard the door close and turned, letting the cloth drop. Rita watched me. She was angry, I could see, that I had stolen a look at her painting, but she said nothing. She turned from me and busied herself cleaning some brushes at the sink.

I longed to speak, to ask about Rachael, to talk about her, but I knew that if I said anything it would come out angrily. I paced about the room for some minutes. Rita did not turn to me. She was tight-lipped, her attention focused on the yellow paint running into the sink as the tap water washed through the bristles of her brushes. I left.

She came around to see me later.

'I'm sorry,' I said.

Rita raised a finger to my lips, silencing me. 'I don't know what you have got against her, it isn't my business.'

'I haven't . . .' I began.

'Don't, Steponas, I don't need you to explain. She, too, is tense when you are around. She told me you knew each other back in the village, but she didn't want to talk about it more. So let's forget it. Leave it.'

We said no more, then. We went for a stroll in the town. At Rita's suggestion we walked to the Dawn Gates. The upstairs grotto was thick with people: peasant women, crying out in Polish and Russian. The warmth of the day, the candles that burned in profusion, the incense and the heavy stench of perspiring bodies made me feel nauseous. The Black Madonna gazed down upon us, impassive, regal. The gold of her gown glowed against her dark skin. The sword-sharp rays of glory, which haloed her inclined head, were at odds with the peaceful grace of her crossed-hand posture.

Rita bent to her knees by the side of a wrinkled Russian woman, who was beating her breasts, and weeping, reciting her petitions to the mysterious, beautiful Mother of God. Rita closed her eyes and I saw her lips stir in silent prayer.

'Come on,' I said, after a few minutes, unable to stand any longer the smell and the heat. Rita looked up and grinned.

'I can never tell if you are serious or not,' I said.

'About what?'

'The pictures, the icons and all this,' I said.

'Do you ask Jerzy if he is serious about his poems?'

'That's different.'

'Because he's obscene to cover his embarrassment?'

There were other times, I knew, when Rachael went to the studio. Her baby was born, a girl, Rita told me one day. Though she didn't tell me when Rachael would be sitting for her, she would at times cautiously suggest I occupy myself for a few hours away from the studio, and, understanding, I would.

Chapter 51

I awoke one morning, the summer sun shining bright through the dirty windows of Rita's studio. For a moment I wondered what had woken me. It was June. June 22 1941. Rita lay sleeping beside me, her hair iridescent in the fresh sunbeams. Abruptly the air was filled with the heart-lurching wail of air raid sirens. I shook Rita awake.

'Forget it,' she said sleepily, not turning over. 'It's just the drill. It was on the radio yesterday.'

I struggled from beneath the thin cotton sheet. The glass in the window had begun to rattle. The air buzzed. I stood and looked out, rubbing a small circle in the dust. The sky was full of planes, flocking like birds in the autumn.

I put some water to boil on the small hob in the corner of the studio and made a coffee. It was Sunday and the church bells were ringing. By the window a new painting stood on Rita's easel, just finished. Madonna and child. Jewish Madonna, with her tumbling dark hair and her soulful almond eyes. Olive-skinned Madonna. Madonna of my childhood. In her arms her little Jewish daughter.

An explosion shook the air from the direction of the airport. It was followed by two more. I jumped up, spilling the black coffee on the wooden floorboards. Rita sat up suddenly in bed. The windows continued to rattle to the rumbling noise of the aircraft.

'It's not a drill,' I said.

'*Partizanai?*'

'Not with planes.'

'The Germans.'

The city was in chaos when later I ventured out. Soviet lorries clogged the streets. Horse-drawn carts wound between them piled high with the hastily packed possessions of Jewish families. People ran backward and forward, panic tightening the skin on their faces. Late into the night the city packed its bags. The air reverberated to the sound of the explosions and the roar of aircraft engines.

It took the Germans just two days to reach Vilnius after invading on the morning of 22 June 1941. The streets were full again. This time the Lithuanian population of the city came out to cheer and salute the liberating army. Pretty young girls ran out into the street pushing flowers into the buttonholes of the uniforms of the young German soldiers. In the bars they celebrated the retreat of the communists.

I was surprised to bump into Fisk. He looked agitated and tired. He was shuffling in the shadows. When he saw me he tried to smile but it came out as a grimace.

'Hello, still here?' I said, taking a little spiteful pleasure in his fear. 'I would have thought you would have got out with your Russian friends.'

'Shh!' He put a finger to his lips and glanced around nervously.

'What's the matter, Fisk, worried somebody might inform on you?' I asked maliciously.

'I tried to escape. The lorry I was travelling on was stopped by a roadblock. The Lithuanian partisans weren't letting people get away. I made a break for the forests and joined up with a small group of Jewish partisans. But there was a lot of fighting going on. We had to get out of there.'

'So you're back here.'

'Just for a couple of days while I sort out transport. Wait for the Lithuanians to calm down.'

* * *

The last time that I saw Fisk he was still flitting around the city, keeping to the shadows. He was not wearing the yellow star that the Germans had enforced on the Jewish population. With a poetic justice that the world generally seems to lack, it was Ira who told me of his fate. Within days of the arrival of the German army there were rumours of the disappearance of Jews. Young Lithuanian thugs boasted in bars that they were being paid ten roubles a day to hunt them out for the Nazis. The Jewish population that had not managed to flee ahead of the Wehrmacht laid low.

I met Ira standing on the cracked paving stones of Wielka. He was looking leaner still and was unshaven. His yellow star was pinned to his chest and despite his smile he looked agitated. 'I'm looking for some work,' he explained, shrugging his sagging shoulders. 'Ei! And did you hear about your friend Fisk, Comrade Fisk?'

I shook my head. 'He wasn't really a friend.'

'Don't worry, I don't feel bad about you, Steponas. Anyway the fucker got his deserts.'

'What happened?'

'Some Lithuanian thugs picked him off the street. They recognised him from the time he was hanging out in the bars with the Russian officers. You know where they took him?'

'Where?'

He grinned. His clean smile was broken by missing teeth. 'To the same place they took me!' He laughed. 'Beat the miserable little creep to a pulp that even his own mama wouldn't be able to identify.'

The Nazi swastika hung from the building recently vacated by the fleeing Soviet army. The dark cells continued to be put to good use.

'Many have taken refuge in the forest,' Ira continued. 'I talk to Rachael about this, but every time I mention the forests she shivers and refuses. Not the forest, she says, just not the forest. And in truth the forest is not a good place for baby. What to do? We keep our heads low and hope that it will pass. It will pass. It has to. There are good times and bad times, it has always been so, the good times give way to bad and then the bad give way to good. Just to keep the head down and weather the storm. After all, they can't kill us all!' His grin was curiously chilling.

'No,' I agreed. 'They can't kill everybody.'

Before the month had ended Einsatzkommando 9, the special action squad, had moved into Vilnius on the heel of the German tanks, and conducted their first Aktion. Five thousand Jewish men were rounded up from the poorer quarter of the city centre, not far from where Jerzy and I were lodging. Jerzy, who had ventured out into the warm sun, came back ranting.

'Why are they not fighting?' he yelled, slamming the table top with his weak fist.

'With what are they going to fight?' I asked. 'The Polish army was steam-rollered, the Russians have retreated, but a group of unarmed Jewish men are going to take on the Wehrmacht?'

'Still!'

Jerzy paced about the untidy room wringing his hands. I sat at the table working on a play, a project Marcin Lunski had suggested about the rout of the German crusaders at Zalgiris – Grunwald – by the intractable Samogitian forces.

The Germans claimed the Jews had been taken to labour camps but within days other rumours began to circulate in the city. There were stories of survivors of a massacre. A young man who had crawled naked from the mountain of corpses in the forest glade just outside the city. Tales whispered in the candlelight. Nightmares perhaps. Perhaps only rumours and nightmares.

In early September more Jewish families were dragged from their homes. With pitiful bundles they were loaded onto trucks and driven away down the avenue of maples, tremulous with autumn's first breath. From imprisonment in Lukiszki they were taken somewhere else. This time the talk of deaths was more open, reprisal for the killing of Germans, the Nazis reported. And the name Ponar began to haunt the lips of young and old. The beautiful thick woods six kilometres beyond the city.

The thinking behind the removal of the poor families from their cramped apartments soon became clear. Two ghettos were established. Around each of the small areas wooden fences were erected to cut them off from the general population of the city. The two ghettos were divided by German Street – Niemiecka. The entrances of the houses facing out were blocked off. There was only one entrance to each of the ghettos. These gates were placed on opposite sides of the ghetto so that it was impossible for the residents of one ghetto to communicate casually with the residents of the other. Though only metres apart they could have been separated by kilometres. At the large wooden gates of the ghetto signs were erected reading, 'Attention! Jewish area. Danger of infection. Non-Jews Keep Out!'

As the narrow streets resounded to the work of the Germans, officials with wads of lists worked door to door. Finding ourselves within the limits of the planned ghetto area Jerzy and I were politely informed we would have to move.

'You are not to worry,' the plump, red-faced Nazi official assured us. 'It is an inconvenience, I know, but heavens, better than living here like rats, heh?' He laughed nervously, flicking through his papers. 'You will be allocated with property vacated by the Jews outside the ghetto area. You will I am sure be pleased.' He was sweating in his uniform which seemed slightly too tight and he looked weary. He clicked his heels smartly when he left, throwing us a respectful salute. Jerzy, however, did not move.

I gathered some boxes and rented a small pony and cart from a friend of Rita's. When I returned with them to our apartment in Rudnicka, Jerzy had disappeared. I swore angrily and began to gather our meagre possessions. I was most concerned to prevent our books and papers from being damaged. As I was carefully packing Jerzy's old typewriter into a small wooden box the door burst open. Jankowski stood in the open doorway ashen faced.

'Alexei! Where the fuck has Jerzy got to?'

'Come and see,' Jankowski said, almost inaudibly.

I followed him out into the dark stairwell. Boxes and packages of belongings were piled deep on the landing and up the stairs; residents coming and going following Nazi orders. Jankowski kept two paces ahead and would not turn when I called. The pony I had hired stood patiently tethered to the old maple. In the low afternoon light I noticed a commotion down the street, sliced by a sharp shaft of heavy afternoon sunlight.

'What's going on?' I asked Jankowski, hurrying to catch up. He stared ahead, pacing quickly down the uneven cobbles.

On the edge of the crowd Rita was stood in a cold slab of shadow. Her face was white and she covered her mouth with her two delicate painter's hands. Lunski stood beside her.

'Rita? What is going on?' I asked, fear knocking heavily from within my chest. She shook her head and Jankowski took my arm and thrust me through the crowd.

The onlookers circled an old tree. An oak. Its leaves had begun to fall and lay golden on the grey cobbles. The tree was gnarled and twisted with age. From its stubby trunk it threw out one particularly impressive limb. The branch reached out across the street, dappling the cobbles in the summer, providing shade for the tired walker. From the sturdy limb Jerzy's emaciated body hung. The body swung in small, slow circles. His hollow eyes gazed down vacantly at the earth. His feet dangled. His poet's fingers curled like claws.

Chapter 52

'Two young German soldiers stopped a mother in the street. An argument started. Jerzy wanted to step forward and intervene then. He was boiling. I held him back. You will cause more trouble than good, I told him. I managed to cool him. And then one of the soldiers grabbed the young mother by her hair and dragged her to the ground.' Marcin Lunski demonstrated, grabbing the air in his fist, twisting and pulling it down. He wiped his eyes. 'As she fell, the baby dropped from her grasp. It was swaddled and bounced on the pavement. Rolled. The young girl let out a scream that stopped my heart. She leapt forward to grab it, but the soldier yanked her back by the hair while the other soldier kicked the bundled baby out of reach of her fingertips.' He paused again. 'They laughed.'

'They laughed?'

'At that moment Jerzy let out such a shriek! Like an animal. Like something non-human. It sent a shiver down my spine. He lunged forward and I was not able to stop him. Before I knew what was happening he was on the soldiers like a wild animal. A tiger. He ripped at their flesh and bit into one of the soldier's necks. They were terrified.'

Lunski paused. I did not turn from the window where I was stood. Outside darkness had fallen. The night was crisp, clear. From the street came the sound of cartwheels scraping on the cobbles, the breath of the horses, occasionally a phrase; low, nervous Yiddish. They made their way quietly to the ghettos.

'More soldiers appeared instantly. They pulled him off kicking and screaming. When they had secured him they took the young woman and stood her against the wall. Right there in the street, beside the doorway. Look, they said, she is not worth fighting for. She is Jewish. She is vermin. They have diseases. Like rats they must be exterminated. A soldier raised his rifle and shot her. She crumpled against the wall. One shot.'

'And the baby?'

'It was dead already. The kick had killed it. They lobbed it over a wall. The soldiers.'

'And then they hung him.'

'I couldn't watch. I buried my face in my hands. A soldier came by and hit me in the ribs with the butt of his gun. Watch, he said. Watch and learn what happens to those who try to defend Jewish scum. I uncovered my eyes, but I did not watch.'

Fear settled on the city like a freezing fog. There was no nook or crevice into which it did not reach its icy fingers. It settled and it did not shift. We lived in the knowledge that it was scraping its broken fingernails against the panes of our windows. Sucking the warmth from our hearths. Bleeding the strength from our limbs.

I moved into the new apartment Jerzy and I had been allocated, but without him I felt lost. I sat alone in the room, a blanket wrapped tight around me, the door locked and bolted. Lunski had suggested I stay with him but I could not. There I would talk and we would drink, we would drink and laugh and then I would turn and Jerzy would not be there. I unpacked his books and poems and placed them neatly on the desk. Alongside them I set his typewriter. Closing my eyes I pressed the keys, listening to its clack as if it was his voice whispering to me, late into the night. When sleep ambushed me I dreamt of him swinging, hollow-eyed, the wind catching the curls of his hair. A pounding on the door woke me. Rita called to me through the keyhole. I did not get up and after a while she left.

Ghetto number one was designated for craftsmen. Ghetto number two was for everyone else. Those with work permits were required to move into Ghetto number one, whilst the elderly, the sick, and orphaned children moved to Ghetto number two. They began the long walk between the two ghettos late in the day on 15 September. Of three thousand sick and elderly, only six hundred walked through the wooden gates. The rest were lost in the night. In the fog that had descended upon the city.

I returned to the hospital, numbing my pain with work. I avoided Lunski and Jankowski and saw little of Rita, who immersed herself in her painting in her small studio. I hid the play I had been working on with Lunski beneath the rug in the flat I had moved into. One night I woke with a start. The fog buffeted the window in the darkness. Scrambling out of bed I gathered the sheets from beneath the rug. One by one I burned them in the flame of a candle.

In February 1942 I heard that Ira had escaped the ghetto. He had joined the FPO, the United Partisans Organisation. Making their way through the sewer system they had taken to the forests to continue the fight from there. A sister in the hospital gave this news to me. She was a Dominican nun and I was aware that their convent was sheltering partisans. Despite the conditions a theatre had been established in the ghetto. Concerts were performed to packed audiences and a lending library, even, had been organised. All this the sister told me. I listened but I did not ask.

Sometimes, in the early evening, despite the debilitating fog, I once again wandered the streets. Here I had first seen her.

Here we had talked. Here I had followed her. Here I saw her, radiant, her curls bursting out from the kerchief, her belly bulging slightly, giving away the reason for her joy. We had stopped by the old birch tree, a lifetime before. It shone silver. At the point where Old Mendle's path forked off the road. Her breath was ragged. We stumbled. Our faces met, in the pale light. Almost lip to lip. Almost.

The sun shone. Day followed night. Winter thawed and spring blossomed. The summer was warm. Autumn turned the leaves and winter froze them on the cobbles beneath my feet as I walked to the hospital tired. Always tired. The hospital overflowed with the sick and wounded. The smell of death filled my nostrils. Having been raised on a farm I was used to the death of our livestock. As a child my grandmother had taken me to sit with the bodies of dead neighbours, in the days before burial, but that was a normal part of the routines of village life. This death I now confronted in the hospital, with its dark corridors, plastered green walls, tiled floors and stench of disinfectant, was coldly industrious. Care of the sick and the dying was a chore and the bodies were removed hastily to make room for others. A typhus epidemic assailed the city population exhausted by war.

One evening Sister Martha found me crouched in a corner with my hands clasped tight over my ears, blocking out the sound of the suffering we could do little to control. She knelt beside me and stroked my forehead softly with the back of her hand.

'How can you stand it?' I asked her.

'If we don't, who will?' she said, simply.

She took me by the hand and lifted me from the floor. I followed her back out into the corridor where the sick sat on narrow benches, waiting for the dead to make room for them in the more comfortable beds.

*   *   *

From December 1941 to early 1943 the city achieved a kind of peace. Nervous peace. Fearful peace. But the fog never entirely dissipated.

The peace lasted until July of 1943 when the Germans captured Wittenberg, head of the FPO. The partisan groups responded immediately, launching a fierce attack on the police station where he was being held, and freed him. Wittenberg went into hiding. The partisans had been carrying out small-scale attacks on the Germans around the city, blowing up rail tracks, murdering smaller isolated groups of German soldiers and stealing supplies. When I arrived at the hospital on the morning of the sixteenth Sister Martha, my Dominican companion, was distraught.

'The Nazis have threatened to liquidate the whole ghetto if they do not hand Wittenberg over,' she told me.

As the hours trickled on towards the deadline, our hands worked and our bodies continued their tasks; our minds, however, gnawed at the news of the ghetto. Ira had, I knew, escaped to the forest and joined the partisans, but Rachael was still inside the walls of the ghetto with her young child. Sister Martha had been a nun for ten years. She was young and good-looking. Her hands were always steady and I never saw her flinch from the most difficult tasks; but when she lit a cigarette, later, in the semi-darkness it shook in her fingers.

We smoked the cigarettes sparingly; they had come from a former factory owner, a patient wanting a little better treatment.

'You puzzle me,' she said, passing the cigarette across to me.

'I do?'

She nodded, waiting for me to draw on the cigarette and hand it back to her before she continued.

She hesitated a moment before she said, 'There is something

strange about the way you behave. You're reserved and you say very little. You are interested in what is going on in the ghetto, though you pretend not be. But you are not with the partisans.'

'You think I'm a Nazi informer?' I said dryly.

'No, but I was wondering whether you had Jewish blood?'

'Jewish? No,' I said quickly, flushing.

She gazed at me fixedly, inhaling the smoke deep into her lungs. 'So?'

For some moments I said nothing. A small window high in the wall let in a sliver of grey light. Sister Martha had deep black rings around her eyes. Her sharp eyes did not leave my own, I felt them searching me. Perspiration beaded my forehead. I felt a sudden overwhelming need to confess to her, to tell her all. The agony of silence broke within me and I felt it rise in my throat, a painful lump. I coughed back a sob. For a moment I could not speak. She reached out a hand and let it rest gently on my knee. It was the first kind touch I had felt in months. I could not hold back my tears then. I wept bitterly. I told her about Rachael. I told her everything from beginning to end while we slowly smoked our precious cigarettes. She did not interrupt me. After the long silence words tumbled out. When I had finished she leant forward and wrapped her arms around me.

A young boy arrived later that evening and asked for Sister Martha. I ran to find her. Martha was weeping when she returned to the ward.

'What is it?' I asked.

'Wittenberg has given himself up to spare the ghetto,' she told me.

Just over a month later the Nazis decided to liquidate the ghetto anyway. When we heard the news we rushed into the streets. I do not know what we thought that we could do. Sister Martha left me to find one of her contacts to see if anything could be done. The streets were full of soldiers. I hurried to the ghetto.

Chapter 53

The closer I walked to the ghetto gates the more soldiers there were. Tanks loomed at corners. The soldiers were tense; their guns held at the ready. A large fair-haired young soldier approached me.

'*Ja?* What you want?' he asked in heavily accented Russian.

'I live that way,' I said, indicating past the ghetto gates.

'Go!' he said. His hand pushed against my chest. Pushing me back down the street away from the large wooden gates. 'Get out of here!'

A sweat broke out on my forehead and my hand began to tremble. 'But I must get home,' I said, aware that he could ask for my papers and check my address.

'Fuck off!' he said aggressively. He was joined by another soldier, slimmer, thin-lipped. He pointed his gun at my chest.

'You heard him,' the second soldier said. 'Get out of here.'

I retreated down the street. The gates to the ghetto had swung open. Soldiers swarmed around a couple of green army trucks. In the distance I could hear shouting. Orders barked. Impotently I stood in the shadows at the corner, looking down the cobbled street to the ghetto gates. They would take her through there. She would be loaded onto a truck. They would take her. My heart thumped and a thin fog appeared before my eyes. Where would they take her? Ponar? I pushed down the images, the pictures that had filled our nightmares. Bodies in ditches. The crack of gunfire startling the birds in the forest.

Bloodied, lonely survivors, lying in stupefied silence beneath the corpses of their friends, families, waiting for darkness to creep away. Rachael oh Rachael, I breathed. Oh God help.

So intent was my attention on the flurry of activity at the gates of the ghetto, I did not hear the quiet footsteps on the cobbles behind me. A hand grabbed my arm and I had to stifle a scream. I wheeled around. Sister Martha held me, indicated for me to be quiet, to follow her.

'I have a message,' she breathed.

'A message?'

'From the ghetto. Come. Quick.' Her attractive face was drawn and hard, the skin taut across her skull. She pulled my arm, turning me from the gates of the ghetto. I ran behind her.

'The girl, your girl, the one you were telling me about. She sent a message through one of our boys.'

'Rachael?'

'Yes, Rachael.'

We ran through the winding narrow lanes, skirting the outside of the ghetto, keeping clear of the guards, who were jittery and suspicious. Ducking into a narrow alley Sister Martha took my hand and put a finger to her lips. At the end of the alley was a blank wall built crudely from poor quality bricks. A portion of the wall had collapsed and had been boarded up tightly with planks. Barbed wire spiralled the top of the fence.

The alley-way was dark and it stank of sewage. In the centre of the street was a manhole and Sister Martha pointed to it. 'From here it is a quick journey into the ghetto. It is the route that our boys take sometimes.'

'We're going into the ghetto?' I asked. My heart froze at the thought. To be caught in the ghetto would mean instant death. The place would be swarming with soldiers. Indeed we could hear their menacing voices echoing in the narrow lanes little more than a few houses away. Sister Martha shook her head.

'She will come. She should be here.' She took a thin, long knife from her pocket and slipped it between two boards. They came apart with remarkable ease. The hole she made was just large enough for someone to slip through. A child perhaps, or a lean, small adult.

Sister Martha was tense. She glanced at the watch on her wrist. Her eyes flicked around the damp alley-way. 'There is a regular patrol,' she said. 'You need to listen.' She waited a few moments more, though I could see her growing increasingly edgy.

'I've got to go,' she said suddenly. 'I've got to give help to the others. You must stay. She will come. I'm sorry.'

I nodded mutely. She turned to go then halted. She turned back and her eyes brimmed with anxious tears. 'Be careful,' she said. 'Be very careful.'

I watched as she dashed down the alley-way. The noise from the ghetto grew louder. Shouting vibrated the air. From somewhere came a scream. A chilling, heart-rending scream. A scream that made my knees tremble with fear. I pressed my forehead against the wall and tried to control my breathing. A vision of Jerzy swinging from the bow of the old oak flickered across my mind. Murdered for helping a Jew.

And suddenly she was there. Pressed against the wooden boarding. Pulling the loose boards out. The small child was quiet in her arms. Her eyes were wide with fear. Her lip was shivering. My heart leapt; she looked painfully fragile.

'Steponas,' she said and her voice trembled so much it was hard to make out my name. The yellow star on her coat was dirty and frayed. Her hair was lifeless, dangling down the sides of her face like a spider's web. Her cheeks were sunken and her skin yellow and tired. My hand reached out to her. She did not move as I touched her cheek. She was deathly cold. I pushed another board from the fence, enlarging the hole she had made.

As the board clattered to the floor, I heard the heavy click of military boots on the cobbles. The ring of barked commands. Shouting. German accents. Rachael trembled so much she could say nothing more. She stared at me a moment in silent supplication, her discoloured teeth rattling.

'Take me,' she stammered.

'Take you?'

Take you where? To the forest where you would be safe. To a molina, a hideaway, beneath the church on Rudnicka where I knew there to be one. To Sister Martha and her convent to find safety with the partisans there. To the village, to my own home hidden in the forests, tucked in the hills. I reached out to her, my own hands shaking as they passed through the fencing.

The boots sounded loud on the road. They echoed in the narrow alley-way. Her eyes reached out to me. The soldiers turned into the small courtyard behind where Rachael was standing. They peered into the gloom, their guns cocked and ready. Rachael glanced back swiftly over her shoulder. One of the soldiers spotted her and called out, his young voice ringing sharply against the stone walls.

'Take my child. Keep her safe. Keep her safe.' She thrust the muzzled child at me. It lay quiet in the threadbare blanket it was wrapped in. It was small and emaciated. Like a little sack of potatoes. A little Russian doll.

The soldier was running, demanding. He raised his gun. I jerked back from the fence.

'Steponas,' she called.

My eyes could not meet hers. Those beautiful eyes. I could not look into them. She thrust the child forward, but my shivering hands did not reach out to take it. Jerzy had swung on the tree, when the wind caught him. His thin body hung so awkwardly. So uncomfortable with its neck wrenched out of place. His eyes were open. They popped from their dark, tired sockets.

'Hey, what is going on? Hey, you!'

'Please,' she said.

God in heaven. Dear God in heaven. My mind shivered between love and fear. My own teeth rattled. The child was close enough to take. The soldiers clattered up behind her.

I turned away.

'Stop!'

I scrambled quickly down the alley-way. She did not cry out or call after me. The soldiers were shouting, cursing. My feet scuffed the cobblestones and in my hurry I stumbled. From behind me I heard a small cry. I did not turn. I picked myself up quickly and lurched on. I did not turn. I ran. I broke out of the gloom into a courtyard. I ran and I did not turn back.

Chapter 54

I threw myself down on the bank of the river. It was dark. A thick layer of cloud hid the moon. I wept. A cold wind blew across the river. My heart burned with pain. Framed by the broken boards she held out the little child. Her eyes caught mine and would not free them. I dared not think where she was. Where she was going. I stood on the edge of the river, the current flowing fast and dark beneath me. Oh God, I thought, what have I done? And that was all. I could allow no other thought. I dared let in no other thought.

When dawn broke timidly over the city spires, my legs trembled still. I pulled myself up from the bank of the river which I had not the courage to throw myself in. I stumbled away from the city, following the serpentine flow of the river out into the forest.

At night I slept in ditches, by day I wandered, begging food in the villages. Crusts of bread, rotten fruit. I drank milk from goats early, before the farmers rose. The villagers were nervous and suspicious. I moved on quickly.

My mother cried when she saw me. She fell to her knees and hugged her stinking, dirty son to her. My father hobbled from the shadows. An old man, fearful and broken.

He held me and I wept.

Epilogue
Lithuania
(Mid 1990s)

Chapter 55

It was dark when I stopped writing. I laid down my pen and picked up the oil lamp. The air was still and cool. I stood in the doorway leaving the memories behind. It was done. There was a light glowing in the cottage across the grass. Egle and Jolanta would be there, I knew, but I did not feel like going over to them. Instead I blew out the small flame in the lamp and left it by the door of the wood-panelled writing room.

Passing the cottage I walked through the thick grass to the trees. The moon shone brilliantly from a clear sky. The woods were silver and black. A thin breeze stirred the leaves. I startled a fox and sent it scurrying through the undergrowth, a cub clamped in its jaws. For fifty years I had buried these memories. When the Soviets returned I was conscripted and served for two years in the Red Army. Despite the efforts of the partisans who fought from the forests, Vilnius became the capital of the Soviet Republic of Lithuania.

The Soviets had no desire to investigate the massacre of the Jews; we were all victims of the fascist oppressor. And so the rubble of the devastated synagogues was slowly cleared. The vacant Jewish homes were reallocated to the needy. Thugs who had gone Jew-hunting for kopecks during the war years wandered the old alleys free and unmolested. We all forgot. We all buried the rubble of war. Hid the sores. Turned our attentions to new enemies, new struggles.

I took a job at the university teaching literature. I wrote poetry in Lithuanian and was celebrated, in a quiet way. My work was not confrontational, it didn't provoke the authorities, but it was Lithuanian verse, it spoke to the Lithuanian people about themselves, of their history, customs, of their place in the world. And for that I gained a reputation I enjoyed, but did not deserve.

I moved into the flat on German Street, not far from the university. But despite walking those streets daily, bathing in the Vilija in the summer, smoking in cafés in the winter, I did not think of her. Each day I forgot her. And forgot and forgot. Buried her under a mountain of words, and cigarette butts, casual affairs with students, drinks with friends. Under poems and novels and two plays. Under study and teaching. Under the mountain of deadness that grew round my heart.

Coming out of the forest, the river shone brilliantly in the moonlight. I sat on the bank and gazed into the rippled light. Bats turned erratically above my head. The breeze carried the sound of drunken singing from the village.

And then the words stopped flowing. The poems dried up and the novels refused to take shape. I've retired, I told them. You've heard enough from me; it's time for the younger generation to make their voice heard. I managed to pen some articles for the newspapers and edited and collated anthologies. The young students stopped reading my work and stopped being impressed. They became more careless of my attentions.

And as the cracks began to appear in the walls of the Soviet system, the whole building began to grumble and totter. As the plaster fell in dusty clouds and the bricks tumbled, I began to feel my own building tremble.

Egle found me sitting by the river. She took my arm and led me back through the woods.

'I've finished my writing,' I told her as we pushed through the thin, supple branches of the pines, trying not to lose our way in the darkness. She pressed my arm but said nothing.

'I would like you to read it,' I said.

'If you would like me to.'

'I think you should know.'

When we returned to the cottage I gathered the papers from my desk and gave them to Egle. She stowed them on a shelf out of the way of the fingers of little Rasa. It was late and we went to bed. For some time I lay beneath the cool sheets, gazing out at the distant silver disc of moon caught in the apple tree's mesh of twigs.

I awoke early and let myself out before either Egle or Jolanta had risen. There was a small chapel on a rise some two kilometres out of the village. I walked across the fields to it. Later I had lunch in the village. In a shallow hollow, beneath a copse of aspen, I slept for an hour. I watched the sun make its slow passage across the sky and the pale ghost of a moon rise from behind the trees.

I walked in the woods, listening to the sound of the birds and my feet rustling through the long grass. The sun sank and silence settled upon the land. Fearful, I still put off going back to the cottage.

It was late when finally I turned and made my way home. In the darkness I stumbled slowly along the rutted road, nervous of the reception awaiting me. How would she feel, knowing? She who could have been Rachael's daughter. She who was saved by a peasant family's courage – a family with more courage than I. The windows were dark, no lamp burned. I pushed open the kitchen door, relieved and disappointed. Moonlight glittered on the window pane but did little to illuminate the interior. I almost tripped over her.

She was sitting silently on one of the wooden stools by the

kitchen table. On the table in front of her were the papers I had left her to read. I cried out, so startled was I to stumble upon her.

'I'm sorry,' she said. 'I didn't mean to startle you.'

'I didn't see you.'

'I was reading.'

'Without a light?'

She looked around as though she had only just noticed that it had grown dark.

'No,' she said. 'Earlier.'

I pulled a stool up to the table and sat down. Taking the cigarettes from my pocket I offered her one. She took the cigarette and we smoked silently for a while, little else visible but the glowing tips of our cigarettes and the moonlight glittering on the glass. The night was warm. She slipped her hand across the table and let it rest gently across my own.

'What can you think of me?' I said finally.

She did not answer immediately. She did not remove her hand from mine. She breathed the smoke out in a long, thoughtful exhalation. 'It should seem closer to me, shouldn't it? As if this was in some way my story, or rather not my story. How my story could have been.' She paused, drawing deeply on her cigarette. 'It doesn't though. It was a long time ago, Steponas. Many people did things they regret. Many people did things they were ashamed of, even if it didn't seem that they were.'

'I thought that if I wrote it down, if I faced up to it after all these years, it would make me feel better.'

'And does it?'

'No. It doesn't. The memory doesn't bring forgiveness.'

'But it is good to remember, even if there is no hope of forgiveness.'

She squeezed my hand and brushed it against her soft cheek. Somewhere in the dark house I heard the baby cough and stir.

It cried out. Jolanta's voice, heavy with sleep, shushed it. The baby quietened a little and I heard Jolanta singing, her voice soft and low.

Shluf Meine Kind,
By dine veegel zitzt dine mame,
Zingt a leed un vaynt.

Sleep, my child, my comfort, my pretty,
By your cradle sits your mama,
Sings a song and weeps.
You'll understand some day most likely,
What is in her mind.

Chapter 56

On that, my last night in the village, I did not sleep. I lay on my bed staring out into the darkness. The earth had shifted, and the long dead had risen. I had looked once more into the eyes of the love I had betrayed. But still, there was so much more left buried. I have not remembered all. Cannot.

One hundred thousand Jews were killed in the Vilnius region, in those few years. Not everyone was marched from the ghetto to their death in the forest glades at Ponar, or at the Ninth Fort, or in the concentration camps in Estonia. Some were left. The inhabitants of a hospital were left. They closed the doors and locked them. Boarded up the windows, and doused the building in fuel and set it alight. They were left. The doctors, the sick, the elderly, the infirm.

When the Russians returned to the streets of Vilnius, the remnants of the Jews trickled into the city from the villages, from their molinas, from their forest hideouts, from the holes beneath floors, secret compartments, tunnels beneath the earth, where they had been forced to live like animals. Several thousands; the thin, harried, destitute leftovers of the Jerusalem of the north.

They established a school on Zigmond and a museum and a memorial to the ones that they had lost. But these were soon to disappear. The communists had no appreciation for a separatist, ethnic counting of the dead. We were all one, neither Jew nor Gentile, bond nor free. We were all communists.

I too became a communist. I was cynical about it. When

I told Rita of my decision we had a furious row. What would Jerzy have said? she demanded. There was one of two choices, I told her, either you were for the communists or for the Nazis; that was how the world stood. There were other choices, of course, but I was not ready to acknowledge them. Splitting the world by this neat division was the easier route. To be communist was to be against the Fascists, and the Fascists were the root of the evil that had overshadowed our nation. Communism was a balm. It allowed us to forget.

And we forgot. Nobody spoke of those years, our lips were sealed. We did not tell our children or our grandchildren what we had done in the war. It was a closed book and best left to the communist texts and teachers in the schools who had been trained to say the right thing. We did not sit in bars and reminisce. We did not chat idly about those times, over beers. The communist Party arranged the days of remembrance and we knew they served political purposes and were not about remembering what happened in the war. Yes, the communists defended us against our pasts. They allowed us to forget. They allowed us to bury the dead beneath slogans and platitudes, beneath the suffocating layers of lies and deception and the rewriting of history.

I saw less and less of Rita. At the time I believed that it was I who had became uncomfortable with her; I avoided going to her studio where she was working hard on a triptych of Madonnas. Perhaps though it was she who withdrew. She was preoccupied and her eyes wore a haunted look. One night after drinking a little too much I told her that she needed to put the past behind her, to get out more. She gazed at me intently, sending a shiver down my spine. I flush with shame now, remembering that moment. It was one of the last times I saw her.

*   *   *

The moon shone through the window of the cottage, and the branches of the apple tree stirred in a light breeze. I did not sleep. I watched through the night, till the new day dawned.

Chapter 57

The television tower soared above the forested hills. The boulevards were busy with cars and trolley buses. The road dipped down a long curving slope and the Old Town emerged from behind the grassed banks, shimmering under a haze, south of the river.

Grigalaviciene was sitting on the wooden bench outside the door to our block. She was sewing. When she saw me she said nothing, just grunted and continued embroidering the pretty little handkerchief. I nodded to her, and smiled. The flat was cold and musty. I dropped my bag inside the door and opened the window. The soft afternoon breeze blew in, stirring the curtains and the photographs pinned to the wall. I boiled some water for a coffee and sat down at my writing table. The Russian girl stared out at me from the photograph.

When I had finished the coffee, I took down the photographs from the wall. The afternoon passed slowly. Grigalaviciene called around to see if I needed anything. She shuffled on the doorstep, but didn't come in when invited. She looked at me out of the corner of her eye, as if she could not trust me. I shut the door on her impatiently.

The next morning I walked across the ghetto to Svetlana's on Sv Stepono, for the small bag of laundry I had left with her and in search of company. She did not answer the door when I knocked. I tried to peer through the windows, but they were opaque with dirt. On a chance I pushed at the door and it creaked open. I stepped into the gloom. The room was empty. On the bed was a picture of the crucifixion. I sat next to it. Dirt obscured the lower part of Christ's face. Vaguely I noticed how feminine the upper half of His face looked.

A voice caused my heart to jump. A figure stood in the doorway. The light was behind her and in the gloom it was impossible to see her features. Her hair shone golden in the sunlight. She stepped forward and the gloom revealed her.

'Oh,' she said, recognising me. Her face flushed.

'Svetlana,' I said, getting up hastily. 'I'm sorry, I knocked and no one answered.'

She was dressed in pink sports clothes, her sleeves rolled up revealing her arms, which were red. She had been working, washing clothes I assumed. I noticed her glance at the sequined dress hung carefully on the wall.

'Please, sit down,' she said, laying a package on the end of the bed.

Clumsily I sat back down. Noticing that I still held in my hands the icon, I held it out to her and she took it. She hung it on a nail on the wall. She seemed nervous, a little embarrassed perhaps.

'Would you like a drink?' she said then.

'I came for the washing,' I said, uncomfortably.

She nodded. It was wrapped neatly in brown paper on a pile of junk in the corner of the room. She took it and handed it to me. She hesitated then turned away.

'I have something else of yours,' she said.

She spoke quietly and I had to strain to hear her. She returned to the pile in the corner and began shifting the layers of clothes that lay on top of it. I was a little bewildered. I was not aware that I had left anything else. I guessed that perhaps it had been a shirt I had left some time before. But she pulled a bag from the jumble. For some moments I did not recognise it.

She sat on the bed beside me, the blue plastic bag on her

lap. It was ripped and dirty. She pulled the thick sheaf of papers out of the bag and they were crumpled and ripped and dirty too.

'Where did you get these?' I said, finally.

She seemed a little embarrassed. 'You left them, in a café. I picked them up meaning to return them to you . . .' Her explanation petered out. She handed them to me.

I stared at the crumpled sheets in my hands, the manuscript finally returned. A little thrill of relief shuddered through my body. I clutched the papers tightly. For some moments we sat in silence.

'I'm sorry,' she said then, perhaps misinterpreting my quietness.

'There's no need to be,' I said. 'I'm just a little confused. I thought somebody else had them.'

There was then a knock at the door. A young girl entered, no older than thirteen. She was a pretty girl, but there was something harsh about her features. The smile on her face dissolved the moment she saw me. She eyed me suspiciously and when Svetlana explained who I was she did not shake my hand. Svetlana got up and boiled some water on the small stove. She made me a cup of tea and I drank it gladly.

'How's Misha?' I asked to break the uncomfortable silence that had descended on us.

'Fine,' Svetlana said. 'They laid him off at the building site. He left yesterday for England.'

'England?' I said, my eyebrows rising.

'To find work. I managed to borrow some money.'

She smiled and it struck me that I could not remember having seen her smile before. As if reading my thoughts she said, 'My husband has gone.'

'He left?'

'The police took him, the day after I saw you last.' She shrugged. 'He was doing the dirty work for some guy called

Kasimov. I don't know. It's just a fucking relief to have him out of the way.'

'Kasimov?'

'Mafia,' she said, her nose wrinkling with contempt.

'A lot has happened since last I was here!'

'A problem doesn't like to walk without company, as they say.' She smiled again, but this time it was tempered with weariness.

As I was leaving, the young girl, whom Svetlana called Ruta, was pulling Svetlana's tub in from the courtyard. She did not smile or acknowledge me when I said goodbye.

'You have a girl working for you?' I asked Svetlana, curiously, as we walked out to the street. She flushed and turned away from me.

'She's living here now that Ivan has gone,' she said. For a moment it seemed that was all she was going to say and I was about to say goodbye when she added, 'She's a good girl. Life has been hard. We live the best way we can.' She held my arm and looked into my face. 'We just do what we can to survive. It's easy to say that it's not right, but sometimes we have little choice . . .'

She looked up at me as if she wished for my concurrence. Her face was lined with doubt, but her head was tilted back as if to suggest she would not care if I disagreed. I was a little confused and unsure how to reply. I took her hand and gripped it.

'Svyeta,' I said, 'God knows I'm not the one to be telling you what is right.'

She pressed my hand and smiled at me.

Chapter 58

The waiter in Markus and Ko did not seem to recognise me. He brought a menu when I sat down at the table by the window. I shook my head and ordered a coffee. My pocket bulged as I sat, Marcinkevicius' dog-eared volume pressing against my side. I did not take it out. I love you with hands black from crying. The waiter brought the coffee and I made a point of laying the money out on the table for him to take. Perhaps then he remembered, for he hesitated as he picked up the coins.

I love you with darkness and death. Forgetfulness and light. Yes, with pain. With guilt. Grass on a sunken grave. In the moonlight, our hands brushed. We stopped by the old birch, which shone silver, at the point where Old Mendle's path forked off the road. Your breath was ragged with nerves. We stumbled and our faces met, almost lip to lip, in the pale light.

I lit a cigarette and brushed away a tear, but another welled up to take its place. I let them fall. The smoke rose blue from my cigarette. My eyes blurred. Through the window I saw a woman pass and then hesitate. Her hair fell dark around her face. In her arms she held a child. She looked in through the glass and I had to rub my eyes to see her clearly. She smiled. My heart jumped with a painful little leap of joy and I beckoned for her to come in. She nodded.

When I had returned from Svetlana's the previous day, I got out the volume on the development of Western art I had borrowed from the library. Clearing a space on the table,

I turned over to Daddi's Triptych. I switched on the small reading lamp. It struck me as I examined the reproduction that in the side panel depicting Christ on the cross, the emotional heart of the picture was in the bottom left corner, where the apostles stand supporting the Holy Mother. They lead her away, her shawl pulled tight around her, as Christ looks on. I took out a cigarette and lit it, taking care not to exhale on the print. The gospel story told by Daddi is the mother's story. The young virgin, the tender mother, the aged widow who has lost her son.

The waiter smiled as the woman pushed through the door into Markus and Ko. She crossed the restaurant and slid into the seat opposite mine. The young child looked at me curiously.

'I wasn't sure I would find it,' Egle said, cradling her granddaughter. I ordered her a glass of wine.

It struck me that there is something uncomfortable about Daddi's portrait of Christ on the cross. The way that the figures reach up to him. There is something a little hysterical about it. Theatrical. As I gazed at the image a thin crease of light ruptured the darkness inside me. It reminded me of something I had read in the manuscript Svetlana had returned to me. It had taken me a while to rearrange the pages. Some were ripped and a couple seemed to be missing altogether.

He wrote,

As he pinned the medal to my breast I had a sudden vision of her standing at the edge of the village, the smoke rising behind her, the charred timbers tilting awkwardly, her scarf pulled tight beneath her eyes so that I could not see the sting of loss on her face. Our truck pulled away and she was lost in the swirl of dust. This medal, I understood then, was earned by her sacrifice – nourished by her suffering.

'It has been a few years since last I was in the city,' Egle said.

'And do you find it changed?'

'Everywhere you go they are painting, rebuilding. It's beautiful.'

'I worry sometimes,' I said. 'I fear that all the memories are being plastered over. They are painting over the cuts and bruises of the city. It may well be pretty when they have finished, but will it have a soul?'

Egle laughed. She laid a hand on my own and looked into my eyes. 'Daumantas the poet!' she mocked. 'Look.' She held up Rasa, in her arms. 'Is it for her that you are wanting to save the rubble?'

Later Jolanta joined us. She looked worn. She drank a coffee and stared out of the window.

'I read your husband's novel,' I said.

She turned to me. As soon as I had arrived home from Svetlana's with the manuscript I had telephoned to let her know I had it. She had been a little short with me on the telephone – had thanked me, and said we would discuss it when we met. I had suspected she had been crying.

'It's good,' I said. 'He writes perceptively about the war, as if he was there.'

She nodded. 'Yes, he served in Afghanistan.' She paused and looked back out through the window. 'He is back in hospital. They have given him some medication and he is calmer.'

'What is the matter with him?'

'He has always been highly strung. After he finished his degree he was conscripted into the Soviet army. He never told us what happened. He came home safely, thank God. Then one day I received a telephone call to say that he had been admitted to hospital. They would not let me see him, nor would they tell me what had happened.

'When he was discharged, on medical grounds, he was

transferred to the psychiatric hospital in New Vilnia for some months. When finally he came home, it was as if he didn't know me. And I did not know him. Sometimes he is in control and there are days when he is almost like the man I used to know. And then . . . Reading the book I feel I can understand a little, but he will not tell me if what he has written is true.'

Egle slipped her arm around her daughter's shoulders. Looking across the table I felt helpless.

'If there is any way that I can help you . . .' I said. 'As to Kestutis' manuscript I will pass it on to a friend, an editor at the Vaga publishing house, if your husband agrees.'

She smiled and reached out her hand to take my own. 'Thank you.'

Later, I suggested we drive out into the country. Some twenty kilometres out of the city, on the road to Trakai, there is a small lane that cuts off the highway. After a few miles it turns to dirt track for the rest of the way to the village. In the centre of the village stands a small church. During Soviet times it was used as a storehouse. The priest lived in a small cottage adjoining it.

I parked the old Moskovich beneath the silver birch. The roots of the tree had toppled the low stone wall around the church. The leaves danced in a gentle gust of wind. Inside the church it was cool and gloomy. It smelled vaguely of hay, of the farm, along with the incense that the priest had burned, cleansing his church once the Russians had gone.

A heavy, autumnal slab of light fell from the windows near the altar. We stood in front of three canvases.

'They're beautiful,' Jolanta said.

'A woman I knew during the war years painted them,' I told her. 'Her name was Rita.'

In the central canvas sat the Mother of God. She sat upon

a throne, resplendently swollen with child. Gently her hands rested upon the bulge under her dress. She was weeping.

Standing beside me, Egle slipped her hand into mine and rested her head upon my shoulder. Jolanta sat on the front pew, cradling her daughter. Rasa. A drop of dew. Fresh as the morning. The small child sang, playing with her mother's fingers.

Outside the church, the birds sang. Down the road was Ponar. In the forest glade the birds would be singing too. The sun, there, would cut across the treetops as it cut across the treetops outside the village church. Grass had grown over the pits, and trees too. They towered, those trees that had been planted at the end of the war. Blackberries, currants, mushrooms. The foxes made their homes and the birds their nests.

Chapter 59

The city is quiet. Somewhere a bell is tolling and a child wanders down the narrow lane singing. She has not seen me. I stand on the corner and watch her as she disappears around the slow twist of the ghetto street. Birds lift from the rooftops and are caught dazzlingly in the net of the sinking sun. A soft breeze.

In the square a woman brushes the leaves. The twig broom scrapes rhythmically. Switch. Switch. Switch. Unhurried. A man sits on the grass and lights a cigarette. He pulls off his battered cap and mops his brow. Beside him his scythe. Patiently the horse waits with the cart.

The city is still. It slips from late afternoon into the evening's blue coolness. A thin haze hangs over the court-yards. A bonfire burns, the blue-yellow flames devouring the leaves and long, dry grass.

The city is calm. Night slides up through the valleys, snaking into the city on the back of the river, and the first star appears. The moon, crisp and distant, balances on the broken-tiled rooftops, with the roosting birds.

The cupolas and the crosses, the onion domes and the ornate spires. I sit alone in my room. The window is open. I have moved the desk so that I can write looking out through the window. The night has come. But I am no longer alone. Outside is the city. And here, on the desk before me, on the left of my typewriter, is a photograph of a mother holding her child. And behind her is her mother, a child plucked from oblivion. And tomorrow I shall see them.